"Charming, sly, and seriously scary"
— Glen Hirshberg

"You're waiting for Mike," he said. Not a question.

I didn't answer. Just looked at him until his mouth twisted in what, for a cop, passes for sympathy. I asked him if it was quick, and he spared me the bullshit.

"It was not," he said.

The drive was way across town, but took barely five minutes. Which might sound impressive to you, but then you're probably someone who doesn't have a siren sitting in your glove compartment for whenever you feel like cutting through traffic.

Mike, or what was left of him, was underneath the pedestrian bridge, mercifully hidden from the sight of casual passers-by. Jesus Christ. It looked like something had clawed its way out of him, something powerful and frenzied. Like someone had force-fed him a mountain lion and then whistled it to come home...

- from *"The Stuff That Dreams Are Made Of"*

By Peter Atkins

NOVELS
Morningstar
Big Thunder
Moontown

COLLECTIONS
Wishmaster & Other Stories
Spook City (with Clive Barker and Ramsey Campbell)
Rumors of the Marvelous
Cemetery Dance Select: Peter Atkins
All Our Hearts Are Ghosts & Other Stories

SCREENPLAYS
Hellbound: Hellraiser II
Hellraiser III: Hell on Earth
Fist of the North Star
Hellraiser: Bloodline
Wishmaster
Prisoners of the Sun

ALL OUR HEARTS ARE GHOSTS

& other stories

PETER ATKINS

A Shadowridge Horror Book
Shadowridge Press

ISBN: 978-1-946808-23-3
shadowridgepress.com

Cover Design: Twilight Hill Graphics
Illustration: *Silver Moonlight* (detail)
by J Atkinson Grimshaw

First Edition

For Dana

CONTENTS

*CONTENT WARNING. This story might be disturbing for
survivors of sexual assault.

ALL OUR HEARTS
ARE GHOSTS

THE STUFF THAT DREAMS ARE MADE OF

San Francisco, 1941

First, I was totally minding my own business.

Second, if the pretty boy behind the bar had shown his hand sooner, maybe we wouldn't have had to wash what was left of two of his customers off the walls.

I'd been nursing a cocktail, the taste of which I like but the name of which I prefer to keep private because it sounds like something Deanna Durbin might order if she was doing the town with the Pope, and I was waiting for Mike Bowman, my business partner. He was already spectacularly late, but that was hardly cause for alarm. With Mike, keeping people waiting is practically an art-form.

I'm not going to lie to you. It's not like I hadn't noticed the blonde when she walked in—there was a lot to notice and hardly any of it was shy—but after that initial glance I'd kept my eyes on the counter and my mind on whether the lead Mike had claimed to be following would turn into an actual case paying actual money. We could use it. It had been a slow month in a long winter.

The blonde wasn't alone anyway; a guy twice her age and certainly more than half her height joined her at the counter after wasting two minutes glad-handing a table of second-stringers from the *Chronicle*.

"Just making sure they're going to cover the opening of the new store," he said to her and to anyone within a hundred yards. "Prime location, Ruby," he added, though I suspect Ruby might have already had that fact mentioned to her once or twice. "Right there on Market."

"Are you going to make a lot of money?" she asked him. I know, I know. I wish I could tell you Ruby didn't actually say that out loud, but she did.

"Well, it's not like I'm hurting now," he said, and pulled something shiny from his coat pocket. It was a small green stone of some kind that hung from a thin gold chain, and he dangled it from his fingers to catch Ruby's eye.

"What is it?" she said.

He waved it in front of her eyes again, twitching his fingers so that it did a little shimmy for her. But he waited to speak until he slipped it back into his pocket, waited in fact until he patted the pocket to be sure his trinket was safely there, as if he feared some last-minute trick from an unseen Magician. Seemed odd. Maybe he was crazy. But what the hell did I know? Maybe he *wasn't* crazy. Maybe Ruby's day-job was Beautiful Assistant to some quick-with-his-hands vaudeville shyster and they were setting this idiot up for a now you see it now you don't routine. Christ knows, wouldn't be the first time.

Done patting, he gave her a wink. "My ship came in," he said. Kind of smug, kind of teasing.

"That's nice, Albie," she said. "But what *is* it?" Flirting with petulant, heading for insistent.

Albie lent his voice as much drama and mystery as he could, which wasn't much but you work with what you've got. "The stuff that dreams are made of…" he said, and his eyes did their rheumy best to twinkle.

"On," said the barman quietly. He was wiping glasses down and not even looking at Ruby and her swain, but the latter believed he knew a challenge when he heard one.

"I beg your pardon?" Albie said. Little spin on it, like he was giving the guy the opportunity to plead insanity.

"On," said the barman again, looking up this time. "It's 'on', not 'of'. It's Shakespeare, isn't it? *The Tempest*, if I remember correctly. 'We are such stuff as dreams are made on'."

His voice was rich with that just-like-us-but-smarter thing that had once had women throwing themselves at John Barrymore. Ruby heard it too. Still worked, apparently. She smiled. "I love your accent," she said. "Are you British?"

"When the occasion calls for it, Madam," the barman said. He gave her a small nod that managed to be both self-satisfied and self-deprecating, and the smile with which he backed it up was a clear signal that should she be looking for male company he was more than willing to step into the breach once she came to her senses about the asshole she rode in on.

Before all interested parties could learn just what the hell Albie was going to do about that, the street door to the bar slammed open, loud enough to make everybody in there look over.

Revealed in the doorway, framed against the rain that was just starting to fall outside, was an odd little fellow who was busy lowering the silver topped cane with which he'd shoved the door open. Really quite splendid in his own bizarre fashion, he was a compact dandy in a formal dress suit, his hair slick with pomade, and only his eyes—slightly protruding, almost batrachian—spoiling his pocket-Adonis ambitions.

Those eyes fixed themselves on Albie and a small and far from pleasant smile twitched across his tight little lips.

"Jerome Cadiz," I heard Albie mutter just before the barman stole my attention by tapping an unobtrusive finger on the counter in front of my stool. He'd laid down a small key—like something for a left luggage locker at a train station or a bus depot—and slid it toward me.

"Got a little something for you, Steve," he said quietly.

I pocketed the key instinctively—what else are you going to do, someone hands you a key?—but it bothered me that he had my name, because as far as I knew I hadn't been handing it out.

"Huh?" I said. And I'll have you know I said it pretty damn incisively. I didn't read those Perry Mason stories every month for nothing.

"I know how much you like your hats," the barman said, as if that explained anything.

"What?" I said. "Have we met before?"

"Depends what you mean by 'before'," he said. And then the world went mad.

Albie suddenly pushed himself back from the counter, stool slamming to the floor behind him, and glared down the length of the bar at the little peacock he'd called Jerome Cadiz.

Whatever trouble Cadiz might have thought he was bringing to the party, it seemed that Albie was determined to head him off at the pass. "*P'hath bar nyleq'h hunq'a!*" he yelled at him. Or, you know, words to that effect.

"*Albie!*" Ruby said sharply, not like she feared for his sanity, but like he was embarrassing her, like he'd just told an off-color joke to a minister's wife or something.

But Albie wasn't done. And he certainly wasn't chastened by Ruby's disapproval. If anything, he looked like this might be the very opportunity he'd been waiting for to impress her.

"Behold the shard of the God!" he shouted, which was at least in English, even if it was still gibberish. He drew out that shimmering green stone from his pocket with his right hand, held it out threateningly at arm's length toward Cadiz, and waved his left hand over it in three consecutive counter-clockwise circles ...

And then nothing happened.

You got to assume that was a bad moment for Albie, and I'm sure the contemptuous giggle that escaped Cadiz's mouth didn't help at all. Like the kind of jerk who sits down at the piano and plays a perfect *Moonlight Sonata* after you've just failed to play *Chopsticks*, Cadiz too put his hand into his pocket and brought something out.

Not much of something, though. All he had in his hand was an unprepossessing mound of ashy grey dust. It looked like he might have scooped up a tablespoon's worth of somebody's dead relative from an unguarded urn, no more than that. It sat there cupped in his palm, doing precisely the same amount of nothing that Albie's shard of the green god had done. Until Cadiz blew on it. At which point it began to behave a little differently from your average pile of crematorium ash.

At first rising up in an arching line, swollen at the head like a King Cobra woken by the charmer's pipe, it then swept upward and outward through the air in a curving arc, trailing more of itself behind it than should have been possible, and roiling at the head like a tidal wave about to break.

"Albie?" Ruby said, her voice small and unsure.

That voice, and Albie's devastated expression, were the last any of the rest of us knew, other than the deafening concussive roar of Cadiz's party favor as it reached critical mass and exploded.

♦ ♦ ♦ ♦

I wasn't the last to wake up, but I wasn't the first either and by the time I did the uniform cops were already taking notes and sharing disbelieving glances.

There were a handful of us left in the bar, but there was no Jerome Cadiz. He'd gone, as had my curious friend the key-dispensing barman. As for Albie and Ruby ... well, they weren't *gone*, exactly, but they were unlikely to be giving statements to the lead Detective. They were nowhere to be seen, unless you counted the two vaguely people-shaped bloodstains that were dripping their way down the back wall, already seeping and staining unpleasantly into the sawdust piles atop the bar's old-school tiled floor.

The lead Detective though—in this case, a one-time beat cop bruiser named Dominic Coughlan whom nobody expected to ever make detective, let alone turn out to be good at it—certainly wanted to hear for himself what the rest of us had to say, no matter how ridiculous. He saved me till last, figuring with the license and all I might actually be of some use to him. On this occasion—and not, I'm sorry to say, for the first time—I was a great disappointment to Dominic, being as unconscious as every other idiot in the room when whatever finally happened finally happened.

The thing about lead Detectives is this; like stallions or bulls, it's never a good idea to put two of them in the paddock at once, so when Tim Loory walked into the bar a few minutes later, I got an unfocused bad feeling. This jacket had clearly landed on Coughlan's desk, not Tim's, so why was he here? I mean, it might've been a coincidence—cops have got to drink *somewhere*—but he was looking right at me like I was the guy he was looking for and while the expression plastered on his big stupid Irish face was perhaps intended to be unreadable I was pretty sure he hadn't shown up here to tell me he'd just heard from Bay Meadows that my horse had come in at twenty to one.

"Steve," he said.

"Tim," I said, and waited for him to tell me I was still the king of the snappy comeback. But he didn't. He didn't say anything, in fact, for a good three seconds, which is a hell of a long time for we who banter.

"You're waiting for Mike," he said eventually. Not a question.

I didn't answer. Just looked at him until his mouth twisted in what, for a cop, passes for sympathy.

Ah hell, I thought, and asked him if it was quick.

He spared me the bullshit. "It was not," he said and pretended to look at the painting behind the bar to prevent me reading just how not quick it had been.

"Out by the old railroad cross?" I said and then, off his nod, "Let's go."

"You don't want to see it," he said.

"The hell I don't," I said. I took a last belt from my drink and reached for my hat.

Tim didn't move, other than to point at my glass, a stunned expression on his face. "What in God's name is that?" he said.

"It's a drink, Tim," I said, planting my hat pointedly on my head. "We're in a bar."

"It's *pink*," he said.

"We should go."

"It looks like something they'd reward Little Lord Fauntleroy with for finishing in first place in his dance recital."

"We should go."

He came out of his trance and looked at me again, sympathy for the loss of my partner back in place. "You don't want to see it," he repeated, and this time there was something in his tone that actually slowed me down.

"On account of...?"

"On account of it makes what happened here look like a pat on the cheek in the kind of third degree we reserve for people with a long history of generous contributions to the Policeman's Benevolent Fund."

I waggled my hand like I was going to have to deduct a point or two. "A little elaborate," I said, not without gratitude for the distraction.

Tim's shrug was implicit. "My wife's cousin?" he said. "The head doctor? Last time he was around for Joan's veal parmesan he volunteered the opinion that I take refuge in colorful simile and metaphor because I'm uncomfortable with my emotions."

I gave it a moment while we headed for the door.

"This cousin of your wife's," I said.

"Yeah?"

"You let him have it once she wasn't looking, right?"

"She knows better than to leave him alone with me," he said, and I followed him out to the street.

As he drove us over to the old railroad station, the one that still did some storage business but hadn't seen a train since they cut the big red ribbon at Downtown Union, Tim did his best to talk about other stuff and I appreciated the effort even though he wasn't very good at it. He didn't have to try for too long; even though we were heading way across town, the trip took barely five minutes. Which might sound impressive to you, but then you're probably someone who doesn't have a siren sitting in your glove compartment for whenever you feel like cutting through traffic.

Mike, or what was left of him, was underneath the pedestrian bridge, mercifully hidden from the sight of casual passers-by. Jesus Christ. It looked like something had clawed its way out of him, something powerful and frenzied. Like someone had force-fed him a mountain lion and then whistled it to come home.

♦ ♦ ♦ ♦

Mike and I had never done well enough to afford an honest to God full-time receptionist, but Mike's sister's youngest came in two afternoons a week for pin-money and to let us look like a going concern for clients to whom that kind of thing mattered. It was she who'd told me yesterday that Mike was following up a lead for a potential new client.

"What kind of client?" I'd asked.

"You know what kind," Valerie had replied, with a sparkle in her seventeen-year-old eye that would have been a great disappointment to the holy sisters back at her parochial school.

"Was it the kind that has a name?"

"It was," she'd said. "Kelly Woodman. *Miss* Kelly Woodman."

"That your stress or hers?"

"Oh, hers," Valerie'd said. "She was *very* emphatic about it."

All of which meant nothing more than that I had a name, which was something, but it wasn't likely to be enough.

Mike had never been great at the administrative side of the

business. Stuff like filing receipts or keeping notes or making entries in a phone-log cramped what he liked to think of as his style. Fortunately, his aristocratic disdain for keeping house also meant he rarely cleared out the trashcan under his desk and I found what I needed in there.

It was a napkin bearing the logo and address of a residential hotel, to which someone had added a hand-written room number. Someone—presumably the same someone—had also left a small and perfectly formed crimson lip-o-graph next to the number. Might've merely been happenstance—napkins were invented because people have to dab their mouths now and then, even people who wear bright red lipstick—but I couldn't help but wonder if it was also something to ensure that Mike was kept at full attention.

◆ ◆ ◆ ◆

The Hotel Montana, which was apparently where Miss Kelly Woodman hung whatever hats she had, was the kind of residential hotel that didn't have lobby security, just a bellboy with his feet up on the front desk. And, if his employers had any of the usual disapproval of gentlemen callers, they certainly hadn't bothered to let him know about it. I made it all the way to the elevator without his eyes once raising from that month's *Terror Tales*.

Her apartment was on the fifth floor and her door had its own little bell. I gave it a push.

When she opened the door, apparently fresh from the shower, she was still tying the satin belt of her satin bathrobe. I couldn't help but feel that that was all part of the floor-show, but that doesn't mean I didn't like it.

She gave me a brief appraising look and then cocked a loaded finger at me. "Mike's partner," she said, like I was not only the answer to the puzzle but the lucky winner's grand prize.

"Steve Donnelly," I said.

"You found me, Steve Donnelly," she said. "Aren't you clever?"

"I don't know about that," I said. "You want to play hard to get, don't leave your address in a detective's office."

"Now don't be cruel, Steve" she said, then cast her eyes down demurely and gave a half-smile. "At least, not yet."

Jesus Christ. Mike must've been putty in this one's hands.

"Come on in," she said, and stepped aside—but not too far aside—to let me pass.

"You'll take a drink?" she said, once we'd managed to reach her living room without anyone getting pregnant. Her question about the drink wasn't really a question. She may have been polite enough to make it sound like one but the door to her cocktail cabinet was open long before I could actually answer.

"It's eleven-thirty in the morning," I said. "Not exactly sundown." It wasn't like I didn't feel that I could use a drink, just that I thought a mild protest was appropriate. After all, I didn't want Miss Kelly Woodman thinking I was easy.

"You know, Steve," she said, "one of the most pleasant revelations of my life was the moment when I found out that all that stuff you can do after sundown, you can do before sundown too."

"Really?" I said. "What was the occasion?"

"I was having my dress taken off by my best friend's husband," she said. "Bourbon or vodka?" She was holding up a bottle in each hand and wiggling them at me.

"Those are my choices?"

"What did you have in mind?" she said. "I like to be accommodating."

I gave a brief hopeful glance into the cabinet.

"Oh, that's right," she said, her voice full of teasing delight. "Mike told me. You like that cute little drink that sounds like—"

"Mike told you what I like to *drink*? How the hell long were you with him? I thought it was a half an hour?"

"Time is relative," she said. "Haven't you heard?" She made a show of looking into the cocktail cabinet. "Anyway, looks like I'm all out of cotton candy or sugar plums so there goes *that* concoction." Her hands made the bottles of vodka and bourbon sway at me again, slow as a hula dancer's hips. "I'm afraid you're just going to have to go for the blonde or the brunette."

"That's fine," I said. "I'll take a vodka rocks."

"There's a big boy," she said and then, while pouring the vodka over the ice, "I heard about what happened to Mike, by the way. I'm so very sorry."

She didn't sound all that broken up about it, to be honest, but I tried not to hold it against her. She'd only known him half an hour, which works out pretty much as half an hour, however relative time might be.

"And all so unnecessary as it turned out," she said, handing me the drink. "If we'd known you were already on the case, we wouldn't have had to approach Mike in the first—"

"Hold on," I said, cutting her off. I put my drink down untasted on a side table next to her white leather sofa. I saw how she threw it a quick glance as if bothered that something wasn't quite going to plan, but I had other questions first. "What are you talking about, I was already on the case? And what makes you think—"

It was her turn to interrupt me. "You were in the *bar*," she said, and gave me a look like I was either screwing with her or had just had a small stroke. "Last night."

Well, that made things interesting. An old-timer from the Confidential Agency whom I'd got to know when he was just a few months shy of retiring had once said to me, "You'll find, kid, that when you're looking into something, there's no such thing as an unrelated incident." It was the kind of observation he liked to toss around when he figured he had a receptive audience, the sort of homily with which canny old operatives in love with their own legend like to dazzle the young and impressionable. The more kindly disposed among us like to call that sort of thing myth-making, though I believe the actual scientific term is horseshit. But maybe the old Confidential Op had been smarter than I thought.

Before I could ask about the bar and what it might have had to do with whatever she'd been to see Mike about, the doorbell of her apartment rang. I felt the germ of a suspicion that it was not an unrelated incident.

Kelly made a tutting noise. "Look at me," she said. "Nearly noon and still half-naked." She turned and headed for what I presumed was her bedroom door. "Could you see who that is, Steve? I need to slip into something a little less comfortable."

I opened the apartment's front door to find that Miss Kelly Woodman of the Hotel Montana had another gentleman caller. That bellboy downstairs, I decided, was really not doing his job.

The new arrival was not much taller than me. He was, however, about three times as wide. And all that width was encased in a coruscating cashmere robe that seemed to billow and undulate around him despite the hotel corridor's surprising lack of gale force winds. It was the kind of thing one would wear to an afternoon soiree at an opium parlor in a Cairo bazaar, I figured, though I should tell you right now that I've never been to Cairo, know nothing of its bazaars, and certainly have no idea whether or not they feature opium parlors. It was just what came to mind at the sight of the fat man and his vast and absurd caftan.

"Garland," he said, smiling at me. "Constantine Garland."

"Steve Donnelly," I said. "You here for Kelly?"

"Indeed," he said. "Aren't you?"

"Sure," I said. "But I didn't know it was a party."

He leaned a little to his right to cast a somewhat theatrical gaze over my shoulder and down into the length of the apartment. "Really?" he said, looking back at me. "Even though you were not the first guest to arrive?"

I half-turned and looked back behind me. Kelly had come out of her bedroom again and had brought a little surprise with her. Jerome Cadiz. The peacock from the bar who'd taught the unfortunate Albie a lesson in magic. Neither of them had a gun on the other, though both of them had guns. Both of them were smiling, too, and Kelly's smile was almost as unsettling as his.

I turned fast, ready to push my way past the fat guy and at least get his bulk between me and whatever bullets might soon start flying, but it turned out I was a tad optimistic. From somewhere within the labyrinthine folds of his ridiculous robe Garland had already pulled out a nasty little hammer, raised it way above his head, and was swinging it heavily down toward the center of my brow.

◆ ◆ ◆ ◆

I didn't even remember the moment of impact, let alone hitting the floor and being carried back into the living room.

By the time things swam back into focus, I was propped up

in a perfectly comfortable chair sitting across from Constantine Garland, who was taking up most of Kelly's white leather sofa and who was beaming at me with the kind of benevolent indulgence he'd show to an old friend with whom he'd been enjoying a quiet hand or three of pinochle and who'd decided to take an unscheduled break to indulge in a little nap.

Kelly was sitting at a small letter bureau. She had the bureau's writing-lid down and was shuffling a pack of cards on it. Her eyes were on Garland and me and she was shuffling blind, but it was smooth and beautiful and expert enough to make it clear that should she ever find herself in Monte Carlo she'd have very little reason to starve. Cadiz was leaning against the door jamb with a kind of louche elegance as if waiting for a society photographer to immortalize his moment and passing the time until that happened by giving me the ambiguous benefit of his fishy stare.

Garland registered my return to the land of the conscious. "*T'reh faghul al aklo?*" he said to me. "*Thepha cantro? Cantro?*" Well, let me be a little clearer: I of course have no idea what the hell he *actually* said, but that's approximately what it sounded like. Once he was done, he looked at me with an optimistic inquisitiveness that was as meaningless to me as the nonsense that had been coming out of his mouth.

"How hard did you hit me with that hammer?" I asked him, tapping at my forehead with a couple of careful fingers. "My Pig Latin skills seem to have deserted me."

His eyes clouded briefly as if he suspected me of either lying or mockery and his fat little fingers twitched instinctively, as if eager to reach for his hammer again. I could imagine how fully at ease he was using it as a tool of persuasion or punishment, so was relieved when I saw the moment pass, saw him choose to believe that I wasn't just playing dumb.

"So you are not of the elect, Mister Donnelly," he said. "One always likes to be sure. I take it then that your interest in the spoils of the *Stella Noctis* is purely financial?"

"You got something against money?" I said. Other than the fact he was now speaking English, what he was talking about was still meaningless to me but I've never found that admitting ignorance is a good way to get people to open up.

He gave a throaty little chuckle. "Against money?" he said "No indeed, sir. It is, after all, what makes the world go round." He gave a sidelong glance to Kelly. "At least for now," he said to her like a stage aside, like they had a little secret, and a glint of excitement came into her eyes, an excitement that didn't have a lot in common with the expert come-hither crap with which she dazzled saps like me or Mike.

"Let's say my interest *is* financial," I said. "How interested are you willing to make me?"

"You *have* it?" he said, suddenly eager. "You have the statue?"

"Never mind what I have or don't have," I said. "Let's just say my ship came in." I was taking a shot. I'd remembered that that's what the late lamented Albie had said to the late lamented Ruby and figured that the *Stella Noctis* that Chubs here had referred to was very possibly the literal ship in question.

The anticipatory sigh that came out of Garland and the way Kelly suddenly set her pack of cards down told me that I was perhaps after all not as dumb as I look. Also, it wasn't as if I *didn't* have something. I just had no idea what it was for and why I had it. But, given that all this circling wasn't doing any of us any good and—as it surely wouldn't have taken them much longer to realize I had absolutely no idea what the hell any of us were talking about—I played the only card I had.

"Lookit, fats," I said, hoping he'd be offended enough to assume I must have a bargaining chip if I was willing to risk mouthing off like that but not offended enough to take another swing with his hammer. "Let's get something straight. I don't give a shit about you or your little green god. I just want to know what you know about the key."

There was a moment of complete silence. Just long enough for me to wonder if I'd over-reached. I'd been playing the same kind of association game that had scored me a significant point with the ship thing. *Shard of the God*, Albie'd called his small fragment of green stone. *You have the statue*, Garland had asked. So the Donnelly brains trust had put two and two together and risked making five by presuming that this week's trigger for the criminal lunatic population of the city to run around trying to kill each other was a green statue of a god of some kind. The silence can't have lasted more than two seconds, but I really felt I owed Kelly an apology for my earlier skepticism about time being relative.

Finally, Garland gave a slight chuckle. The amusement in it wasn't of the nicest kind, but I'd take it. "Oh, Mister Donnelly," he said. "It's extremely unlikely we'd be having this conversation— delightful though it is—if I had the key or knew where it was."

"You wouldn't mind me wanting independent corroboration of that, would you?" I said, though I tried to make my tone suggest I really didn't give a damn whether he minded or not.

He blinked once as if to pardon my rudeness but stayed polite, stayed amused. "Not at all," he said. "Not at all."

Cadiz was still lounging against the door-jamb giving me

the benefit of a lazy eye that was supposed to tell me something. He needed to work on his act a little; I couldn't tell if he wanted to kill me or kiss me. At the sound of Garland's snapped fingers, though, he looked over like he was about to be let off the leash.

"Jerome," the fat man said. "Do I have the locker key in question?"

"You do not."

"Do *you*, perhaps, have it?"

"I do not."

Garland turned back to look at me, spreading his hands in a 'what more can I do?' manner, but Cadiz had apparently been enjoying the game and wanted to throw in a new wrinkle.

"Perhaps *she* has it," he said, and nodded in Kelly's direction.

"Miss Woodman?" Garland asked him.

"Yeah," Cadiz said. "Perhaps *she* has it." He paused, letting his eyes take a good long look. "About her person."

"And who's going to search me?" Kelly said. "You?" The contempt was withering, but Cadiz just shrugged and gave a half-smile. It was wry and boyish and, though I hate to admit it, almost goddam charming.

"Nobody needs to search anybody," I said. "*I've* got the key."

That got their attention. In fact, it was kind of unsettling the way all three pairs of eyes swung as one to lock on my face.

"More importantly," I said, "I know where the locker is. Which means I can get whatever's in there. Which means, unless I miss my guess, that I'm the only son of a bitch who can get his hands on this statue you're all in such a dither about."

♦ ♦ ♦ ♦

Thing is, I *did* know where the locker was. I hadn't realized

I did until remembering the key reminded me of the bartender and remembering the bartender reminded me of his crack about my hats. How he knew whatever he knew about me was still a mystery to me, but he'd used it to give me a clue. *I know how much you like your hats*, he'd said. Well, I do like my hats. And I don't like them from five and dime chain-stores. I like them custom-made by an honest to God hat guy, and my particular hat guy was Stavros The Hat Guy—no kidding, that's actually what it says on his shingle—who runs his business out of one of those little store-front franchises on the west concourse at Downtown Union. He's sandwiched in between the shoe-shine stand and the cigar store. And directly opposite the bank of left luggage lockers.

Being polite about it—asking permission of my new friends before I stood up to cross the room and use the phone—I called Valerie, told her to get the key out of my desk drawer, head to Downtown Union, and bring whatever she found in the locker to the Hotel Montana.

"Really, Steve?" she said, like I'd brought Christmas to her early. "An assignment?"

She sounded thrilled. And then, when I told her to give the package to the pulp-reading bellboy in the lobby rather than bring it up to the room herself, she sounded devastated. If I got a chance, I'd make it up to her one day but right now she'd have to stay devastated; I didn't want her within spitting distance of these people.

I paused at the cocktail cabinet on my way back from the phone, took out the bottle of vodka, and raised an eyebrow at Kelly.

"Help yourself," she said.

"Not drugged after all?" I said.

"Well, not the *bottle*," she said, like I was stupid. "You think I'm an amateur?"

"I do not," I said, pouring myself a shot. "It was you, wasn't it? You killed Mike."

She gave it a beat or two, wondered if the lie was worth it. "Not personally," she said.

I believed her—I'd seen the body—but that didn't stop her being guilty as sin. I swallowed the vodka and sat back down opposite Garland.

"What is it about this thing?" I asked him. "This statue. That makes people like you do things like that."

"Are you *fond* of anything, Mister Donnelly?" he said, interlacing his pudgy little fingers across his great fat belly as if settling in for Mommy to tell him a story.

"Kind of question is that?" I said.

"Oh, I mean no offense, I assure you," he said, though he seemed mildly amused at any offense he might actually have caused. "I have no interest in whatever worldly pleasures may delight you. I assume, for example, that like any vigorous man of your age, you find that wine, women, and song—or the equivalents thereof—have their inevitable attraction. I refer instead to the fascination that some of us feel for the artifacts of history with their cargo of mystery and the ineluctable. There are some objects, some mysteries, for which—to those of us who are already on the journey—no price is too great.

"This statue, Mister Donnelly, was old before Atlantis drowned. It has been the stuff of legends and the destroyer of empires. Thrones have been traded for it and thousands slaughtered. It is valued both for what it is—a thing of dreadful beauty carved from a stone not seen on this earth for millennia—and for what it represents: The shining path to the Other Kingdoms."

The bell to the apartment rang and Garland nodded to Cadiz who, moments later, was laying a newspaper-wrapped object on Kelly's kitchenette counter. Without waiting on Garland's permission, he whipped the wrappings away, letting them litter Kelly's floor, and revealing what was to my eyes a frankly not very impressive statuette of a squid-like but strangely regal monster squatting on a throne.

"Well, you tell a good story," I said to Garland, and nodded at the tarnished thing on the counter. "And this is it?"

"I rather fear that it is," Garland said, which seemed an odd response. He was on his feet faster than I'd have given him credit for and the nasty little hammer was out of wherever it hid and in his hand before he reached the object.

"No!" Kelly shouted, but there was no time. The thing was in fragments before she or Cadiz could do anything.

"Calm yourselves!" Garland shouted at both of them. "Look!"

Nobody seemed to be too bothered about me anymore so I stood up to take a look as well. Apparently, the statuette was important not for itself, but for what it contained. Within its shattered ruins, there was some kind of loamy earth. And within *that*, there were nine small objects. For one nauseating moment, I could have sworn they were wriggling in the stinking soil as if the decay-filled thing had bred worms within itself over the centuries. But, as Garland's eager hands swept the soil away from around them, I saw the objects were inanimate and stationary.

Figurines, I guess you'd call them. Small ornaments in jade which put me in mind of Albie's sad little fake, although these things had a milky translucency that made them seem ... I don't know ... *denser*, somehow.

"*Ni'ib shuggarath bah'im*," Garland said, in an awed whisper.

"*Ni'ib shuggarath bah'im*," Kelly and Cadiz repeated, in unsettling synchronicity, like congregants echoing a priest's invocation.

Sharing a glance of mutual understanding, their eyes glittering with the fervency of religious lunacy, each of them reached down and picked up one of the figurines and then, stepping away from the ruins of their octopus god as if by unspoken assent, they moved back into the room, each of them pinning their figure to their clothes; to a shirt, a robe, a blouse.

Brooches? I thought. Jesus Christ. This was all for ornamental jewelry?

"Sit down, Mister Donnelly," Garland said. "Please. This won't take long."

I sat—I didn't mistake that 'please' for anything other than the order it was—and he sat too. He resumed talking, making no reference to the odd little ritual he'd just shared with his colleagues, instead moving on to a new theme—I'll spare you the circumlocutions and euphemisms—which was essentially the unfortunate necessity of removing the inconvenient mister Steve Donnelly from the picture.

The ornament in his lapel shimmered a little, catching the light, and giving the strangest illusion of movement.

Garland continued to talk—was there ever a circumstance in which he didn't?—but I wasn't really hearing anything anymore. Because the movement I thought I'd seen revealed itself to be no illusion at all and I watched, appalled, as the small leg of the figure pinned to his lapel twitched spastically, as if in pain or shock. It wasn't shimmering. It was writhing.

Jesus Christ. This fat bastard had pinned to his chest, like some vile cross between a medal and a trophy, a living thing. Living at least until it could be released from its agony.

I'd had very little doubt that these were terrible people, but this seemed awful even for them.

Garland saw me staring at his wretched ornament, and must have read the horror on my face. His own face contorted in a small grimace, not apologetic, hardly even embarrassed, more a sort of facial shrug, like somebody caught doing something not discussed in polite society but entirely natural.

I looked quickly at Jerome and Kelly. Their figurines, too. Pinned, dying, twitching, wriggling.

"You think it a cruel affectation, Mister Donnelly?" the fat man asked.

I just looked at him.

"It's an optical illusion," Kelly said, her voice constrained and tight in a way that I didn't yet recognize as pain.

"Bullshit," I said. "Those things are—"

"That's not what she means," Cadiz said, and I heard something new in his voice too. Half terror, half wonder. I looked to Garland.

"While I never like to correct a lady," he said, "the illusion is not actually *optical*. Your eyes do not deceive you, Mister Donnelly. The movement you see is real and the agony, I confess, is alarming. Your mistake is in assuming which is the pinner, and which the pinned."

His head twitched involuntarily as he finished speaking and suddenly all three of them were jerking spasmodically, jaws loose and limbs twitching.

Something else was happening too. Their faces—no, not

just their faces but everywhere their skin was exposed—were becoming suffused with a hideous soft green pallor. An involuntary shudder from Garland rolled his robe's sleeve back from his forearm and I saw the veins pulsing against the skin, the deep green veins.

I looked from face to face and while, for the first few seconds, there was an atavistic horror etched in each of them, it was slowly, horribly, replaced by what can only be described as delight. Unearthly delight.

It was a matter of moments before the possessions, the transmutations, were complete.

And then it got far too personal as, one by one, those inhuman faces turned to find mine and they each stood, still twitching, and moved in my direction, Garland's caftan now rippling and pulsing as if it concealed beneath it a writhing array of soft new limbs.

They advanced on me with a shuffling step as if whatever they now were had yet to fully learn the intricacies of human anatomy. But, however contorted, the expressions on their faces were alarmingly readable. Cruel. Eager. Hungry.

There was a sudden rising sound from somewhere around us all. It sounded vaguely familiar as it surged to a climax. I assumed it was their doing until there was a brief second where what used to be Garland looked at what used to be Cadiz with a mutual incomprehension before a concussive roar similar to what had put paid to Albie's ambitions the night before turned out my lights.

♦ ♦ ♦ ♦

I don't know if there's an actual law about it, but being

pummeled into unconsciousness by one means or another three times in two days seemed to me to be pushing the limits of reasonableness if not legality.

But seeing the face of yesterday's barman looking down at me with benign concern was certainly preferable to the faces I'd been looking at before this last blackout.

He was holding a briefcase, which seemed a little incongruous, and was the only person in the room apart from me. There was no sign of the three impostors that used to be Garland, Cadiz, and Kelly, though I saw that the wreckage of the statuette was still on the counter, along with the remaining six figurines.

"Wha...," I managed.

"The Old Fellowes never see me coming," he said, just as if I'd asked an actual question, one that made sense. "Don't quite understand why. Perhaps because I'm a *very* old fellow." He paused, as if puzzled by something. "Though not as old as I used to be," he eventually said, more to himself than to me.

I'd have asked what the hell he was talking about except that I'd already decided to give myself a break from shit that makes my brain hurt for a couple of days at least. So I stuck to more practical matters.

"They're gone?" I said.

"Unfortunately, yes," he said. "They managed to fold themselves into a gap in the continuum before I could complete the harrowing."

Well, who could argue with *that* explanation? I elected to focus on the fact that they were gone. It helped me breathe.

"This can't have been easy for you," he said, which showed what a very perceptive fellow he was. "Why don't we fix you a drink?"

He crossed to Kelly's cocktail cabinet and took out the vodka bottle, though I noticed he held it to the light and turned it a couple of times as if he wanted to be sure that it was, you know, actually of this Earth. It seemed to pass the test and he proceeded to fill, quite generously, a crystal tumbler.

"Sorry," he said as he handed it to me. "The former Miss Woodman doesn't appear to have kept in stock the ingredients for a Pink Princess."

"You know, a barman is supposed to be a confidante," I said, as I threw the vodka down gratefully, "not someone who goes around giving away the name of someone's preferred poison."

"You don't like to name it?" he said. "Can't say I blame you. It sounds like—"

I raised a hand. "I've heard every possible riff on what it sounds like," I said and looked at him. "You *are* British, aren't you? You told our friend in the bar that you weren't."

"Come on," he said. "I work for the government. Can't trust a thing I say."

He moved to the kitchenette counter and opened the briefcase. I stood—I think the vodka had helped—and walked over to take a look at what he was doing. The briefcase had been customized, the inside fitted with a bank of specialized housings. Three rows of three. Nine in total. My friend—I really needed to remember to ask his name at some point—swept the remaining six figurines into their ready-made nests. I noticed that his movements were as quick as he could make them and that he almost unconsciously dry-wiped his fingers against each other once he was done.

"Sticky?" I said.

"No."

"Wet?"

"No."

"Dusty?"

"No."

"I can do this all day."

"Fair enough," he said. "Malevolent. They're malevolent. And persuasive."

I'd've asked if he was kidding but everything I'd seen in the last thirty-six hours made me fairly sure that he wasn't. "You came prepared, though," I said, nodding at the briefcase as he snapped it shut. "You knew what you were looking for."

He shrugged. "Playing a hunch," he said, which was obviously horseshit but, what the hell, I wasn't going to break his balls about the fine details. He'd saved my life.

"You saved my life," I said out loud, in case he'd failed to notice in all the excitement.

He wavered for a moment as if not sure exactly how to respond, and then smiled. "I know your granddaughter," he said.

What the hell? "Granddaughter?" I said. "I'm thirty-three years old."

"You won't always be," he said, and then looked to the window a second before a car-horn sounded from outside. "Our friends from Washington," he said. "Impatient already."

"F.B.I?"

"No."

"O.S.S?"

"No."

"D.A.R?"

"No."

"We work on this a little harder and I can get us six nights and a Sunday matinee at the Orpheum."

He actually looked like he might have been interested in discussing that idea further. But the car-horn sounded again. Twice.

He hoisted the briefcase from the table and gave me a wink, like it was all just a fun day at the office. I looked at the briefcase swinging from his insouciant hand, thought about the terrible things that were in it, and decided I needed to work a little harder on my brio.

"You're handing them over to them?" I asked.

"Somewhat reluctantly," he said. "They assure me they'll be safe." He didn't sound entirely convinced. "I'd like to take them back with me. Keep them out of the wrong hands. There's a war on, you know."

"Yeah," I said. "Last couple of days have given me that impression."

"No," he said. "I mean the other one. The one that makes the papers." He gave the case another shake. "And I hear Herr Hitler is rather fond of things like this."

I let him get to the apartment's front door and open it before I asked him.

"Jesus Christ," I said. "What *are* they?"

He gave me a look, like he couldn't believe how ready I was to be the Abbott to his Costello.

"Were you not paying attention?" he said. "The stuff that dreams are made of."

Z.O.A.

Time-Code Imprint: 08:32:01

The thing about county roads, even way out in the back of beyond, is you can always find a strip-mall, and the thing about strip-malls is you can always find a Radio Shack, and the thing about strip-mall Radio Shacks is that what you can always find *there* is shit that everybody else stopped selling at least a decade ago.

Like the cute little fossil into which I'm currently speaking. It's a Digital Dictaphone. Says so right there on the box, along with the boast "Completely Tape-Free!" as if that was still a big selling point in the second decade of the twenty-first century.

The Digital Dictaphone is a pretty good example of the kind of crap nobody wanted even before there was an app that made it obsolete, but I guess it gets the last laugh now: It runs on batteries and doesn't need an Internet server to function. It's still what it always was but, like the only blonde left at the bar when they call Last Orders, all of a sudden it ain't so ugly.

The other thing about strip-mall Radio Shacks, or at least

strip-mall Radio Shacks during the end of the world, is that the clerks have all either gone home, gone to Jesus, or gone to Hell. Nobody's minding the store. Nobody wants your money. You can help yourself to as many Digital Dictaphones as you want.

Oh, and—whether it's the end of the world or not the end of the world—the thing about strip-mall Radio Shacks in the *south* is you can pretty much count on there being a Guns 'n' Ammo Outlet right next door.

Time-Code Imprint: 08:34:54

Okay, I stopped and played that back to make sure it's working—I mean, you know, Radio Shack—but it seems to be fine.

I'm leaving this record of what happened not because I think anybody else will care, and not because I care what anybody else will think. I'm just leaving it for you, Jess.

I'm going to see you at least one more time before you get to hear this, but I can't be sure what condition I'll be in by then so—while I can still think clearly and talk straight, while I'm still *me*—I want you to know that I love you and that I spent this day coming to get you back.

I'm shutting this thing off again for a while. Gotta go steal a faster car.

Time-Code Imprint: 10:11:37

Here's what's happened before I hit the road and found the Radio Shack:

I woke up about four, four-and-a-half, hours ago and had no idea where I was.

Well, that's stupid. I knew where I *was*. I could see where I was. I was in some back alley somewhere. What I mean is I had no memory of why I was there or what had happened. That was a bad feeling.

And then the memories flooded in.

And that was so much fucking worse.

Because I remembered that you were gone, Jess. I remembered that they'd taken you and that I hadn't been able to stop them. I don't know if they'd been stalking us, targeting us specifically, or if we just won the worst place worst time lottery, but either way we didn't see them coming. *We.* Jesus Christ, what's wrong with me? You're fifteen years old. It's not your job to see anything coming. *I* didn't see them coming. Not until it was too late and I was on my back with a monster's teeth buried in my arm and you were being dragged into the shadows . . .

Yeah. Those were the morning headlines, Denny O'Brian edition.

My daughter was gone.

And I had less than twenty-four hours before I turned into a zombie.

So I figured it was probably best to skip breakfast.

Time-Code Imprint: 10:47:15

A lot of people who'd never seen a gun, let alone used one, had to get familiar with them real quick once this shit started going down.

And the thing is, people didn't just need to get used to shooting guns, they needed to get used to shooting them accurately. Zombies don't share the finer feelings of muggers, stalkers, or burglars. They don't have a fight or flight response. You're not going to scare them with a near miss or a warning shot and you're not going to stop them even if you blow a hole in their chest. With zombies, you have to pay a little attention. You have to shoot them in the head.

So, if you were one of those people who didn't previously know how to point a gun so that the bullet went where you wanted it to go, then you had to develop a certain degree of skill and had to develop it fast. The ones who didn't develop it fast were soon finding themselves getting shot in the head by the ones who did.

Now, as it happens, I'm not one of those people who needed to learn how to shoot straight but, ironically enough, putting the bullet exactly where you want it isn't going to be that big of an issue when it comes to today's little adventure.

Zombies, you have to shoot in the head. Humans are easier. You can shoot *them* anywhere the fuck you want.

Time-Code Imprint: 11:32:43

You're going to hear this, Jess. After whatever goes down goes down, I'm going to make sure somebody gets it to you.

Here's what I want you to know, what I hope you already know:

Your father loves you. Always has. Always will.

But you'll have to accept that by the time you hear this, I'm not going to be around anymore. There's going to be a thing shambling around tomorrow that's going to *look* like me. But it won't be me, Jess. I'll already be gone. So if it ever crosses your path and if—or, please God, *when*—somebody shoots it in the head, you are not going to be upset. You, Jessica Judith O'Brian, are going to be cool. Because you're my girl. You're gonna shrug at whoever's with you and say, "Dude, that last zombie kinda looked like my old man. Weird." And then you're going to raise your own gun and you're going to keep shooting.

So that's what you know.

Here's what *they* know, those lunatic survivalist mother-fuckers who took you from me:

One: They've captured themselves a beautiful piece of breed-ing stock. That's you, sweetheart, in case your new friends are trying to put a prettier face on the situation and not tell you how things really are.

Two: Nobody's going to do a goddam thing about it, because the last person left in the world who gave a shit about you was your dumb asshole of a father and . . .

Three: They left your dumb asshole of a father in the dust after they'd sucker-punched him in that alley and banged the dinner gong for a zombie the size of LeBron fucking James to come finish him off.

Yeah. That's what they know. Here's what they *don't* know:

One: LeBron might've gotten a pretty good chunk out of my left arm but, before I passed out, LeBron also got a railroad spike through his forehead.

Two: Tomorrow morning won't be the first time I'm going to wake up as a different person.

Honey, I probably should have mentioned this before, but your dad hasn't always been an insurance salesman.

You always knew me and your Mom only moved to the south a year or so before you were born, Jess—I mean, how could you not, with the accent and everything?—but I guess we never made it clear to you that the move was . . . how shall I put it? . . . gov-ernment assisted. And it wasn't your Mom—God rest her soul, six years now, can you believe it?—who was in need of relocation.

Look, there's a bunch of stuff I did back in my former life

that I'm not proud of, sweetheart, but at least it means that today isn't the first time I've had to track people down in order to take an unfinished conversation to the next level.

And with these guys, it's not like tracking them is going to be difficult.

First of all, they think I'm dead.

Second, they ain't fucking hiding. Not from me or anybody.

Time-Code Imprint: 16:11:32

So about two hours ago I'm in another abandoned convenience store, this one a KWIK-SHOP. Didn't even realize the franchise was state-wide, thought it was strictly local.

Remember it, Jess? The name, I mean. Remember how even *before* the world went to hell I used to find that name really depressing? A mash-up—no, not a mash-up, that would imply artistic intent—a lazy rip-off of two of its rivals, KWIK-PIK and STOP'N'SHOP. Which, Christ knows, were bad enough, but look: KWIK-PIK; Okay, it's stupid and cutesy and apparently proud of its inability to spell but at least it fucking rhymes. STOP'N'SHOP, the same.

But KWIK-SHOP. Jesus. Such a lack of effort. Like it's not even worth pretending to try. The franchise name equivalent of going out for lunch in your pajama bottoms and Crocs. So yeah, depressing enough then. But *now*. Now it looks like the kind of precursor we all should've been paying attention to. *Check it out*, it says in its gleeful brain-dead way. *We were zombies already.*

Anyway, I'm in there, I've already thrown some batteries in my pockets, and I'm chewing on some string cheese, trying to persuade my body to pretend it still gets hungry, when I hear the shotgun cock behind me.

I put both my hands out to the side slowly, fingers spread. "Can I turn around?" I say.

"It's *may* I," a voice says.

Female, and just free enough of spin that I really can't tell where she was coming from with that schoolmarm correction. Like, is she being funny or is it truly her first concern when she's got the drop on someone that they watch their fucking grammar?

"I'm sorry," I say. "May I turn around?"

"Long as it's slow and easy."

So I make sure it was and, once I'm facing her, I risk an apologetic smile.

"I really thought there was no-one here," I say. "If money's still any use to you, I've still got money." I've also still got my hands up, but I waggle a finger to point down at my pants pocket.

She's somewhere in her forties, running to fat, but she gives great deadpan and she's holding that shotgun like she and it are far from strangers.

"What else you got in that pocket?" she says.

"I'm not gonna lie to you," I say. "I have three handguns on me right now, two in back of my belt, one in a sock-holster. But that pocket, just a billfold, I promise."

She nods toward the front window, at the car I parked outside, but her eyes stay on me.

"Just handguns?" she says.

"No, Ma'am," I say. "Shotguns and semi-automatics in the trunk."

"Huh," she says. "Loaded for bear."

"Something like that," I say, and then, off her silence, "It's my daughter. She's in trouble."

She nods her head at me, still no expression. "You don't look so good yourself," she says.

Making no fast moves, I roll back my left sleeve and show her my arm, no point in pretending. The infection is radiating out eagerly from the wound now, got the run of the whole forearm and half the bicep. The bite itself, by this stage, doesn't look so bad. Which is, of course, very very bad. The necrosis is complete, ready for its mutation and its next life.

She's like, "How long?" and I tell her the truth, probably got fifteen, sixteen hours left.

She nods. "Come back here after those sixteen hours, and I won't waste time asking how you're doing," she says, and then she cocks the shotgun in case the sympathetic delicacy of her phrasing caused me to miss her point.

I nod, letting her know I understand. Can't hold it against her. It's just the way the world is now.

"So you say your daughter's in trouble," she says. "She bit too?"

"No," I say. "Taken."

"Taken?"

"Survivalists, I guess."

"Preppers, they been calling themselves the last few years," she says. "You know, from 'prepared'? Didn't want to be caught with their pants down at the end of the world. Always thought they were mental cases. Pisses me off that it turns out they were right. Wasn't quite the apocalypse they were expecting, of course, but I guess they'll settle."

"These particular guys had a whole Christian thing going on, too," I say, remembering their stupid flag and the painted sign on their truck. "Called themselves the Children of the New Jerusalem."

She doesn't actually bite her tongue—like anybody actually bites their tongue, ridiculous fucking expression—but I can tell from the tiny flicker of sympathy in her eyes that what she's stopping herself from saying is that it might have been better for you if you *had* been bitten.

"You know them," I say.

"Not socially," she says, and I still can't tell if what she's got is a nice line in very dry delivery or a simple case of tone-deaf and stupid.

"But you know where they are."

"I can point you in their direction," she says. "But I wouldn't advise you go there."

"They have my daughter."

"Uh-huh," she says, like that information's not new so why am I repeating it.

"You got any kids?" I say.

"Two boys," she says. "Both gone now."

And I'm like, "Zombies? Or with *them*?" I found a gentler way to say it, actually, but I can't remember what it was.

She shrugs, says, "What's the difference between a zombie and a Child of New Jerusalem?"

"Seriously?" I say. She's like telling a *joke* here? Man, she had that stay-detached thing down pat. We could've used this lady back in Brooklyn.

"One's a mindless shell that used to be a human being," she says, "And the other one's a zombie."

Not a good joke, but I give her a nod and a half-smile. She gives it a beat, and then half-lowers the shotgun.

"Help yourself to anything you need," she says, "and then be on your way."

Time-Code Imprint: 18:28:47

This'll be the last update before I see you, Jess. I'm inside the Compound right now, less than a half-mile from the main house.

Like I'd thought, Brother Zebulon—the KWIK-SHOP lady gave me his name—isn't much on hiding. Isn't much on fortification, either, though I guess he and his Children of the New Jerusalem figure that unless and until the zombies learn to use tools the razor wire and log-buttress perimeter fence is going to keep their party private.

Now I, of course, *do* know how to use tools, so the fence didn't bother me. It wasn't meant to bother me. What was meant to bother me, or any other inquisitive human, was the *Duck Dynasty* wannabes patrolling the inside of the perimeter. But the thing about armed guards—particularly the amateur type, and particularly the *God is on our side so He'll pick up the slack* type—is that, with a little patience, you'll eventually locate the jack-off ones.

I got here about a half-hour ago and it took me twenty minutes to find my jack-offs. There were two of them, and they'd paused in their patrol duties long enough to indulge in what must pass for sport for these sons of the Confederacy when it's Off Season for Deer.

Somehow, they'd lured a dozen or so zombies to the razor-wire and got them nicely tangled in it. And now they were taking their sweet time shooting chunks off them.

One of them, the one with a rifle, was lying on his belly like he'd seen real soldiers do in basic training in the movies, and the other was just sitting up by a tree, back against the trunk, and blasting away with a handgun.

"Hardly seems sporting, fellas," I said.

Yeah, I'd got close enough to them to talk at a conversational level without them hearing or sensing me beforehand. This did not say good things about their life expectancy in this changed world.

For one of them, the handgun one, bluster, as usual, was the way out of embarrassed surprise. He's all, "What the hell's it to *you*?" pretending he hadn't half-jumped out his skin at the sound of my voice.

The other one hadn't flinched, hadn't jumped, and doesn't crack wise. He just looks at me. More significantly, he looks past and around me, taking measure, making sure. Okay, I think, him I might have to keep an eye on.

"It's nothing to me," I say in answer to Handgun's question. "Nothing at all."

"What do you want?" says the other one. Smarter. Focused.

"I want you to tell me how to get into the main house," I say.

"You think there's some kinda *password*?" says Handgun. "Like what?"

"I wouldn't know," I say, giving him a shrug like I've no idea but I'm willing to take a shot at it. "*Praise the Lord and Pass the Ammunition*? Or some other stupid shit that mashes up Jesus and guns?"

"Is he trying to insult us, Garrett?" says Handgun. "You think he's trying to insult us?"

Garrett doesn't say anything. Keeps his eye on me, still not sure where this is going.

Handgun's on a roll, though. "I think he's goddam insulting us," he says, and then, directly to me, "You looking to get killed, brother?"

"Already dead, brother," I say, and hold my left forearm

forward to let him and Garrett see the splendors of its blue and transmutating flesh.

"Holy shit!" Handgun shouts, "He's one of them!"

He starts to raise his gun. Garrett's quicker, of course, but neither of them are fast enough. The two from the back of my belt are already head-height, one pointed straight at each of them.

Hashtag, Never Got Rusty.

"Whoa," I say, off their stunned expressions. "It's like *magic*, isn't it?" Bragging is unseemly, Jess, and you should try not to develop the habit. But sometimes—especially when dealing with douchebags—you just have to rub it in.

I look at Handgun. "I'm not one of them," I say. "Not yet. Don't you even know how this shit *works*?"

"I know it's the Lord's judgment on a sinful world," he says.

"Yeah?" I say. "That what Zebulon tells you?"

"*Brother* Zebulon," says Garrett, and the sour tone of his correction makes me kind of sad because I realize Garrett is a True Believer too and I'd been hoping he was a little smarter than that. A smart soldier knows when to stand down. A True Believer will die for his leader. I can't take the risk of that happening when his willingness to die might matter so I cut to the chase and shoot him. One. Two. Head. Heart.

It was quick and he didn't suffer, and Handgun sees that that's all I got in the way of mercy. "Christ almighty!" he shouts, and drops his gun without even being asked.

"Let me ask you something," I say. "You think the Lord protects His own?"

He doesn't want to answer, thinks it's a trick question, but eventually gives a guarded and frightened nod.

"Let's find out," I say. "Go cut the fence."

"*There?*" he says, pointing to the zombies he's recently been having fun with and looking at me like I'm fucking crazy.

"There," I say.

"You want me to let them in?"

"I want you to let them in."

"What am I supposed to do then?" he says.

"You're supposed to run, asshole," I say. "You're supposed to run."

♦ ♦ ♦ ♦

Thing is, *he* runs—like he needed telling twice—but I don't. I stand there, letting those things shuffle up toward me and hoping to Christ that I've figured this right.

My smell confuses them. I'm getting pale enough that I sort of look like them, but I don't *smell* like them. Not quite. Not yet. Fortunately for me, I don't smell like food anymore either.

One of them growls at me and shakes its head aggressively, but it's nothing. An animal thing. Territorial. Alpha-male jostling.

Other than that, it's pretty clear pretty quickly that they'd be prepared to leave me alone.

But that's not what I want.

Time-Code Imprint: 04:22:17

The thing about Witness Protection is, before they give you the new Drivers' License, Social Security, and everything, before they drive you to your new house in your new state and tell you your new name, you do have to go through the embarrassment of actually sitting in court and presenting the testimony for which they're giving you that shiny new identity.

Which means all the defense attorneys of all your former colleagues get to call you all kinds of names.

One of them, for example, in an attempt to persuade a jury that they should perhaps take everything I had to say with a pinch of salt, pointed out that I was "a merciless killing machine, with no feelings, no remorse, and no humanity," which was not only way melodramatic but a bit fucking rich given the murderous scumbag of a client he was representing. But the point is this: Couple of short hours from now, I'm finally going to be what that little drama queen said I was.

So if I believed in karma, or poetic justice, or anything, I'd be able to draw a moral lesson here for us. But I'm not going to do that. I'm just going to give tomorrow's me a name. Like The Wrath of God. Or He Who Lays Waste.

Or Harry.

I've always liked the name Harry. Well out of fashion now, of course. But I have a feeling Harry's not gonna give two shits about fashion. Gonna be too fucking busy Laying Waste, isn't he?

♦ ♦ ♦ ♦

I'd wondered if I'd catch Brother Zebulon mid-sermon or something, but by the time I walk right into the Great Room of the main house, he and all his Dukes and Duchesses of Hazzard are just hanging around drinking cold ones, like it was any other redneck jamboree.

Couple of his boys, drunk or not, have their guns up fast, so I'll have to give them that. Zebulon himself, though, waves them down, like he's actually kind of interested that I've managed to show up.

"Do I have some sentries to chastise?" he asks me, in a slow and frankly over-stylized drawl, but at least it jumps us past all that *how'd you get in here* shit.

"They're in no position to notice," I say.

"Then, sir, you have not only my gratitude for thinning my flock of those clearly unworthy to be in it—"

"Amen!" comes a knee-jerk interruption from some Gomer Pyle dickhead, which Brother Z doesn't even acknowledge.

"—but also my admiration for the courage it must have taken for you to come here on your own."

"Oh, I wasn't on my own," I say.

I whip out the guns, take out the two or three who look like they could do anything about it and then take a moment to watch and enjoy.

Because that's when the doors and windows give way and Harry's future tribe-members join the party and all those Jeds, Jethros, and Ellie fucking Maes realize their God has abandoned them.

Hashtag, Worst Posse Ever.

◆ ◆ ◆ ◆

Here's what happened, Jess. When I found you in that back room and realized you were alive and that I was going to get you out of there, I felt the last good feeling of my life, an overwhelming rush of love, the thing I'm going to choose to remember when I close my eyes for the last time a few moments from now.

You're not with me now, of course. I left you with the people inside the safety zone the KWIK-SHOP lady told me about. They seem like decent people. So decent they were prepared to let me stay, too. Provided I let them chain me up so that I could die in peace among my own kind and they'd have a sharpshooter ready to end it once I woke up. But I said no. Partly because I don't want you seeing any of those last moments.

And partly because I owe Harry. The imminence of his arrival is what allowed me to walk among his kind and save you. So I'm choosing to wake up somewhere back where Harry can have whatever passes for a life.

There's a third reason, too. But I'll get to that in a moment . . .

♦ ♦ ♦

I'm pretty much done now, Sweetheart. Next time I close my eyes, it'll be the last time. So I'm going to say goodbye and tell you again that I love you and that that's all I want you to remember. Then I'm going to turn this thing off and hide it somewhere to keep it safe until someone finds it and gets it to you.

Then I'm going to take a moment, not a long one, to remind myself that my last day on Earth wasn't entirely a bad one, that the parts that *were* bad—you getting taken, me getting bitten—weren't my fault, and that I managed to put right what I could.

Then I'm going to settle back down and not fight it anymore. My limbs are going to numb up, my tongue's going to stop working, I'm going to lose consciousness, and I'm going to die.

I'm so glad you're not here to see it.

I'm so glad Brother Zebulon is.

You've probably been noticing those annoying noises in the background, right? Scrabbling feet? Whimpering? You weren't the only one I brought out of the Zombie Jamboree with me, Jess.

Brother Zebulon is here in the barn with me, just the two of us. He's tied up pretty good, and probably more than a little scared right now. It has, after all, become clear to him in the last few hours that your dad's got quite a fucking temper on him. But he shouldn't feel too bad. I'm not going to lay a finger on him.

I'm just going to lie down here and die.

And then Harry's going to wake up.

And then Harry and Brother Zebulon are going to investigate the possibilities of breakfast.

ALL OUR HEARTS
ARE GHOSTS

Los Angeles, 1934

First time Henry Burgess saw Addison Steele, the guy was getting himself shot.

Henry, first day on the job and excited to be sent from the production office on Melrose out to the Placerita Canyon studio ranch, parked his Austin Roadster—tiny amongst the big Plymouths and Fleetwoods favored by the cast and crew—and made his way across to where everybody was working hard on bringing *Outlaws of Calico Creek* to life.

People and equipment were gathered in front of one of the ranch's standing sets: a segment of an old west's main street; a general store, a corral, and a one-storey chapel. Henry walked toward them, glancing beyond the fragment of a town to where the canyon stretched plain and clear between its low hills and offered a view in the far distance of the Sierra Nevada, still snow-topped in late April.

"Quiet on set!" a voice yelled, and Henry froze in place like everyone else not actively involved in the shot. From a few yards behind the director's chair he watched as, up on the chapel roof and on the shout of *action*, an older man—lean, wiry, wearing a black coat and black hat—jerked his hand to his chest and staggered like he'd just taken a bullet between the ribs. Henry turned to see who'd shot him and felt like a rube when he saw that the actor playing the good guy, knowing he was out of frame, was simply standing and watching like everybody else.

The older man's body went limp and he fell from the roof, playing dead all the way down until hitting the bunched mattresses piled below the camera line.

At a nod from the director, an assistant yelled, "Cut! Moving on," and Henry waited for applause from the crew for the stunt but none came; they were all already busy shifting the camera and the other equipment across to where the next set-up was to be.

Henry moved after them in the direction of a scrub-covered hill with a narrow cave mouth at its base, waving the batch of revised script pages at the assistant director to get his attention.

The AD hung back to let Henry catch up. "Who are you?" he said, glancing at the pages but not taking them—Henry wondering if he was used to dodging process servers or something—and turned to wave the camera crew on.

"Henry Burgess," Henry said. "From the production office. New revisions." He fluttered the pages again. "From the writers."

"Oh, yeah," the AD said, and then turned again to shout across to the crew. "Grant! Get the damn horse inside!"

Outside the cave mouth, a wrangler, presumably Grant—a big guy in his early thirties, ruddy-faced, with scowl-lines permanently etched in his brow—was standing tugging at the reins of a roan horse which was refusing to be led into the narrow darkness of the cave.

Even Henry—no farm-boy, Boston born and bred, and fresh out of Princeton—could see that the horse was afraid. Could see too that Grant wasn't helping; taking a tighter grip on the reins, jerking them, trying to get the horse's head down as if he could simply drag its thousand pounds inside.

"God damn it," Grant shouted. "Get in there!" He reached out his other hand and swished a tight leather riding crop hard against the roan's flank. The horse reared and he cut at it again.

"While there's still daylight, Grant!" the AD shouted.

The older man Henry had watched make the fall from the chapel roof walked out and around the crew to stand in front of the horse. "Mind if I try?" he said to Grant, holding his hand out for the crop.

Grant gave it to him, and the man held it low and loose at his side, Henry wondering if he was letting the horse see it was no longer any immediate threat. "Let go the reins," the man said to Grant, though his eyes stayed on the horse.

"Don't be crazy, Addison," Grant said.

"Let go the reins," the man, Addison, repeated, with only a shade more emphasis.

As Grant dropped the reins, the horse shivered and flexed as if ready to buck again. Grant stepped back sharply but Addison moved closer to the roan and breathed out through his nose into its flaring nostrils, murmuring softly and reaching a confident hand to stroke the animal's brow. A few seconds later, he'd walked the calmed horse into the cave and come back out to rejoin Grant.

The wrangler nodded a slightly resentful acknowledgement. "Shoot," he said. "You didn't even need the crop." He held out his hand for its return.

"Sure I did," said Addison, and slashed it across the younger man's face—once, twice, left, right—before dropping it to the ground. "But I'm all done with it now."

Henry was as silent and still as everyone else as Grant stepped forward, the welts already forming on each of his cheeks. Addison stood perfectly still, letting the man come ahead if he was going to.

But he wasn't, Henry found himself realizing, and wondered why—the wrangler had fifty pounds on Addison and was half his age. The director stood up from his chair and shouted, "Save it for wrap, both of you. We've got work to do."

"I'll let it go, old man," Grant said to Addison. "You're lucky we're on a tight schedule."

"Right," said Addison. "That's why." He turned to look at the director, gave him a wink, and walked away, Henry turning his head to watch him go until the AD's voice brought him back to business.

"Pages?" the guy said, with a show of impatience, like he hadn't been just as fascinated as Henry. Henry placed the revisions in his outstretched hand and asked if he could stay to watch a couple more shots.

"Don't you have phones to answer back at the office?" the AD said, and Henry wished he had a riding crop.

◆ ◆ ◆ ◆

Second time Henry saw him, he was getting quietly and elegantly drunk.

The residential hotel on the eastern reaches of Wilshire was hardly the Waldorf Astoria but Henry liked it enough. He'd been there four days now, the cute redhead in the production office having found it for him after he'd spent a few minutes whining to her about how the apartment he'd been promised—hell, put down a deposit on—had fallen through. She'd said that several members of the company were rooming there. "Including you?" he'd asked—you know, taking a shot—but she'd wiggled her engagement ring at him with a seasoned efficiency and he'd retired gracefully.

The hotel's bar looked like it had never heard of the Volstead act nor its repeal, like it had been quietly open for business all through prohibition, though Henry assumed that that couldn't actually be true. He hadn't given it his custom yet but on this fourth night decided to treat himself to a beer. He'd got his first week's wages earlier that morning and had had a long day.

Addison Steele was standing there, in the same black outfit he'd worn on set, one booted foot on the bar's brass rail. There was a shot glass full of whiskey in front of him, and two empty beside it.

"I'd like to pay for that, if you'd let me," Henry said, walking up to stand beside the older man and gesturing at his glass.

Addison gave him a look. "Man's a fool to refuse a free drink," he said. "But a bigger one if he doesn't ask the reason."

"I liked the way you looked out for that horse," Henry said, and saw a slow recognition come into Addison's eyes.

"Right," he said. "You were over to the Canyon Monday last."

"Henry Burgess," Henry said, putting out his hand. "From the production office."

"Henry," Addison said, after he'd shaken his hand. Not addressing Henry, simply weighing the word in his mouth and finding it not entirely to his taste. "Anybody ever call you Hank?"

Henry told him that no, nobody ever had, and Addison nodded like that was perfectly understandable. "I'd like to call you Hank," he said. "Unless you have any objection to that?"

"No," Henry said, amused, kind of pleased, but keeping it to himself. "None that I can think of."

"Well, alright," Addison said, and raised the shot glass in Henry's direction before throwing the whiskey down in one and flicking an upraised finger at the bartender to bring him another.

"My friend Hank will be paying for that one," Addison said to the bartender, "but I don't want him held accountable for the several more with which I intend to chase it."

The bartender nodded, and Henry waited till he'd walked away. "Talking about names..." he said, letting it hang.

"Yeah?"

"Addison Steele?"

"What about it?"

"It's a stage name, right?"

"A *stage* name?" Addison said, like the very idea of such a thing was bizarre. "No, Hank. It's not a stage name. I've worn it close to forty years now."

"So you weren't born with it?" *Born* with it? Henry being polite. If the guy'd worn it for forty years, he must've been twenty-five when he first tried it on.

Addison cocked his head. "Full of questions, aren't you, Hank?" he said.

"I don't mean any offense."

"None taken, son." Addison took a sip of his next shot, staring at the mirror behind the bar. Staring *through* it, Henry thought, to somewhere very far away in time. He'd just about given up on getting an answer when Addison turned back to him.

"It was given to me by a friend," he said. "At a time when I had sufficient reason to let go of the one my people had christened me with."

"Oh," Henry said, wondering what *that* story was but not ready to ask. "Because it's a ... well, not a *pun*, exactly ... a play on words, I guess." Desperately avoiding the word joke. "A literary *jeu d'esprit*." Jesus Christ.

"A *jeu d'esprit*, huh?" Addison said, a little glint in his eye. Amused by the words but pronouncing them perfectly.

"It's the names of two eighteenth century writers. Addison and Steele. Editors of *The Tatler*. And *The Spectator*."

"Is that right?"

"It is."

"Huh," Addison said, and was silent for a moment, looking through Henry like he'd looked through the mirror. "Well, the friend in question was an educated lady," he finally said. "And her sense of humor always favored the sly."

"It's a good name," Henry said. "Must read well on the posters."

Addison smiled, kind of. "I don't get my name on movie posters, son. I'm just another bad guy in black. Someone for the hero to pick off. I get shot for a goddam living, Hank. Been doing it a long time. Been shot by Bill Hart and Bronco Anderson, been doing it since before the movies learned to talk."

Henry was eager to ask him about his life before Hollywood started paying him to die, because he could smell real western history on the man, but Addison—perhaps mindful of his manners, perhaps for reasons of his own—turned the conversation to Henry's own story and how a kid with a degree from a fancy school back east could think it a good idea to come out and work as a glorified errand boy for the hacks at a B-movie factory, a move Addison plainly, albeit politely indirect about it, thought of as a symptom of a sadly undiagnosed mental illness.

They continued to talk, and Addison continued to drink—the impressiveness of his intake matched only by the impressiveness of how little it seemed to affect him—and Henry thought he'd heard the last of the man's secret history until they were almost done for the night.

"Know what she said to me once?" Addison suddenly said, out of nowhere, out of a conversation about gunfights and wasted bullets—*you do it right, it only takes one*, he'd thrilled Henry by saying—and the other ways in which the movies got it wrong.

"Your friend, you mean? The educated lady?"

Addison nodded, and Henry asked him what it was she'd said.

"She said, 'All our hearts are ghosts'."

Way he said it, it sounded like a quote from something, Henry thought. Thought too that it sounded like the saddest thing in the world, but he was, after all, a little drunk himself. "What does it mean?" he said.

Addison paused before replying, covering it by throwing down his last shot. "Damned if I know, Hank," he said, slamming his emptied glass down onto the bar like an unseen director had told him it was a good way to end the scene.

Henry was damned if he knew either, but he watched Addison stare again into the bar's mirror after he said it and figured it for the first lie his new friend had told him.

◆ ◆ ◆

Third time he saw him, he drove him upstate to kill the richest man in Houghton County.

Henry'd been taking sandwich orders in the office when he was urgently re-assigned. It was the last day of the *Outlaws of Calico Creek* shoot and Addison Steele had ruined everybody's morning by not showing up for work at the ranch location. Henry was told to drive back to their hotel and get him out to Placerita as fast as he could.

There was no answer to Henry's repeated knocking on Addison's door but—a phone call from an enraged studio executive overcoming any scruples the hotel management felt about letting anyone short of a cop into the room—a bellman eventually unlocked it for Henry.

The room wasn't empty, but clearly deserted. The belongings were few, but were all tied in neat and ready-to-be-disposed-of bundles in a way that suggested Addison had no intention of ever returning for them.

On a circular occasional table, two items had been bound together with a thin red ribbon and stood beside a newspaper clipping and the envelope it had been mailed in, the envelope bearing the previous day's postmark. The clipping itself was from a Lake Tahoe daily and was an obituary notice for a woman, a Mrs. Lester Cutter, who had died in Northern California's Houghton County the previous week at the age of sixty-three. Survived by her husband, it said, the founder of Cutter township and three times its Mayor.

Untying the bundle beside the clipping, Henry looked at the two things Addison had thought worthy of a red ribbon rather than the twine with which he'd bound everything else he'd left behind. The first was an old photograph—so old that it was not on paper but on tin, its silvered image seeming so fragile that Henry feared his fingers could wipe it clean—and was a formally posed portrait of a beautiful young woman. Hardly more than a girl when the picture was made, Henry saw but knew—if only from the fierce and eager intelligence glowing from her dark eyes—that he was looking at an educated lady.

The other item was a book—published, Henry saw from the title page, back in 1894 and by an author with the unlikely name of Lafcadio Hearn. It was called *Shadows in Running Water; tales and verse from the Japanese*, and there was an inscription on its fly-page in a beautifully neat copperplate. *To my dear friend Addison Steele*, it read, *who knew me well when both our hearts were alive. In affectionate remembrance, Marianne Cutter (nee Ryan).*

A worn leather bookmark protruded from the text-block and, at a gentle touch from Henry's hand, the book fell naturally open there, as if the bookmarked page had been looked at many times over the years. There were four three-line verses on the page and the last line of the third *haiku*, underlined long ago in pencil, read; *all our hearts are ghosts.*

◆ ◆ ◆ ◆

"Let me spare you the suspense, Hank," Addison said, when Henry's roadster pulled up at the bench outside the Pasadena train station. "You are not going to succeed in your mission."

"You're not going to come back?"

"The prospect seems unlikely."

"I gathered that when I saw your room. Even though you left everything behind."

"Not everything," Addison said, and Henry knew at once what he meant, though Addison's coat was roomy enough to conceal whatever he might have been wearing at his waist.

"At least let me give you a ride," Henry said. "Train to Tahoe stops every damn half hour. And you'll still be twenty miles from Cutter when you get off."

Addison looked almost impressed. "Well, Hank," he said. "You've been busy with your research. And quick, too. You know, once you've got this picture business crap out your system, you should head up to San Francisco; I believe Pinkerton's still hiring."

Henry didn't say anything, just leant across to spring the passenger door. Addison didn't say anything either, just got in, and Henry let him stay silent for almost the first hour of the long drive, before opening with what he figured was his best way in.

"The book and the picture," he said. "Everything else, sure. But I don't get leaving them behind."

"I didn't want them buried with me," Addison said, and let that sink in for a minute. Then, in a gentler voice, "Besides, I figured it'd be you that found them."

Henry felt a rush of sentiment, but didn't surrender to it. "They're in the trunk," he said.

"Well, you look after them then."

"I'm hoping I won't need to," Henry said. "I don't know how this story's going to end."

"Oh, you know how it's going to end, Hank," Addison said.

"I do?"

Addison looked at him like he was stupid. "I thought you liked those western pictures," he said.

"Sure, but—"

"Then you know they all end the same way. Two guys pull down on each other and one of them dies."

"*One* of them dies," Henry said.

"That's something else the movies get wrong," Addison said. "Real life, both those idiots usually wound up dead. Unless one of them got real fucking lucky."

Henry waited another half-mile or so before saying, "Okay,

enough about the ending. I want to know the beginning."

Addison looked out to the side of the road for a moment or two, to where the Southern California topography was slowly giving way to the harsher and less forgiving look of the north, and then back to Henry.

"Price of the ride?"

"Price of the ride."

So Henry heard a story from the tail-end of the boomtown days, from when tiny communities would grow a hundredfold in three years when the gold was leaping out of the hills and dwindle back to nothing in two when the seams were exhausted. But truth was this particular story could have happened almost anywhere because it was a story about people, about a young girl and her dreams and the young hothead who loved her for them and how she was lost to him and became another man's wife.

"Rich guy from the big city?" Henry said, thinking he knew how this part went. "Turned her head with fancy jewelry and fine manners?"

"Big city? Fine manners?" Addison said and Henry, ashamed, heard the older man struggle to keep the contempt out of his voice. "Jesus Christ, Hank, maybe you *are* dumb enough to be in the goddam movie business. I believe he may have been born back east, yes, but Lester Cutter had killed three men before he was twenty-one. And enjoyed it. Poor as dirt, mean as they come, and fast enough to back it up."

"So why did she—"

"She didn't," Addison said, and his voice got very flat and very cold and he told it quickly lest the scars of the ancient wounds start bleeding anew. "He raped her. Got her pregnant.

And I'd've killed him the day I found out if her people hadn't forced a wedding the previous night."

"My God, Addison," Henry said, not knowing what else to say.

"God wasn't paying much attention," Addison said. "I've found that to be the case more often than not."

Henry gave him a moment. "And the child?" he finally asked.

"Lost almost at full term, along with the chance of others," Addison said. "But I was long gone by then. It was my last promise to her, that I'd pay no visit to her husband while she was still alive."

"And now, what, you're just going to *kill* him? Just find him and kill him?"

"We've been over this, Hank. I'm not going to *bushwhack* the guy. I'm doing her memory the courtesy of facing him down properly."

"You're going to knock on his damn door or something?"

"No need," Addison said. "He knows I'm coming."

"He *knows*? That's ridiculous. How does he *know*? Some old gunfighter instinct?"

Addison just looked at him, letting him start to believe that that was in fact exactly right, before giving a little snort of amusement. "The modern world has its conveniences," he said. "I called him up on the telephone. Made a date."

"Christ almighty. And he *agreed*?"

"Of course he did, Hank," Addison said. "Lester always appreciated the opportunity to kill someone. And it don't matter how much money he's made, how sleek he's got. Guys don't change. Not guys like me and him."

Henry had nothing to say, just shook his head and stared out at the road ahead. Who the hell *were* these people, he thought.

He knew the wild ones were still out there, of course. Papers were full of them. Pretty Boy Floyd, Baby Face Nelson. Dillinger. And it was they, Henry thought, with a stab of something lost, who were the true heirs to the men of the old west, not the shiny-suited heroes of the silver screen with their guitars and good manners. They were just pretty lies made for boys like him. He had a wild animal in his car, he realized. A wild animal, no matter its charm and elegance. He really didn't have much to say for the rest of the drive.

◆ ◆ ◆ ◆

They could as well have been back on the *Outlaws of Calico Creek* set, Henry thought. They were more than a mile from the modern township with its stoplights and paved streets and Woolworths and, yes, movie theater. This was the slowly decaying old town, long abandoned, a ruined thing left to rot out of sight of all those people with their eyes on the glittering American future and no mind for its past. Chroniclers of his country's recent history had already coined a phrase for places like this, Henry knew; *Ghost towns*, they called them. And, standing here, he knew that they'd named them well.

Lester Cutter, though, was fully alive. Unlike Addison, he'd grown fatter with the years and the fedora hat he wore, unlike Addison's, paid no homage to the days of their youth. But his eyes were feral and excited and Henry was instinctively afraid of him on sight.

"This is Hank Burgess," Addison said, before Cutter could ask. "He's got no dog in this fight and I trust you'll respect that. He's just here to take me home. You know, one way or another."

Cutter's half nod was unpleasantly amused. "Appreciate your

thoughtfulness, Addison," he said. "I'd hate to have to call out the fire station boys to clean up my mess."

Henry wondered if there'd be some kind of formal countdown, some kind of etiquette and stated rules of engagement, but they both slipped into it like old boxers back in the ring, old gladiators back in the arena, pausing instinctively about fifteen feet from each other on the dry neglected dirt that used to be a Main Street. There was no right or wrong left in their scenario, Henry realized. No good or evil, no black hats or white hats, nothing but mutual appetite and excitement. They both waited a second or two, their atavistic clocks perfectly synchronized. Savoring it, Henry realized. Jesus Christ. *Savoring* it.

And then—without a word, without a gesture—it happened.

Cutter was fast, just as fast as Addison had said, fast on the draw and fast to fire, and his eye was as good as if the years between had never happened. Three bullets had slammed into his opponent before Addison's Colt had even cleared the holster. All in the chest. At least one in the heart.

Henry's own heart lurched in despair as if he, not Addison, had been the target. No, not despair. A terrible sadness, perhaps, but not despair. Because Henry knew something that Cutter didn't; Addison Steele got shot for a goddam living.

Addison didn't fall, didn't falter, taking Cutter's bullets like they were no more real than the many he'd mimed taking in the movies. His gun was in his hand, his arm was up and straight, and his aim was cold and true.

The man in the black suit may have already been dead, already been as much of a ghost as the town he'd come back to, but this ghost had its finger on the trigger of its colt and enough will—or its memory—to squeeze it.

You do it right, it only takes one, he'd said to Henry. And, one last time, Addison Steele did it right.

The entrance wound was nothing, Henry saw, through eyes already wet with tears—a small, elegantly centered hole in Cutter's forehead—but the exit tore half the fucker's skull off and Henry watched Addison's old enemy hit the dirt before he did. Whether Addison's eyes saw it or not, though, was something Henry was never able to say.

POSTCARDS FROM ABROAD

The house was nothing special, just another Liverpool semi-detached, one of those blink-and-there'll-be-ten-more-of-the-fuckers types of places. If *you* don't have a Granny who lives in one, you've got a mate who does, know what I mean?

There were a lot of them strung along the half-mile drag of Woolton Road as it fled Wavertree for pastures snootier, most of them dating from the dull and deco-free end of the nineteen-thirties. This one hadn't even kept the stained glass fanlights that were one of the few things that gave them any character at all, but at least it didn't have a name—you know, *Dunroamin* or something equally witty—so there was that.

I rang the bell and waited and, eventually, the front door swung open. The look that the little old lady in the hall gave me once she'd blinked away the glare of the sunlight was neither suspicious nor welcoming, just mildly surprised as if she thought her life had long ago run out of visitors.

"Mornin', luv," I said. "I'm from the Council." Which is lower middle class for *Open Sesame*.

"Oh," she said, as if already worried she'd done something wrong. "You'd better come in."

She stepped back, ushering me past her into the hall. It was narrow, of course, and made narrower halfway down its length by the stairs that led up to the bedrooms. I stopped before reaching any of the doors to the downstairs rooms and turned back to her, figuring I needed to do me bit for civic responsibility. "You know," I said. "You really should ask to see some identification before you let someone in your house."

"Why?" she said. "Are you a murderer?" Very deadpan. Not even a twinkle in the eyes. I liked her.

"No," I said. "I'm not a murderer."

"And you've not come to read the meter, have you?"

"I've not, luv. No."

"Then you must have come about the Banshee," she said. "Kettle's boiling. Go and sit down."

♦ ♦ ♦ ♦

I hadn't reckoned to be out in the field when the day'd started. Morning had found me down by the Pier Head getting slapped around by a nasty wind off the Mersey as I made my way to the Liver Buildings.

Like a lot of government jobs these days, mine didn't really *need* me to show up at the office—even the paperwork can be done via telecommute and, given the nature of the department, anything that didn't draw attention to our existence was considered a score—but I'd been told to come in for a face-to-face with a visiting Higher Grade up from London.

We're on the seventh floor of the Liver Buildings and, while there's no specific *rule* about not using the big flashy main entrance that fronts the river, the standing policy is keep your fucking heads down whenever possible and so we're encouraged to enter through one of the various smaller side entrances, all of which have the benefit of relative anonymity. I like the one opposite the India Buildings because there's a lift right the other side of it that doesn't get as stop and starty as those in the main bank in the front lobby.

If it's still start-of-the-working-day sort of time, the lift can be packed with a bunch of the Internal Revenue birds from the fourth floor but it was already gone half nine when I got in it so my only fellow passenger was Toni from our mob, on her way back up from Records in the basement. She'd fetched a folder that must've been down there since before Victoria died—yellowed, damp-stained, all-but-cobwebbed—and was holding it face in as per policy. Surprising how a glimpse of file-names like *Necromancy/Mossley Hill/1897* can start rumors among the civilians.

Toni, who I'm not sure was even twenty yet, wore her hair like Barbara Stanwyck in *Ball of Fire* and dressed like it had never stopped being 1942. In Manhattan. But have a conversation with her and there's no mistaking where she's from. I'd once made the mistake of asking if her name was short for Antoinette.

"Antoinette?" she'd said. "What are you, fucking stupid? Me mum likes Toni Braxton." Winsome and delicate, these Liverpool girls. It's why we love 'em.

"Mornin', Tone," I said now.

She tutted at me. "Could've worn a tie," she said. "Top Brass coming in special to see you. What're you like?"

"I don't think I own a tie," I said. "Tell you what; give his mobile a jingle. Ask him to pick me one up on his way in."

"He's already here," Toni said, and I resented the hushed and impressed tone in her voice. I'd met James Arcadia before and I was a lot less fond of him than he was.

♦ ♦ ♦ ♦

The parlour—that's what the old lady called the front room, like me Nan used to—was clean and tidy but it had a bit of a musty smell like it had kept its windows closed on the world a little too long.

Her mantelpiece ornaments—probably only Woolworth's to begin with but chosen with taste and now improved with the accidental gravitas of age—sat below a big oval mirror in a genuinely impressive gilded frame. Between the ornaments and the mirror, tacked across the wall in a ribboning sprawl, were dozens of postcards.

"Our Carol," she said, when she saw me looking at them. "She's in the diplomatic service. All over the world, she's been."

"Very nice," I said. "She ever anywhere long enough for her Mum to visit?"

"Ooh, yes, luv," she said, and I could hear the pride and wonder in her voice at what her daughter's life had allowed for her—world travel hadn't been for the likes of her when she herself was young. "I've been to America, you know. And Sardinia. Very nice. Most recently the Caribbean. That was probably me last trip though. Can't take those long flights anymore, I were running a fever all the way back on this last one. Ooh, and Berlin. Had a lovely time there, I did. Almost forgave 'em for the Blitz. I don't know if—"

"I don't mean to cut you off," I said. "But you know what it's like—they've got me on a clock back at the office. Can we get back to this Banshee you mentioned?"

"Well, I thought you'd know all about them," she said. "You're here to take care of it, aren't you?"

"Well, possibly, luv, possibly," I said. "Look, I'll be honest with you." I lowered my voice a bit like I was letting her in on government secrets. "We *have* had a few ... well, I don't want to say complaints ... let's say expressions of concern. From the neighbors. About the noises. But I don't think anybody said *Banshee*, specifically."

"Well, perhaps they're not as well read as me," she said. "To be honest, I'm not sure some of them *can* read. That Mrs. Bennett in number forty-seven, she—"

"Again," I said, as gently as I could. "If we could stay on—"

"Isn't it Banshees that howl?"

"Aye, I think so."

"Well, *something's* howling," she said, as if that was that. "So what do you do?"

"Eh?"

"With a Banshee. What do you do? What's the procedure?"

She didn't come over as pushy, just interested. And she seemed much more alive than when she had opened the front door. Like most civilians, she found this shit fascinating as long as it stayed on the other side of scary.

"Well," I said. "It'd be your garden that'd be the issue. If it was a Banshee, I mean. And I'd ... well, I'd spray it. The bushes. The hedgerows."

"Spray it?" she said, all disappointed, like her date had shown up with a tandem instead of a Bentley. "No bell, book, and candle and all that stuff?"

"Well, it—"

"*Spray.* Tch. What sort of spray?" she asked. "Is it like poison? Like rat poison?"

"No," I said. "It's—"

"'Cause if there's something dead there in the morning, *I* won't be the one shifting it."

"There wouldn't be anything dead," I said. "It's not poison. It's more like a warning."

"Oh," she said. "*Keep off the grass* sort of thing?"

I smiled at her. "A little more aggressive," I said. "*Get out of Town* sort of thing."

"How does it work?"

"Can I be indelicate?"

"I was a nurse, luv. Seen it all, heard it all."

"Fair enough. It's like piss-marking territory. Spraying the area to tell a smaller predator that it's had its fun. That it can sling its hook now, because something bigger and nastier is claiming the manor."

She gave me a pointed up and down. "You don't *look* big and nasty," she said.

"Day's not over," I said, and winked.

♦ ♦ ♦ ♦

When the lift opened on the seventh floor, Arcadia had been standing there. Three-piece suit. Pocket watch. Trademark grey leather gloves. That handsome forty-ish face, and those ancient eyes within it.

"Antoinette," he said, as if just the sight of Toni had saved him from suicide. "As radiant as ever."

Not a word of objection from not-Antoinette. Just a smile that was almost a simper and a little wiggle that was almost a fucking curtsey. He took her hand, raising it to his lips as he glided her elegantly out of the lift and gestured her down the corridor.

"Go and further brighten the lives of your lucky colleagues," he said, "while I take our young friend here topside."

He stepped into the lift with me and we rode to the top floor, or to what I'd always believed to be the top floor until—via an obscure door that looked like it should lead only to a closet and the spiral staircase that actually lay behind it—we came to a small circular room that I guessed was inside one of the towers that, from the street twenty flights below, appeared to be purely ornamental.

"One of my favorite rooms in the place," he said.

"You've been to Liverpool before, then?" I said. Which was really stupid. He'd obviously been to Liverpool before; he apparently knew Toni well enough to get away with shit that would have had some poor local bastard up on sexual harassment charges.

"Oh, many times," he said. "I was actually based here for nearly a year." He paused for a half-smile. "During the War."

I nearly bit. I'd heard what he'd said—*the War*, not *the Falklands war*, not *the recent unpleasantness in Iraq*, just *the War*—but I was buggered if I was going to play his let's-flirt-with-my-legend game this early in the day.

Apart from a couple of chairs, the room contained only a large circular white table set below a brass and mahogany contraption that disappeared into the ceiling.

"It's a *Camera Obscura*," Arcadia said. "A shadow cabinet. Do you know what that is?"

"Of course I know what that is," I said. Bit of a spin on the tone, I admit. I hadn't liked the way he'd used a foreign accent for the Latin phrase. Bad enough when people do that with

French or Spanish, but at least we know what they sound like. Nobody knows what *Latin* sounded like so, you know, fuck-off. It annoyed me that he could well have been simply making the accent up, confident that no one up here in the barbarous north would challenge him on it, him being such a toff and all. But it annoyed me more that he might *not* have been making it up, that he might very well have heard it spoken and spoken it himself.

"A device to capture images via light," he said, like he wasn't going to let the inconvenience of any pre-existing knowledge on my part slow his gallop. Arcadia's one of those blokes who regards a conversation as a good lecture spoiled. "The name came from Kepler, of course, but the Chinese and the Greeks knew the principle long before."

"Shame they had to wait two thousand years for someone to invent celluloid," I said.

"That *was* inconvenient," Arcadia said, and I could tell from the delight in his voice that I'd just played straight man to his coming punch-line. "Of course, not everyone was as patient as they should have been. Chap who made *this* one, for example." He patted the curved housing of the device with the kind of proprietorial affection a well-heeled Victorian roué might have shown a chorus girl's bottom. "It's from the early Seventeenth century," he said. "There've been whispers it was once owned by John Dee, but we can't be sure."

His eyes lost focus for a second or two, and I knew he was remembering the old days when, if the fancy took him, he could have popped off for a minute or two to find John Dee and just fucking ask him. But Mr. Sweets was dead and, though Arcadia still had plenty of tricks up his impeccably tailored sleeve, Time was as closed to him now as it was to the rest of us.

"So it's a *magic* Camera Obscura," I said. "It takes pictures. Well, no offense, but these days so does me fucking cell phone."

"No, it doesn't take pictures," Arcadia said. "Not as we understand it. But, still, it's unique."

"So what *does* it do?"

"It remembers," he said, and my eyes snapped back instantly to the machine.

"Ah," said Arcadia. "There it is." He was looking at me rather than the machine, and he sounded genuinely pleased. And not just with himself for once.

"There what is?" I asked.

"The first of my three Cs," he said. "Curiosity."

"Oh," I said. "Cars? Cancer?"

"I'm sorry?"

"Are we not playing *Things that Killed the Cat*, then?"

"No, we're playing things that make us good at our job. Not, you understand, things we need to *do* the job. Lots of people can *do* the job. The three Cs are what I consider vital to doing it *well*."

"Oh, aye?" I said. "So what are the other two?"

"Well, the second is Competence. You've already demonstrated that. I read the report on that mass clearing you did in Wavertree Playground a couple of weeks ago."

"The Mystery," I said, and then, off his questioning look, "nobody local calls it Wavertree Playground. It's The Mystery."

"Oh," he said, like he'd just had a hit of something good. "How ... apt."

"Aye," I said. "What's the third C?"

"The most important one of all."

"Which is ... ?

He gave me his half-smile again. "That would be telling," he said.

♦ ♦ ♦ ♦

"So these noises," I said. "This *howling*. Is it constant?"

She pursed her lips, thinking about it. "No," she said. "No, not constant."

"Is it daytime, nighttime? Both?"

"I'm not sure. I hear it sometimes, but not others."

"Are you hearing it now?"

"Eh? Don't be daft. Are *you* hearing it now?"

"I'm asking if *you* are," I said, and glanced around the room as if only now appreciating its architectural splendors. "From the thirties, isn't it, the house?"

"Aye," she said. "Just like me."

"But you weren't *born* here or anything," I said. "Weren't here as a little girl?"

"Oh, no. No. Me husband bought it just after the war—he were a bit older than me, been gone near enough twenty years now—and just moved me in once he'd made an honest woman of me. Our *Carol* was born here. Well, I mean, she was born in the hospital, but we were living here when—"

"But the house is as it was?" I said. I didn't like to keep interrupting her but, you know, meant to be working here.

"How d'you mean, *as it was*?" she said, ready to be insulted, like I was saying she hadn't once redecorated or something.

"No, I just mean, you know, original features and fittings and things."

"What, like banisters and windows and stuff?"

"Like the coal cellar," I said.

"Coal cellar?"

"Yeah. Is there still a coal cellar down there? Hasn't been bricked up or anything?"

"*Coal*," she said, like I was an idiot. "It hasn't had coal in it for forty years."

"Then what *has* it got in it?"

"Eh?"

I stood up. The racket was getting fucking unbearable. "What is it in the coal cellar," I said, "that's making all that noise?"

◆ ◆ ◆ ◆

Arcadia hadn't had a lot more to say. Pulled a few further details out of me about the job in The Mystery, congratulated me on it again, handed me the file on the Woolton Road semi, and that was it.

"Off you pop then," he said. "Got everything you might need?" He raised an eyebrow and mimed an example, his left hand sketching in the air in a way that no passer-by would have put down to anything more than an unusually elegant Tourette's spasm but which I recognized as an Assyrian scattering spell known as much for its difficulty as for its usefulness. I suppose he wasn't *just* showing off, but it's so fucking hard to tell with him.

"Well, I've got me charm and me good looks," I said. "See how far they get me, eh?"

"Quite," Arcadia said, and smiled like he was comfortable with a certain degree of humor from among the enlisted men. I was just turning to go when he spoke again.

"Actually," he said. "There's something else I think you should take." He reached into a desk drawer and handed me something from it.

I weighed it in my hand and gave him a look. "Hardly standard issue," I said.

He shrugged. "I just have a hunch about this one," he said.

◆ ◆ ◆ ◆

The roars from below only increased in intensity and ferocity as I approached the little three-quarter door at the top of the steps that led down to the coal cellar. But the second I slammed back the top and bottom bolts that had been holding the door shut, the sounds stopped dead. Something knew I was up there and had no wish to discourage my descent.

Banshee, my arse.

I suppose the old lady had been technically right to have called them howls, but howls always suggest an element of the plaintive to me, dizzy young romantic that I am, and these things hadn't had a trace of melancholy in them. They were feral, angry, and—not a comfortable concept as I made my crouched way down the cramped wooden stairs—hungry.

The cellar was long but low—its ceiling not even high enough to let me stand upright—and if there'd ever been a light down there, it was long gone. There was a little residual spill coming down from the house, but whatever it was that was in the cellar had moved way back into the shadows at the rear. Its silence and its retreat didn't mean that it was hiding, though. They meant that it was trying to draw me in.

Fuck. I froze for a moment, trying to get my breathing under control and pondering my choice of career, and then I stepped in. One yard. Two. A third, and suddenly the thing lurched out of the shadows and came at me.

It was the old lady from upstairs. Or used to be.

The rot of the dead flesh had left one hand entirely skeletal and half the chin was naked jawbone. From what I'd heard, these things didn't breathe but I'd swear those gray desiccated nostrils twitched as if catching a whiff of the warm meat I was wearing on my bones.

It raced towards me. Not graceful, but fucking fast. Much faster than the manual says. I thought about writing the editors a stern letter, but I didn't think about it for long.

Fuck knows, if I'd come here with just the standard issue kit, this undead thing would have had half my face off while I was still trying to weave a circle round it thrice and say something in Phoenician. But Arcadia'd had a hunch. I was pissed off that I owed him one, but I can't deny the tingle of gratitude and admiration I felt as I lifted the ancient service Webley and aimed for the head.

◆ ◆ ◆ ◆

She was sitting on the couch looking up at her postcards from abroad when I came back into the parlour.

"Everything all right?" she said.

"It will be," I said, and sat down next to her. I took her hand and closed mine around it gently. Still stuns me how solid they can feel.

"Ooh," she said. "Getting a bit familiar, aren't we? It's not grab-a-granny night down at the Grafton Rooms, you know."

"The Grafton Rooms?" I said, smiling. "Before my time. Been closed for nigh on thirty years now."

"Christ," she said. "That long? It all goes so fast."

I gave her hand a gentle pat. It was a little more yielding now, like water within a thin membrane trying to maintain a half-remembered shape.

"Are you starting to get a handle on what's going on, luv?" I asked her.

She sighed. "I think I knew as soon as I bolted the cellar door on it," she said. "I just didn't want to admit it to meself."

She looked up above the mantelpiece to the postcards from her daughter again and was silent for a while. I kept stroking her hand, less substantial by the minute.

"Downstairs," she said, suddenly. "Will someone tidy—"

"They'll send a team," I said.

"When?"

"Once I call them."

"You should call them," she said. "You're on the clock."

"Bugger the clock," I said, still holding where her hand used to be. "I'm right here. You just relax, love. Take as long as you need."

She didn't need long. And I had nowhere better to be.

LORD BYRON'S
NOVEL OF THE FRAGMENTS

The Taviani Pass, 1824

I am to tell you, or so the muse instructs me, of the curious adventure that befell me during my wanderings in that mist-shrouded region of hills and caverns—nestled between two neighboring kingdoms and long the source of their centuries-old enmity—which our unimaginative guidebooks call merely The Taviani Pass (after the Venetian botanist who first mapped it) but which is known to one of its reclusive mountain tribes in their strangely beautiful mongrel tongue as *Draumestauch*, or The Place of Gentle Misfortune.

I was descending a south-facing slope, aware already of how low the sun was to my right, when I grew conscious of a whistled air, high and lilting and tantalizingly faint. At first convinced it was nought but the wind itself, transmuted into accidental melody by its passage through crevice and crevasse, I was forced to revise my opinion when a sudden sour note in a trilling climb within the tune prefaced a pause and then a renewed attempt at the melodic ascent. Neither wind nor accident then, I realized, and was at once—distance and nightfall be damned—determined to find the mysterious whistler. For you see, the air was not unknown to me; it was in fact one of those 'Hebrew Melodies' composed by Mr. Nathan some years earlier as settings for lyrics of my own invention.

A turn or two within the rocky bypaths brought me ere long to the narrow mouth of a cave hidden from the casual glances of most who would brave the mountain, and a walk of but a hundred feet or so within its shadowed reaches brought me to the source of the whistled refrain:

Illuminated by the dancing flame of a torch mounted on the cave-wall, a solitary Hermit in monk-like robes and cowl sat beneath a primitive looking glass of polished obsidian. As I stepped into the pool of light cast by the torch, the fellow stopped his whistling.

"Welcome, my Lord," he said, and beckoned me forward.

"You have the advantage of me, Sir," I said. "In whose company do I find myself?"

"I am the Guardian of the Fragments," he said, with a certain haughtiness not generally associated with—nor, to my understanding, encouraged in—those of the monkish persuasion.

"Fragments?" said I. For, I confess, curiosity had triumphed over my disdain for his cheap Mummers' Show theatrics.

"Fragments of Time, my Lord," he said. "Glimpses of worlds that were, worlds that will be, and even worlds that are."

Well, the damned fellow had my attention. I had to give him that.

"Do we see them in the glass?" I said, nodding at the obsidian pane behind him.

There was a pause before his reply—"Alas, no," he eventually said—and I realized I'd inadvertently knocked a chip out of his self-importance. Missed a trick there, he was probably thinking, while no doubt planning a quick bit of redecoration before the next punter wandered in.

Making the best of it, however, he reached within the copious folds of his robe and removed a document.

"From the distant past," he said, and held the thing out for me to take, which I did.

It was a single sheet of a fine antique parchment and it was folded in half. On the outside of the fold, as one addressing an envelope, someone had written a three-word title in a decent copperplate while the inside, once unfolded, contained a prose passage of some two or three hundred words:

ONLY DEATH, SIR

When the King of all the lands that were fair asked for berries, berries were brought. When his thirst sought sweet water, sweet water was found. So when he asked for wisdom, it was not long before his courtiers brought to him a man of whom no question had been asked for which he had not found an answer.

And the King made the man his servant and bade him walk with him all his days so that wisdom was ever at hand.

And the Servant showed him all the pleasures of the world and how to partake wisely thereof.

And many years passed and the King, grown old with wandering, spoke again to his servant.

"And after this, what then? After flesh and fruit and song, what more remains?"

And the Servant made him an answer and the answer was kind.

And the King, who by now was not himself unwise, accepted the answer but, seeking consolation, went to his window and looked out at his people below.

"That sweet girl who runs eagerly, summer on her cheek, to find a faithful lover: Who will receive her embrace?"

And the Servant made him an answer and the answer was the same.

"And that young man whose heart seeks glory, be he poet or soldier: What will he find?"

And the Servant made him an answer and the answer was the same.

"And those trees, those flowers: To what end do they blossom? Those birds: To what end do they sing?"

And the Servant made him an answer and the answer was the same.

And the King looked at his Servant and saw him for the first time and his heart was heavy in his chest and all his joys were ash. And he gave to his Servant one more question.

"And who are you, o most faithful servant, who has shown me all these wonders, who has walked always beside me, thy footsteps planted next to mine down all my days e'en like those of my own shadow?"

The Servant smiled. And he made him an answer and the answer was the same.

I refolded the paper, handed it back to the hermit, and watched it disappear into the hollows of his monkish robe.

"A lesson the learning of which is hardly the exclusive prerogative of the past," I said. "Nor one reserved solely for Kings."

"I know nothing of lessons, my Lord," he said. "I am merely the Guardian."

His routine could plainly benefit from better dialogue, and I felt a moment's temptation to offer my services in that regard but I feared it might bruise his feelings. He was, in any case, getting on with the show.

"From the distant future," he said, producing the second fragment for my perusal:

THE LAST TIME I ALMOST WENT HOME

The guy we'd actually been hired by, the guy who rounded us up from the club, was just some flunky in a tough-guy suit, spending government money. Nicer than he needed to be, though. "Ladies," he'd said, as he held the limo door and waved the three of us into the back seat. Not a trace of spin on it. You learn to appreciate the little things, believe me.

The guy we've been hired *for* is quiet, naked, and not great on eye-contact. It's hardly surprising that he doesn't understand the subtleties, that his hand is limp and unresponsive when we shake, that he answers honestly when Brigid asks if he likes her hair. It's hardly surprising at all. I mean, *how* far has he come?

The guy with the clipboard and the ugly machine had tried to explain, but I couldn't even. I'm like, "Wait, what?" Mind *blown*.

"C'mon, Caitlin," Jeannie says to me, like she hears

this sort of shit every day. "Like David Bowie. You know, in that movie."

And Brigid's like, "Right, the one where his eyes are weird."

And Jeannie, very offended, is all, "Those are Bowie's actual *eyes*, Brigid."

But she's forgetting the scene with the tweezers, I think, and besides, that was a metaphor. This is a man.

The ugly machine can't make up its mind about its numbers.

Jeannie's tongue is at the corner of her mouth and none of us are sure what to do now.

"Perhaps you could dance," Clipboard says. "Perhaps he'd like that."

Fragment, indeed. Somewhat shorter, even, than the first. And certainly more perplexing; full of words which one could understand singly but which, woven together, produced a tapestry so baffling as to court madness. I would not, however, have this fellow—of whom I had come to think, for all his affectation of a monkish spiritual rigour, as being too pleased with himself by half—believe me to be without opinion or insight.

"A machine that works with numbers," I said. "A sophistication, I assume, of Herr Leibniz's Stepped Reckoner?"

"Were Herr Leibniz to fall asleep and dream himself into a world of mechanical wonders unguessed-at in our present day and then, within that dreaming world of splendours, to fall asleep and dream of a world whose inventions put those of the first to shame, he would still be some distance from comprehending the ..."

Good God. I know that I've been accused of as much myself,

but it seemed to me that my monastic friend was making his point with an inordinate amount of excessive elaboration. I pretended to stifle a yawn but hints, it appeared, were not to be taken.

"... enormous strides in computational capabilities that await us in—"

"That's as maybe," I said, finally cutting him off. "But I suspect two and two will probably still make four. In any case, there's a far more important lesson to be learned from this little curiosity of yours."

"Indeed?" said the Hermit, raising an eyebrow.

"Indeed," said I. "It appears that, in the future, ladies shall still dance?"

"It appears so," he admitted.

"Then the world shall not entirely have gone to Hell," I said, and held out my hand for the third fragment.

"Past. Future," I mused. "This next will, I take it, enlighten me regarding the present?"

A solemn nod was his only reply as he placed the document in my hand.

As with its companions, it was a single sheet of paper folded in half. As before, a title was on the outer fold:

HOW LONG DOES THE MAYFLY LIVE?

But the paper, once unfolded, was completely blank.

For a brief moment, I felt a chill of fear, its source unclear to me and its strength disturbingly disproportionate to the circumstance.

My second thought was that this was merely some ill-judged

whimsy of the Guardian and that, upon renewed demand, he would provide the real document.

And then I understood. Or thought so, at least.

"The present is not ordained," I said confidently, as one who has understood a clever puzzle. "It is ours for the writing."

I looked to my cowled companion for what I fully expected to be an approving nod. But neither word nor gesture escaped him. How could it?

The Guardian was a statue. Man and robe alike hewn by some masterful ancient hand from the very walls of the cavern that appeared to be its home.

I snatched up the flaming torch from its niche in the wall and held it near my former companion. With every second, the thing seemed to be less well wrought until I began to wonder how I could ever have thought it the semblance of a man. A series of natural folds in the rock, and nothing more.

The flicker of the flame's reflection in the obsidian panel above me drew my attention to the looking glass. Holding the torch aloft and close to my own face, I stared into the glass's darkling surface.

There was absolutely nothing to be seen within.

ETERNAL DELIGHT

Energy is eternal delight —William Blake
A Wop Bop a Loo Bop a Lop Bam Boom! —Little Richard

Liverpool, 1985

It was only when all his friends had betrayed him that David Holloway became an unusual person.

The signs of this collective betrayal had been various but invariably vicious, had been sometimes subtle but mostly ruthlessly overt: Andy selling his guitar; Paul's conversation turning inexorably from boxing and blowjobs to babies and bathroom extensions; Tracy marrying a confectionery representative; Maurice—a man obsessed with style from the age of fourteen—allowing his *girlfriend* to take over the cutting of his hair; and so on, and so on.

What happened in the face of all this sociological reconstruction was that David too found his life remade.

What happened was that he saw such visions and did such

things that, had he lived in less civilized times, he would have been hung by the neck until he was dead.

What happened was this.

1. Mystery Train

The plate shattered.

David blamed the fancy washing up liquid. He was accustomed to cheaper brands but there'd been a special at the Tesco's on Picton Road, so he'd indulged. And now look. Fucking stuff was so slick that the dishes had needed a good tight grip, much tighter than he was used to, and his Elvis Presley commemorative plate had slid out from his fingers, cracked against the side of the sink, fallen to the floor, and smashed into five pieces.

"Shit," said David. The King had only been dead seven and a half years. This was disrespectful. He slapped at the detergent bottle to teach it some manners and, gathering the broken pieces of the plate, turned to the pedal bin at his side.

The bin, the fragments, and David himself were in the relatively large kitchen of the relatively small Housing Association flat that took up half of the ground floor of an early 20th century terrace house at the Smithdown Road end of Wavertree.

The flat had been home to David for the last three years, ever since he dropped out of the Poly. Well, not dropped out so much as just stopped fucking going and not bothering to tell anyone. The combination of his DHSS rent allowance and the occasional income from his freelance journalism (of which the DHSS were ignorant) would actually have allowed him to find a slightly larger living space by now, but his position here at the back of the ground floor gave him access to what amounted to a private garden—theoretically, his fellow tenants could knock on his flat door and ask to be allowed through to the garden but fortunately no one was that much of a knobhead—and, in the summer months at least, he found this sufficient compensation for having dominion over only a bed-sitting room and a kitchen.

But this was not summer. David was into the autumn of his twenty-third year, in the literal sense, and, in the metaphoric, deep into the autumn of his youth. His perception of his life as something for which ripeness was a memory colored his perception of everything else around him: The view through his kitchen window of the garden in the afternoon light seemed to him neither mellow nor fruitful but merely dull and brown, a conscious entropic insult by a nature grown not merely senile but malicious with it; the fragments in his hand seemed evidence not of a simple domestic accident, but of a continuing campaign to confirm the willful transience of life and its pleasures.

David shook his head to free it from the gathering of depression and, at a touch from his left foot on the pedal, the lid of the bin flew back. Without bothering to bend down, David dropped the shards of Elvis onto the yielding mass of yesterday's excess prawn curry.

"There you go, mate," he said. "One more for the mystery train."

And then he froze, standing very still as a small and speedy rush of fear jetted through his system, leaving his arms and legs tingling and paralyzed.

Something had slithered.

Something was in the bin.

It had been the tiniest of movements and David couldn't

be sure what he had *seen* exactly—indeed, couldn't be sure that he had actually seen anything. Perhaps, in fact, had seen effect only, not cause at all; just the rising and subsiding of the trash as something unseen had probed and retreated. But the path of that rise and fall had nevertheless managed to suggest a shape, and a quite specific one. Something long and thin and pliable. Something like a tail. Something like a rat's tail. Jesus Christ, there was a rat in his fucking bin!

With an involuntary cry of terror and disgust, David threw himself back towards his kitchen door as the lid of the bin snapped shut. For a long and bowel-loosening five seconds, David simply stood quite still by his door and stared at the stained steel tube of his bin. If you'd asked him what he was waiting for, he might have said that he was waiting for a rattle or squeak or some other sound from within the bin to confirm the problem. Or he might have said that he was waiting for inspiration as to how to deal with the matter. But the truth is that he wasn't waiting for either of those things. He was simply waiting for it not to be true anymore.

And after these five seconds, after this silence and this immobility, the notion of a rat actually being in there—though not empirically proven to be untrue—nevertheless began to seem farfetched enough for David to feel he could perhaps try a little test or two. He seized the long-handled brush which rested against the fridge and, from the safety of the other end of its four foot length, he struck it against the side of the bin.

Irritatingly, the dull thud of wood on metal awoke his ears not just to any new aural evidence of an unwanted inhabitant of the bin but to the entire sonic life of the kitchen, which he had previously managed to tune out. The rhythmic dripping of water from the tap, the low humming of the fridge, the high-pitched keening of the wind in the ventilator above the cooker; across the entire range of his hearing swelled an orchestra of conspiracy that almost succeeded in blocking out the other noise he'd heard. Thought he'd heard. Wondered if he'd heard. Knew damn well he'd heard.

Tiny, ungraspable, a third-generation analog recording of an echo of a whisper, but there it had been.

And there, therefore, it was.

Something in the bin.

This time David acted on instinct and slapped the far end of the brush onto the closed lid of the bin. A rat *in* a bin was considerably better, in the confines of David Holloway's kitchen, then a rat being given the opportunity to get *out* of a bin should it so desire and circumstance permit. Indeed, a monster contained is almost pleasurable. David remembered pressing his nine-year-old palm against the thick museum glass that had, by an all-important quarter of an inch, separated his flesh from that of a very black, very hairy, and very large bird-eating spider.

The sensation had been, if not exactly nice, then not exactly nasty. The fear had been there inside him, granted, but he'd been the one in control of the fear. Like the times he had used the electric-shock slot machines that you no longer saw in the seaside towns, he was his own torturer. His was the decision as to how many volts of electricity or terror he would allow inside his body before letting go. But today's quota had been made, thank you very much, and, if it was all the same to the great arcade proprietor in the sky, he was getting off this particular machine right the fuck now.

He had a plan. Not a complicated plan. A very do-able plan.

He was going to pick up the bin, holding the lid tightly shut, and he was going to walk into the back garden. There, he was going to fling the bin and its contents as far away from himself as he possibly could. And if curry, cigarette butts, Elvis Presley, or a very confused rat landed in anyone else's garden, then sorry mate but tough shit.

It was a good plan, and the first two or three stages of its execution went exactly as they should. David picked the bin up. He held the lid tightly shut. He began walking to the back door that would let him into the garden. He was eight feet from it. Then he was six feet from it. Then he was two feet from it. And then something landed on his foot.

It was at this point that David wasn't in control anymore.

First, he lost control of his fear which, grateful for the opportunity, swept through his body in a triumphant tingling wave, roaring in his ears, clouding his sight in a yellow and black haze, and stopping his lungs. Then he lost control of his voice, which celebrated its escape in a wordless song of rising pitch. Almost simultaneously he lost control of his arms, which demonstrated their independence by losing control of the bin. And, finally, he lost control of his life—though this last was not to be made fully apparent for another five or six seconds.

In the first of those seconds, David looked down at his foot. What had landed on it was an empty tin can. In the second second, David realized that this meant there must be a hole in the bottom of his bin. In the third second, he looked back over his shoulder to where the bin had been. There was a small hole in his kitchen floor and, protruding from it, there was a tiny pink wriggling thing standing upright like a worm making claims on evolution.

In the fourth second, David found time to realize several things; whatever this was, it was not a rat's tail; whatever this was, it seemed to sense that he was looking at it; whatever this was, there was a lot more of it than he could at that point see, because—for a diameter of several feet around the hole—his kitchen floor was pulsing upwards and throbbing like a pustule about to burst.

There were also several things David didn't realize; he didn't hear himself moan, he didn't see himself shake, he didn't feel the sudden pool of saliva that cascaded from his shock-slackened jaw to run over his chin.

In the fifth second, David's kitchen floor exploded. And in the sixth second—in what all his upbringing led him to assume was in fact his last second on earth—David saw rushing toward him through the dust and debris with all the malevolence of inevitability, an absolute fucking absurdity.

It was big and it was round and, in a last and unwilled piece of analogy drawing, David thought of it as an enormously large golf ball with all the hard white casing ripped off to reveal not rubber bands but an infernal knot of tightly packed and intertwined worms, all wriggling feverishly in a collective rage to escape collectivism. Its pinkness was the pinkness of newly flayed flesh and in those few areas of its surface not covered by its squirming appendages there shone a gray and glistening mucus.

It moved astonishingly swiftly but nevertheless, in the fraction of a second it took to reach him, David saw several of the thousands of twitching wormlike miniature limbs extend and stiffen, each of them growing impossibly—and impossibly quickly—to a threatening length of several feet.

The sight of this was David's last sight of all. Three of these extended limbs rammed into his face, one slipping into his mouth and down his throat and the second and third through each of his eyes and into his brain. At the same time, another tentacular explorer crept between his legs and rammed itself into his gut via his anus, bursting cloth, flesh, blood vessels, and intestinal walls easily and indiscriminately, like a first-time sodomite, charmingly over-eager but hideously over-endowed.

As if some kind of decision had been reached, the other probes withdrew and, instantly, the entire mass of the creature catapulted itself after its scouting limb and began to squeeze itself inward, forcing its enormous mass into David's body, contorting itself, twisting and stretching to ease its passage.

The holes made in David's face, along with his other remaining natural orifices, allowed for the exit of his body's former contents with surprisingly little damage to their fleshy container. Of course, as it was leaving under fairly severe pressure through fairly small holes, the thick liquor that consisted of pulped organ, powdered bone, and plain blood did add quite considerably to the aesthetic disaster that the kitchen had become, jetting out like streams of tomato puree from a pressurized tube and decorating the walls and ceiling like a meeting of the minds between Jackson Pollock and Charles Manson.

When it had completed its occupation, when what was left of David's innards did nothing else but slither and steam, the creature, like a fussy customer in the shop of a ready-to-wear tailor, proceeded to the fine fitting, to the adjustments and the alterations. One by one the body's flaccid fingers were filled, one by one the toes. Only one tip—that of the second finger of the right hand—had burst and later, when it had learned to use needle and thread, the creature would repair that. The scrotum, the penis, the nose, the ears—carefully and gradually all the nooks and crannies, all the highways and byways, of the creature's new property were explored, exploited, and inflated.

All things considered, it really didn't take very long. Two or three minutes and a lot of wriggling and rippling later, a quick glance would have led you to believe that David Holloway was standing in the middle of his kitchen floor. A second look, one which took in the fact that his Sergeant Bilko T-shirt and his Levi 501s were completely covered in blood, would have led you inevitably to a third and to the sickening realization that what appeared to be a small worm was hanging out of each eye-socket. You'd probably not have needed any more prompting than that to leave the flat rapidly, call the Police, and thus save several lives but, as you weren't there, that isn't what happened.

What *did* happen was that the creature—having spent some time and considerable concentration on getting the fit just right—decided in a moment of pique that it found the entire style unsuitable and sprang back instantly to its globular appearance, stretching its new flesh with it. It began to bounce rapidly around the kitchen and then into the bed-sitting room adjoining it, where it hurled itself from wall to wall and between ceiling and floor for an energetic few minutes until it finally settled, wobbling slightly, on David's bed.

Whatever else the creature was, however, it wasn't stupid. It realized that most of the pleasures of this world came with triggers designed for the human frame and the human finger and so, having taken these moments to reassure itself of its independent nature, it resumed its David shape, a little more quickly this time, and set about learning what to do with it.

As if some genetic memory in the borrowed skin aided the

creature's learning curve, walking was a problem soon overcome, the manipulation of the taps in the sink of the wrecked kitchen a lesson soon mastered. The elasticity of the T shirt and jeans had proven less accommodating than that of human flesh and so the shredded clothes were now simply part of the debris that the David thing had stepped delicately over on its way to the sink, and it was an already naked body that carefully washed all the blood off itself and out of its hair before returning to the other room to dress itself.

Apart from the bed—which, covered by day in cushions of varied shapes and sizes, also served as the main sitting or slouching area—the bed-sitting room contained one deckchair of wood and bright red canvas, one large beanbag, one wardrobe, one chest of drawers, one desk plus stool, and a wall of entertainment—a complicated and jerry-rigged shelf unit providing homes for various stereo components, a TV, a VCR, hundreds of LPs, and a few dozen books. Ashtrays, magazines, and an acoustic guitar lived on the floor.

On top of the chest of drawers was a line of toiletries; talcum powders, colognes, aftershaves, and antiperspirants. The David-thing tried them all, spraying, rolling, splashing, and patting its clean new body with a heady cocktail of scents before selecting, from an extensive range of clothes, the only actual suit in David's wardrobe, a jet-black narrow-lapelled two-piece which David had bought to wear at a '60s theme party a year or so earlier, claiming variously to have come as a CIA operative or as an R'n'B musician, depending upon the sensibilities of the person to whom he was talking at the time.

Finding the necessary white shirt and thin black tie in the chest of drawers, the David-thing dressed itself, adding a pair of black suede winkle-pickers it found in the bottom of the wardrobe and completing the look by donning the Ray-ban sunglasses which had perched stylishly on the polystyrene nose of a milliner's bust atop the shelf unit. This last was an entirely aesthetic decision but it did have the concomitant advantage of not revealing that those were worms which were his eyes.

The sharp looking figure in the black suit lowered itself casually into the red canvas deckchair and picked up the various remotes that were scattered on the floor about the base of the chair. It hit several buttons and brought several machines to life. Music filled the air and images flickered to life on the screen. Eddie Cochran's *Something Else* segued into Elvis Costello's *Stranger in the House* while Mister Ed got the better of Wilbur once again. Had the creature learned how to smile yet, it would have done so.

♦ ♦ ♦ ♦

The thing veiled in David's flesh spent the ensuing thirty-six hours watching TV shows and videos, listening to records and tapes, and reading books and magazines, more often than not all at the same time. Finally, at 3:00 o'clock in the morning of the day after the day after the day it had arrived, it decided to have a word.

"David," it said, in a pleasantly resonant Mid-Atlantic voice.

"David," it repeated in a guttural Scouse twang.

"David," it growled, like Pazuzu from *The Exorcist*.

"David," it giggled, like *Laugh-In* period Goldie Hawn getting availably playful.

From somewhere deep inside itself, the creature sensed an answering groan.

"Ah, David. Splendid." Donald Pleasance.

Oh, God. Where...

"Where are you?" The creature said. "Where you've always been, I suppose. Somewhere inside. It's just that you're not alone anymore."

But I... Oh God. Oh God.

"David, please. You've had a very traumatic experience. That's why I let you sleep so long. Try not to get excited."

Who are you?

"Me? Oh, I don't know. What do you think? The Monster from the Id, maybe? The Lump of Goo from Outer Space? The Innocent Young Virus Mutated by Chemical Pollutants? The Devil? Take your pick, David. Whatever floats your boat, mate. I don't give a shit."

Who am I?

"Who are you? You're David. Just as you've always been. You're still here."

Yes. But—

"You're still here, and you're starting to get boring."

But I—

"Do you want to go back to sleep?"

No.

"Good. Now—"

Where do I go when I ... sleep?

"Where do you go? How the fuck do *I* know where you go? You go where Larry Talbot goes when the wolfbane blooms. You go where Billy Batson goes when the Thunder speaks. Where do you go? Who knows? Who gives a damn? Frankly, my dear, I'm a little disappointed by this consistently selfish way of looking at the interesting situation in which we currently find ourselves.

Where am *I*? Who am *I*? Where do *I* go? Come on, David. We're in this thing together. Try and think of yourself as part of a team."

Who are we?

"Ah, now that's a *much* more interesting question."

The David-thing got up from the deckchair, stretched itself, and laughed. The laugh was deep, rich, and attractive.

"Who are we?" it said. "We're the Bruise Brothers, my man. And we're gonna boogie."

2. Love is Strange

Lisette Connaught was having a bad night. She lay, naked and alone, beneath the lime green and shocking pink duvet. It was her first night on her own since she'd married Charles six months earlier and the first night ever that she had been alone in this house.

Both she and Charles had realized that his latest promotion, while giving with one hand the wherewithal to buy this, their first home, would with the other take away occasional nights together in a kind of modern-day *droit de seigneur*, requiring Charles's presence at the odd course or conference while his wife welcomed loneliness and silence into her bed. They had realized it—but that didn't mean she had to like it.

"If you're going to join the rat race, Mister Connaught," she had joked when he first joined the company eighteen months earlier, "just make damn sure you're the fastest rat." And their laughter had dissolved into lovemaking and her worries had dissolved into warmth. But now she was beginning to wonder if the undeniable speed that Charles had since demonstrated really did compensate for all the other trappings of an upwardly mobile urban rodent.

It wasn't as if she actually *missed* life amongst the educated unemployed. It wasn't as if she yearned for mac and cheese three nights out of every seven or dwelled nostalgically on the days of one movie a month and a show every six. She would *kill* rather than ever have to share a bathroom again. It was just that if the hypocrisy, paranoia, and mask-wearing that seemed to be an inescapable part of Charles's new life ("Our new life," she heard him automatically correct her) were to fly from her tomorrow, then she wouldn't actually miss *them* either.

But she would miss the house. And the car. And the central heating. And the big new bed, and the money.

"Shit," she said aloud, as she changed position for the thirty-fourth time that night. Not a wink so far. She looked up at the radio alarm clock on the unit next to Charles's side of the bed. The warm green figures of the LCD told her it was 3:55.

"Three fifty-five. Three fifty-five. That's five to fucking *four*!" she told the room.

"Oh, Christ!" Lisette slammed her hands petulantly against the mattress and then, the little explosion of anger having diffused some of her tension, she folded her arms behind her head and breathed out slowly, enjoying the relaxation of her body. She even managed a passable imitation of a languorous stretch, and suddenly she was amused rather than angry at her inability to sleep—'cause, Jesus, it wasn't like she had anything to actually *do* now that Charles had transformed himself into such a convincing likeness of Mister Happy Breadwinner with a Semi-Detached in Mossley Hill, so who cared how late she fell asleep or how late she got up? She pushed the duvet down to her waist in order to let her body feel cooler and lighter.

Idly, she toyed with her dark brown hair, long and newly permed. "It makes you look younger," Charles had said in a tone that suggested, astonishingly, that this was not perhaps altogether a good thing. Lisette liked it, though. It reminded her of the Pre-Raphaelite paintings that she had always, in their student days, guiltily preferred to the abstract and kinetics that had won the approval of her peers (and the *affection*? she had often wondered—but never out loud).

She dropped her hair over her not insignificant breasts, (now, to her relief, prominently back in fashion) and slowly pulled it back, brushing it gently over her nipples which, happily asleep unlike their mistress, were at first slow to rise but after a few more hairy caresses were fully alert and eager for activity.

"Oh," said Lisette. "That was a bit bloody silly."

She started to giggle but then paused, attentive to the eager pulse of their silent argument.

"Well, what do you think?" She asked the room. "Should I have a wank, or what?"

"That won't be necessary," said a voice from behind the bedroom door.

Lisette shot up in bed, clutching the duvet to her body, her eyes wide in shock and fear. But the scream conceived as she watched the door handle turn was stillborn because, as the door was flung open and the main bedroom lights switched on, the grinning figure revealed in the doorway was familiar to her.

"Surprise," it said.

Lisette's lungs grabbed gratefully at the mouthful of air she drew in as she allowed herself to breathe again. She held the breath less than a second, though, before exhaling it in a shouted torrent composed half of anger and half of relief.

"David! Jesus fucking Christ! Do you have any idea what… I … My God… I nearly *died*, you fucking prick! What is this?"

"This? What is this? This is this," said the tall figure in the black suit and shades. The voice was a pretty perfect Robert De Niro and Lisette was about to congratulate David on a heretofore unrevealed talent when he continued, in a pretty perfect David Holloway. "And this is *this*."

Lisette froze.

The intruder had pulled a gun from his pants pocket and was aiming it at her.

"Now do as you're told, and maybe you won't get hurt," he said, as he crossed the room to the bed and, keeping the gun trained on her with his right hand, threw the duvet onto the floor with his left.

"David, what are you—"

"Quiet!" he said, and unzipped his pants. "Got a little job for you. Make this hard in ten seconds or I'll decorate the walls with your brains."

Lisette bent her face forward towards his groin and succeeded within the appointed time limit, the cold firm pressure of the gun barrel against her temple helping to make easy the necessary moist slackness of her mouth. She fell back onto the bed, staring silently up at the impassive set of his mouth, the implacable blackness of his shades,

"That was very good, Lisette," he said. "Very good. You're a talented girl. Now—what do you want me to do with this?" He gestured at the fully engorged cock.

Lisette swallowed, bit her lip, and spoke. Her voice was a hollow whisper. "Oh, God," she said. "Please don't do this."

"What do you want me to do with this?" he said again.

"I... I..."

"Tell me!"

"I want you to..."

"Go on."

"...to fuck me."

"Properly," he said. "Say it properly."

"I want you to fuck me," she said, in a very small voice.

"Well," he said. "Seeing that you ask so nicely, I'd be delighted to oblige."

He dropped his pants and clambered out of them and the black suede winkle-pickers. He kept his jacket on. He mounted Lisette swiftly and brutally, placing the back of her knees against his shoulders and pressing down on her. For two minutes, he moved in silence, the gun held constantly at her head, and then he spoke again.

"In ten seconds," he said, "I'm going to pull this trigger."

At Lisette's answering gasp, he began to thrust into her more rapidly and more violently, counting down as he did so.

"Ten, nine, eight, seven—"

Lisette stared up at the face of her husband's friend, at the unfamiliar black glasses.

"Six, five, four, three—"

He dropped his face to hers and kissed her. His tongue felt swollen and invasive in her mouth.

"Two, one—"

The gun found the precise center of her temple.

"Zero," he said. And pulled the trigger.

They came together, explosively, the click of the gun's empty chamber lost to both of them in the mutual orgasmic roar.

They clutched at each other for a few more seconds, sweating and slick, before her visitor in the sunglasses rolled sideways and away, laughing with pleasure as he lay on his back on the cool side of the bed, a few inches separating him from Lisette's warm body.

Lisette lay silent for a little longer and then turned her head toward him, a small smile playing about her lips.

"The shades were a nice touch," she said. "Bit of variety." Her tone was relaxed and sated, and she snuggled in closer to him, laying her head on his shoulder and leaning her arm across his chest. "You still play that really well. Was that Robert de Niro you were doing? You know, the accent bit?"

"I couldn't find the gun at first," he said, ignoring her question. "I was wandering around downstairs for at least five minutes. Surprised you didn't hear me. I was looking everywhere. Began to think you'd thrown it away, now that you're a respectable married woman and everything."

She laughed.

"But the *worst* bit," her lover continued, "the worst bit was when I started the countdown. I suddenly realized I hadn't checked the gun and I thought, what if Charles has started taking home security seriously? What if this fucking thing's *loaded*?"

This time, they laughed together. Lisette raised herself on one elbow and looked down at the grinning face beneath her. She tried for a stern expression.

"Never mind laughing," she said. "I'm very annoyed with you. First of all, you nearly gave me a bloody heart attack. I didn't know you knew Charles was away—I thought somebody else had got inside somehow. I was terrified."

The face below her smirked upwards as if to say it all added to the fun, but Lisette ignored it and carried on. "And, secondly, I told you this would all have to stop when I got married, didn't I?"

Her visitor's grin didn't waver. Lisette paused for a moment and then spoke in a different tone; relaxed, inquisitive. "Anyway, how did *you* get in?"

"Love laughs at locksmiths."

"Fuck off. How'd you get in?"

"Through the letterbox."

"Bit of a tight squeeze, wasn't it?"

"Yeah, it was. But then I'm good at squeezing into tight places, aren't I?"

They laughed together again. But Lisette had the sense that somehow the joke was twice as funny for him as it was for her. She shook her head at him, sighed in an exasperation that was only half playful and, turning the light off from the secondary switch by her side of the bed, wriggled in close again, so that they could lay together in the warmth of post-coital silence.

◆ ◆ ◆ ◆

It was about five o'clock in the morning, and Lisette was just beginning to drift into sleep, when she heard David's voice in the dark.

"Isn't it scary?" he said. "Being in a big house all on your own?"

"You're here," she murmured, snuggling deeper against him, reluctant to be pulled back into the world of words.

"Yeah, yeah," he said. "But what if I *wasn't*? Could you sleep alright on your own? I mean, you were awake when I got here."

"Yes, I was awake," she said. "But that was... other stuff. I was just thinking. I wasn't scared. I don't have bad dreams or anything. I haven't had bad dreams since I was a kid."

He shifted position, apparently interested. "What was the worst dream you ever had?" he asked.

Lisette knew he'd won, now. His interest was infectious, and she liked telling this story anyway.

"The worst?" she said. "No question about it. It was a long time ago now. I was still a little girl. About six, I think... maybe seven... I don't know. Anyway, it started in a big room in a house I'd never seen..."

She raised her head towards David's, her storytelling tone suddenly replaced by an explanatory one. "Well, in the dream it was *my* house, of course. What I mean is that it wasn't a house I knew in real li—"

He interrupted her. "Tell it," he said. "Just tell it. Straight through."

Lisette smiled. She nodded and shifted position slightly so that they were both lying on their backs, staring upwards. On the ceiling, the light from a moon very low in the sky threw a distorted black and blue reflection of the half-closed Venetian blinds. As clouds drifted over the distant moon, diffusing its light, the clarity of this image would wax and wane. Lisette found herself focusing on these small and slowly shifting patterns of precision as she narrated her nightmare.

"There were four or five of us," she said, "all gathered in this one room. I think they were all adults apart from me. I knew that they were family or close friends, though I didn't know their faces at all.

"We were all grouped around a big black-and-white telly in the corner of the room, two or three people on chairs and me and a couple of others on the floor. The room seemed sort of empty, or unfinished or something, like there wasn't enough furniture in it, or that what there was wasn't big enough. Anyway, I asked somebody what was coming on the telly, what we were going to watch, and they told me it was *The New Adventures of Jesus*—which, in the dream, didn't seem odd to me at all—and I looked over at the screen. Sure enough, the titles were just rolling up and the scene was fading up beneath them. I think it was Jesus with his cross on his shoulder, but I couldn't be sure because there was interference on the telly and the picture went all wobbly. As soon as that happened, there was a knock on the front door.

"Nobody else moved or said anything, just stayed there watching the screen even though it was just static and snow by now, and I got this sense that I had to answer the door. That it was expected of me. It was around then that I started to feel scared, I think, and also then that it all began to feel... I don't know... *pre-destined*, I suppose. It wasn't as if I knew what was going to happen, more that I knew that what was going to happen was going to happen, if you know what I mean. And that it was going to be bad. But even though I knew it was going to be bad, I didn't say or do anything to show that I knew. I just played along as if I didn't understand anything. I suppose I was hoping not to stand out, or something. Hoping that if I played along and saw the game through then there wouldn't be any special punishment for me, that I'd just be one of the crowd.

"Anyway, I stood up and left the room and went out into a dark hallway. I sort of recognize it now, when I think about it—I think it was the dream country's version of the hallway in the house we lived in when I was *really* small—but in the dream I didn't. It didn't seem odd to me or anything. Just scary.

"The knocking was still going on. Hadn't ever stopped, just carried on, slow and steady, like it knew it was going to be answered. Not *patient*, exactly. More... expectant. The front door was at the far end of this hallway, and I made my way toward it, still frightened but still acting as if everything was alright even though there was no one else in the hallway to watch me. The knocking stopped at the moment I reached the door—as if whatever was on the other side of it knew exactly where I was—and I opened it.

"It was only a man. To look at, I mean. Very big, though; tall and broad. His hair was thick and black. It was balding on top but he had a beard as if to compensate, short but thick and it rose up on each cheek to within an inch of his lower eyelids. His arms were bare and muscular, and they were covered in hair, too. Now, okay, I was a little girl—maybe *all* adult males look big, broad, and hairy to us—but I don't know. This was different. *He* was different.

"He was walking up the five grey stone steps that rose to the front door—I didn't stop to wonder how he'd knocked on the door if he'd been at the bottom of the steps, I didn't want to make any guesses, didn't want to know—and his eyes were fixed on me as he came up. I couldn't meet his gaze and I looked out behind him as I stood back to let him pass. The landscape out there was... I don't know... *simultaneous*. I don't know how else to describe it. It was a long English front garden ending in a hedge and a wooden gate and the sun had just set. And at the same time, it was brown and barren, spoiled land with patches of thick mist coalescing and diffusing, hovering over it. It was both of those things together. It didn't fade from one and into the other. It was more like seeing the result of two negatives printed onto the same photo paper. I was very glad to close the door on it.

"But of course, I'd let the worst part in.

"He looked down at me for a second or two as he stood in the hallway by the closed door and then he turned his head in the direction of the room where the others were before looking back at me and nodding. That nod meant lots of things. It meant 'Yes, we're going to that room'. It meant 'Yes, it had to be you who opened the door'. It meant 'Yes, I know you're just playing along'. It meant 'Yes, I am what you think I am'.

"I walked ahead of him in the dark, leading the way back to the television room. I went into the room but realized he hadn't followed me in, so I stopped a few feet inside, not sure what to do or say. I think the telly was still on, I'm not sure. They all turned to face me, and somebody said, 'Who is it, Lisette?' and I didn't say anything and somebody else said 'Who is it, Lisette?' and I still didn't say anything and then they were all saying, 'Who is it, Lisette?', 'Who is it, Lisette?', 'Who is it, Lisette?' And then, from outside the room, he laughed, and they all stopped talking and he walked into the room to stand behind me.

"His voice was like coal. 'Yes,' he said. 'She's brought someone in with her, hasn't she?' And then it all began to go dark. Not slowly. Not quickly. Not normally. The darkness slid down from the ceiling like something almost solid, blacking out the wallpaper and the light inch by inch. People say, 'Darkness fell', don't they? But they don't really mean it. But that's just what was happening. Darkness was falling on us, oozing down the walls like something solid and hungry, something conscious and malicious. It felt... terminal.

"It's hard to tell people your nightmares because the details aren't enough to convey what it felt like. It's the *feeling* that counts, and you can never really tell them the feeling, can you? And this felt so awful, like everything was over. Not like the end of the world, but like the world had never really been there in the first place.

"The darkness didn't stop falling and, as it got about halfway down the room, as all the grownups' heads disappeared inside it, I began to scream. And scream. And scream."

Lisette stopped.

"God," said David's voice. "What happened then?"

"Then I woke up still screaming and my mother came in and held me and told me it was alright."

Lisette exhaled and, for the first time since she began her story, turned her head slightly to look at the man beside her. His face was still turned to the ceiling. He nodded his head slowly.

"Mmm," he said. "A good one. Definitely a good one." His voice had a strange musing quality to it. He reached over Lisette and, from the unit on her side of the bed, helped himself to a cigarette from the packet of Benson & Hedges that was lying there.

"Good job your mum was there, eh?" he said. He put the cigarette in his mouth but remained raised on one elbow, looking down at her. His question had been couched rhetorically but before Lisette could make even a token answer he spoke again. "Where's your mum now?"

Lisette gave him a puzzled look. "She's in Toronto," she said. "Visiting my... don't you want a light for that?"

"No." The cigarette disappeared whole into David's mouth, which began chewing on it.

Lisette giggled, but she could hear the nervous edge to it and stopped herself. "What are you—" she began to say, but David's voice interrupted her.

"*Yes. She's brought someone in with her,*" he said. "Scary. Very scary. Lisette, would you like to see who I've brought in with *me*?"

"David. Don't mess," Lisette said. Telling the story had, as always, both thrilled and frightened her and she felt a little too receptive to enjoy playing any spooky games.

"I'm not messing, Lisette," he said. "Look. Look at me."

Alright, now he was pissing her off. She looked up, annoyed and unafraid. "David!" she snapped. "I'm not fucking kidding!"

"Nor am I," he said. And then he took his shades off.

Lisette began to scream. And scream. And scream.

3. Yakety-Yak (Don't Talk Back)

On an early morning bus containing seven or eight early-shift weekend laborers making their way to factories and offices and one or two Friday night adulterers making their way to tears and excuses, the thing with the black suit and blood on its collar found a seat halfway down the length of the lower deck. In its hand was a bus ticket, in its jacket pocket one or two grisly souvenirs, and in its head the ceaseless sound of a young man's anguish.

The cuckoo spirit in David's body had amused itself during the course of its adventure with Lisette by switching its host's perceptions on and off at random intervals, so that for David the experience had been like taking part in a movie which had been edited by an impatient drunk and then censored by some hypothetical antithesis of the moral majority.

The whole episode, in David's perceived time, had lasted just over a minute and, apart from an establishing view of the outside of Charles's house, had consisted entirely of jump-cuts between acts of sex and violence: a few seconds of Lisette's beautiful head sliding up and down his erection; her face in the contortion of her climax; random sentences from her telling of what sounded like a creepy story; frightened eyes; a lot of blood. Finally, from the viewpoint of the bedroom door, like a last long-shot needing only closing music and end credits to place it in the sole context he could recognize for it, David had been granted a lingering glimpse of what had once been a girl he had known for four years.

She lay on the bed on her back. On her back, but face-down; her head had been twisted around to an absurdly unnatural degree and her face was pressed into the pillow. A large red stain on the pillow seemed to issue directly from her mouth.

She had been opened from sternum to *mons veneris*. It was not a neat job, though it was clear that a tidy mind had been involved afterwards; several of the internal organs, removed from their home of twenty-three years, were displayed as an orderly though bloody group on a white sheet spread on the floor at the foot of the bed. Taking their place inside Lisette and staring back at David in dumb reproach, its once pristine fur soaked in its mistress's blood, was a large cuddly Garfield cat, the head and shoulders of which alone were visible over the edges of the torn and tortured flesh.

The thing had taken David out of the house before it woke him again and it was only on a wooden bench near the bus stop at the corner of Dovedale road and Rose Lane that David was allowed time to fully realize the enormity of what had happened.

Even as separate predators, grief, fear, and horror can render the wisest philosopher incoherent. Attacking as a pack, they can silence angels and still the mouths of gods. David Holloway was neither angelic nor divine, and such wisdom as he owned was a small and fragile thing which had fled before the fury of this assault, leaving David to stare unaided into the abyss. To describe him as dumbstruck would be accurate but far from adequate. *Gutted*—a word in vogue among David and his friends for the last year or so and used humorously and fecklessly for the most part—began to bounce itself around his mind. The remnants of his sanity seized upon it as a point of focus, as sanity will when catastrophe capers. How the mind gets busy when the world dissolves. How the eye is drawn—in the face of bankruptcy, infidelity, death—to the insignificant detail; to the poor spelling of the bank's typist, to the mole on the faithless cheek, to the scratch on the coffin's handle.

Gutted, David began to repeat to himself. *Gutted. I'm gutted.* And then the other's voice emerged from David's mouth to correct him.

"No, no, David," it said, like a chiding but compassionate teacher who feels your pain but insists on maintaining standards of accuracy. "Let's get it right. *She's* gutted. *You're...* well, I don't really know. Flabbergasted, perhaps?" The voice altered itself before continuing, "Ooh, your gast has never been so flabbered."

The Frankie Howerd imitation was pretty spot-on, but David was neither impressed nor amused. Somewhere inside his head, behind his silent lips, his own voice replied.

You fucking bastard. How could you do that? Why?

"How could *I*? I didn't do anything, David. The sooner you disabuse yourself of that notion, the better. I mean, nobody's going to find *my* fingerprints on the lovely Lisette, are they?"

But—

"No buts, dear boy. It's about time you started facing up

to your responsibilities. When the Constabulary come, David, they'll be coming for *you*."

But—

"But *what*? You'll explain? Oh, well, that's alright then. That'll make everything just hunky dory, won't it? I can see it now. *It wasn't me, officer, it was this large glutinous mass of malice that has of recent date taken over my poor innocent body.* 'Oh, I see, Sir. Well, in that case, we'll say no more about it. You're free to go. Only—if you don't mind?—before you pop off and enjoy the rest of your day, would you just rest your testicles on my note-pad here while I take a brief moment to express my disgust with the thick end of me truncheon?' Yes indeed, that'll go down a storm, David. A *storm*."

The bus had arrived during the silence the that followed this exchange and David, beyond questions, merely wept silently behind the blank facade of his borrowed face as the creature went through a pantomime of politeness and normality, paying its fare, taking its ticket, nodding at one or two of its fellow passengers, and finding its seat.

The bus drove a circuitous route from the fringes of Mossley Hill to the students and dole-ites section of Wavertree where David's flat was—they could have walked home quicker—and for more than ten minutes of the journey the creature left David alone with his shock, apart from an occasional fondle of the ear and two fingers which were in the pocket of their jacket.

They were still several stops away from home when something caught whatever passed for the creature's eye. Several of the windows on the bus, including the one by which they sat, boasted a transfer stuck on the glass. The transfer, in bright red print, bore a message about vandalism and its consequences:

WILFUL DAMAGE TO SEATS, ETC.
THE EXECUTIVE WILL PRESS
FOR HEAVIEST PENALTIES
AGAINST OFFENDERS.

The creature began to giggle, though David at first couldn't tell why. Reaching their hand into a trouser pocket, the creature produced David's front door key and set about amending the Corporation's message by removing certain letters with a scraping action. David's hand worked diligently and neatly and, after a couple of minute's effort, had succeeded in revealing—as if it had always been the hidden subtext of the first—an infinitely more ominous warning:

WILFUL DAMAGE TO SEATS, ETC.
THE EXECUTIVE WILL PRESS
H   IS PEN I S
AGAINST OFFENDERS.

The creature sat back, beaming with pride at its work. A low chuckle began to escape from its borrowed mouth as it dwelt on the images conjured up by the revised message. David too, against his will and against the claims of despair, found it rather funny and began to add a second silent laugh to the one already issuing from his mouth. The more he thought about it, the funnier it became. Inside his head he spoke, between giggles, to his tenant.

Hey, maybe there's a special room, he said. *Somewhere at the dark end of the depot. Where they take transgressors. Probably got a little plaque outside: Office of her Majesty's Penis Presser.*

The creature burst out into a huge belly laugh, gasping for air and grasping at the seat. Suddenly it realized that the sound of its mirth had drawn attention from the front of the of the bus, that the driver was staring back along its length via the rear-view mirror in his compartment.

"Hey!" the driver shouted. "You in the suit! Keep it down!"

Keep it down? David said internally. *Tell that to the Executive. He's the one waving his fucking nudger about.* The creature let out a fresh guffaw and the driver, feeling his authority challenged by this, adopted a harsher tone.

"I told you to shut it, mate!" he shouted.

"He's been writing on the window," said a helpful female voice from the back of the bus a couple of rows behind the troublemaker. The driver instantly pulled the bus to a halt.

"Right, you. Off!" he said, opening the front door automatically from his seat and gesturing dramatically with his left arm.

The creature, by now nearly helpless with laughter, stood up and walked obediently toward the indicated exit.

"Go on. Gerrout of it," the driver said as his passenger disembarked. "Think yourself lucky I don't report you."

David's body turned around on the pavement and his face grinned back through the open door at the driver.

"Yeah? Who to?" he said. "The executive? What will he do? Stick his dick in my ear?"

The very accurate Richard Pryor was lost on the driver, but the self-congratulatory laughter was not. "Piss off, you little yob," he said from the safety of his seat.

"Tell you what, mate," said the creature. "I'll leave it with you. Tell him to give it a good press."

The driver felt something hit his face and fall, to land in his lap.

He was still staring, stunned and sickened, at the severed human ear that lay on his knees as the vandal disappeared running down a side street, his hysterical laughter ringing in the air.

4. At the Hop

Seen from the outside, the social club was a large one-storey rectangle of gray concrete. It was set, as if by chance, in an uncared-for field with only its own car park and gravel driveway for company and was several hundred yards away from the last of the tower blocks of the large working-class estate which it had been built to serve.

The club's only external concession to the decorative impulse was the presence of an illuminated sign over each of the two doors which were let into the one of its longer walls that faced west. One of these signs, in a triumph of minimalism, said simply *Bar*, while the other, in happy ignorance of the incongruity of its implicit promise and its actual potential, said *Gaiety Lounge*.

Beyond this second door you would find a small lobby where, should you not be a member of the district social club, you would be asked to pay a nominal sum of money in order to be admitted through a further door into the palace of pleasure itself.

The Gaiety Lounge was of simple design. At one end of its rectangular shape was a stage, at the other a bar, and in the middle were long rows of narrow tables with seats running up and down their length. By half past nine on this particular

Saturday night nearly all of those seats were occupied and the temporary owners of those seats who were not at that moment sitting down were either busy in the collecting of liquid or busy in the disposing of it.

The air was full of music and chatter as the jukebox competed with various exchanges of the week's gossip. Like most clubs of its type—and unlike the more sophisticated nightclubs in the heart of the city which drew an almost exclusively young crowd—the clientele of this place ranged in years from teenagers to pensioners and this lack of segregation continued even down to the seating arrangements at the tables. Girlfriends rubbed shoulders with grandmothers and elderly widowers discussed football with boys only just getting used to the taste of beer.

Ahead of all of them was an evening of reassuring familiarity. There'd be the Bingo, there'd be the live entertainment, there'd be a little dancing, and there'd be drunkenness sufficient to convince them that they were all having a good time.

It was generally a friendly place and, unlike some superficially similar clubs, strangers were ignored more for reasons of tact than for reasons of hostility. Furthermore, once two or three people had recognized the weirdo at the bar as Jimmy Holloway's lad, David and his parasite were doubly safe from any unprovoked harassment. Jimmy'd been a good drinking companion and a tough bugger to beat on the snooker table, and his move to the greener fields of Wales following his widowing at the hands of a cruel and leisurely cancer was regretted but not resented by the normally aggressive parochialism of the people among whom he had spent his callow years.

One of the regulars, a contemporary of Jimmy's who had recognized his son when the latter first came in, found himself standing next to him at the bar later in the evening. The Bingo was being cleared away and the turn was about to come on.

"Alright, lad," the man said in greeting, along with a nod and a smile. "How's your dad?"

For a moment, the young man appeared to stiffen and hesitate, and the older man wondered if for some reason he was afraid to speak.

It was not, of course, the act of speaking that David was afraid of, but of what his mouth might say. For the moment, though, his fears proved groundless. "Fine, fine," he heard his voice say. "Haven't seen him for a while, actually. But, you know, we talk on the phone and everything." The imitation was faultless, even down to the nodding and bobbing of the head as the kind of vague signal of friendliness that was entirely appropriate to the situation. "I'll... er... I'll send him your best, eh?"

"Yeah, yeah," said the older man. "Send him me best. Definitely. Definitely. Yeah. And... er... how about yourself, like? Doing alright and everything?"

It was becoming difficult. The divisive specter of Further Education hovered above their conversation and the older man was plainly as relieved as David when his voice replied with a universally acknowledged polite method of excusing oneself. "Oh, I'm fine too, thanks. Yeah. Look, I'm just going to have a quick burst before the band comes on, alright? I'll see you later, yeah?"

"Yeah, alright, lad," the man said. "Take care now." He turned his attention back to trying to catch the barmaid's eye.

By the time the band did come on, David had been fully assimilated into everybody's perception of the evening. Bit of a wanker in the fucking suit and everything, but no skin off anyone's arse. Consequently, no eyes followed him more than casually as he wandered, apparently aimlessly, around and around the internal perimeter of the lounge, sipping at his pint and occasionally standing still and studying the evening's act.

The act in question was a small combo of organ, electric bass, and drums. The vocals were shared out pretty evenly between the bassist and the keyboard player. All three musicians were in their late thirties and all three were inevitably dressed like teenagers, though the energy of teenagers was sadly lacking from their performance. Competent professionalism compensated as much as it ever does and the audience's predisposition to enjoy themselves helped a great deal.

The material the band was offering was the predictable mix. Some current chart successes, several old rock and roll songs and, scattered throughout the set, both types of sentimental ballad—the irresistibly beautiful and the nauseatingly contrived. Both types were being performed on this occasion with a depressingly fair-minded equality of enthusiasm.

After he and his colleagues had been performing for about twenty-five minutes or so, the bassist graciously surrendered his microphone to a septuagenarian who had arisen unbidden from his place amidst the tables and, advancing to the foot of the stage and turning to face what had been his fellows and were now his audience, had announced that he was going to sing *The Yellow Rose of Texas*. Sing it he undeniably did, though his particular arrangement of it, idiosyncratic to say the least, ensured that the musicians worked harder in their accompaniment of him than they had worked all night. It was no surprise to them, seasoned veterans of the Social Club circuit as they were, that it also received the warmest applause of the set so far.

Harry—for such, judging by the cries of encouragement

during his performance, was his name—returned to his proud table-mates while wolf-whistles still pierced the air and glasses still thudded against tabletops in rhythmic approbation. The keyboard player, years of experience having granted him an ability to judge accurately the mood of an audience, shouted through his microphone over the cheers.

"Brilliant! Brilliant!" he said. "Fantastic! Nice one, Harry. Pride of Cantril Farm!" The drummer shot him a look like he'd just played the opening chords of *The Rising of the Green* at an Orange Lodge party.

"Netherly, you fucking tosser!" shouted someone from the audience, and a couple of hard cases rose to their feet from a table at the rear like maybe the evening was going to turn out a little better than they'd hoped.

Wisely, the keyboard player instantly locked eyes with a blue haired matriarch near the front. "Ah, 'ey, love," he said, still into the microphone. "You'll have to forgive me. I don't half get confused. I'm in agony 'ere." He gestured to his piano stool and twitched his bottom in wounded fashion. "It's the hemorrhoids, you know what I mean?"

The old woman chuckled sympathetically. "Are they giving you gyp, love?" she shouted up at the stage.

"Ah, I'm not messing, darlin'," he said. "Honest. Me arse is like a plate of frigging spaghetti."

The old woman laughed uproariously, and the rest of the crowd followed her lead. Crisis averted, the keyboard player made to get the evening back on track. "Anybody else out there got a song they wanna do?" he shouted. "Or are youse all gonna let Harry walk away with it?"

While all around the club would-be performers wasted

precious time in false modesty, a figure in black ran forward, jumped up onto the stage, and had a quick whispered conversation with the bass player. The bass player then turned to cue the other musicians while the new member of the line-up adjusted the mic-stand for height and spoke to the audience.

Said audience was somewhat nonplussed. This kind of thing was normally considered entirely the province of regulars, and the general mood was that it was rather unseemly that a stranger should usurp it. Further, it suggested a kind of seriousness of intent that was entirely out of keeping with the spirit of the thing, and the intruder's introductory remarks did little to lessen the incongruity.

"Right!" he shouted into the mic in an authoritative voice which wouldn't have been out of place for a headline act in a major concert hall. "We're going to start off..."

What are you doing?! I can't fucking sing! What is this!?

"...with what they call a rave from the grave. Let's..."

Oh Christ. Don't. Please don't.

"...see some dancing out there! Let's hear some hands clapping! Let's have..."

I'm shitting meself!

"...a good time! HIT IT!"

This last was of course to the band—who were very nearly as bemused as the punters by this breathtaking pushiness. The guy was clearly a knobhead, they thought, and almost certainly an insane knobhead. That said, he was at least a confident insane knobhead, So, what the fuck, they hit it.

BAM!

Dum-dum-dum-dum

BAM-BAM!

With the first explosive staccato chord the figure in black leapt into the air and began a vigorous, flailing dance, a kind of choreographic collage of steps from the Mashed Potato, the Twist, the Pony, the Hand-Jive, and any other hideously outdated dance routine you could care to mention. And all enmeshed within something of his own creation which, even as he was seizing the mic for his vocal debut, he was already christening the Happy Spastic.

"Here she come now, say Mony Mony!"

BAM!

Dum-dum-dum-dum

BAM-BAM!

From the first barked syllable it was clear that he was brilliant. The audience knew it, sensed it the way an audience can, and responded instantly and unselfconsciously, pulled en masse into the magic. Throughout the entire Lounge spontaneous clapping broke out, astonishingly in time, miraculously on the off-beat. Several brave couples were on the dance floor in front of the stage before the end of the song's first line. Women whistled, young men howled, mothers taught daughters the Twist, people shook their heads and bodies in wild celebration. It was great. The band members found each other's eyes, exchanged delighted grins, and began to play—for the first time in years—like they actually gave a shit.

He growled. He howled. He twisted and turned. He did the knee drop, the hip flip, the pelvic thrust. He strutted. He strolled. He fell to the floor. And all the time mouthing the nonsense syllables in the perfect manic frenzy, dripping with psychosis and sincerity. He was wilder than Little Richard, more beautifully insane than Jerry Lee. He was *there*. He was *it*. He was the uncrowned King of Garbage. He *was* Tommy James & the Shondells.

And then it was over. With an imperious yanking gesture of his right arm, he stopped the band cleanly on a downbeat, allowing no post-orgasmic trills or rolls to come between him and his audience's gratitude. And even as this gratitude expressed itself in whistles and roars, even as men of forty-five raised clenched fists in victory salutes, even as sixteen-year-old girls pressed against the front of the stage with promises in their eyes, he was gone. One sharp bow and then off the stage in a rush, flinging himself into the closet-with-a-mirror that passed for a dressing room.

David stared in the mirror and saw his fingers run through his sweat-soaked hair, flicking it back and up into a kind of James Dean goes punk. The huge grin came perilously close to vitiating the cool that the black shades conveyed, but it was undeniably charming. From behind him, resonating through the club, he could hear the chanted demands for more. He saw his lips move in the mirror.

"What do you think, David?" he heard his voice say.

Yeah. Yeah! That was great!

"Right. Let's go back out, then. Give the people what they want." The creature paused and David saw his reflection cast an appraising eye up and down his body. "Tell you what," his voice said. "Why don't I twist around a bit inside here? Just to aid the charisma, know what I mean? Slimmer hips, maybe? Broader shoulders? Bigger cock-bulge? What do you think?"

David thought.

I think you've got a fucking big mouth for something made out of pink spaghetti and snot. Let's go.

The creature laughed with delight and affection and ran back on stage. The audience greeted him with louder whistles, louder cheers, and renewed applause. The band was smiling.

"Whatever you want, mate," said the drummer. "You call it, we'll play it."

Requests were being shouted from the floor as the star of the evening took hold of the microphone again, but all of them were ignored. David spoke to the creature.

How about "I've got you under my skin"?

"Nice one, David," the creature replied. "But I've got a better idea."

The audience—who had of course heard only the second part of this exchange—were only allowed a moment or two to be confused by it, because suddenly, deafeningly, in a hoarse scream like that of a laryngitic Hitler, the figure at the microphone proclaimed:

"I AM THE GOD OF HELLFIRE AND I BRING YOU... FIRE!!!"

This was unexpected.

The crowd quietened. The bass player looked at the drummer and shrugged. The drummer looked at his cowbell and sniffed. The keyboard player, unlike his partners, did in fact have a hazy recollection of The Crazy World of Arthur Brown and of their one hit single—the opening line of which the guy at the mic had just howled—but he didn't have a clue as to how to play it and he was frankly unconvinced that it was altogether an inspired choice of encore anyway.

There was a pregnant silence, aborted by a repeated scream from the front of the stage.

"I AM THE GOD OF HELLFIRE AND I BRING YOU—"

And this time, directly on cue...

"—FIRE!"

...in a massive, searing, blinding explosion of color, heat, and horror, the Gaiety Lounge burst into flames.

◆ ◆ ◆ ◆

Some survivors—for there were some survivors—stated later to the Police that the madman had been seen wandering around the edges of the Lounge at an earlier point in the evening, and more than one of them ventured the suggestion that what he must have been doing, for some obscure insane reason, was laying trails of kerosene or something similar all about the place, intending all along to wreak the havoc he wrought. This was one school of thought.

The survivors counted two among their number, however, who espoused a quite different theory. They were both older women, both Roman Catholics, and they both swore that the flames had issued spontaneously and diabolically from the boy's mouth, nose, eyes, and fingertips and had spread almost instantaneously into circles of Hellfire that engulfed the whole of the club's interior and all of its helpless inhabitants.

Whether the ultimate source was human malice or demonic magic, however, the one thing that was certain was that the flames had seized the Lounge in a rapid, virulent, and all but unshakable grasp.

Not a single one of the exits from the place was reachable without first passing through the fire and only those people driven enough by instinct to waste no time in dismay or speculation were able to run through doors or jump through windows without finding on arriving outside that they had brought the fire with them, still forcing its attentions in a more intimate but no less agonizing embrace.

The musicians alone were able to reach the open air completely unscathed as there was a fire door at the rear of the stage area which gave directly onto the car park.

The drummer, whose brother and sister-in-law were in the audience, held his ground for a few seconds longer than his fellows, his panic temporarily held at bay by a murderous rage directed at the person responsible for the carnage.

One look at the singer's face, however, one heart-stopping glance at the unholy glee that lit his features, one moment's listening to the unbalanced laughter, rich in perverse joy, that emanated from his mouth, changed the drummer's attitude. Putting revenge on hold, he threw himself after his colleagues.

On the main floor of the Lounge people screamed, ran, stumbled, and burned. People cried for help, choked on smoke, wept with terror, and burned. People tripped over tables, they tripped over chairs, they tripped over the dead and the dying, and they burned. Hairs raced for scalps like terrified fuses, sweat turned to steam, skin bubbled and burst.

Everywhere was fire and chaos. Hungry flame ate at the oxygen for which panicked lungs were gasping. People ran blind, the eyes clouded both by the tears they were producing in useless defense against the smoke and by the smoke itself. Shattering screams of terminal terror competed for airspace with howls of blistered agony and with hideous racking choking coughs.

The crowd melted into disparate and desperate smaller sections. Some of these were miniature crowds themselves that ran in groups, surrendering individual reaction to the mass mind— which is no mind at all but instinct at its most pathetic and pernicious—and paid the price by discovering, as weaker members fell beneath the feet of stronger, that pressed and panicked flesh can suffocate you just as efficiently as can smoke. Others ran alone, self-determined but still vulnerable.

One woman, sensibly throwing a chair rather than herself through a window, foolishly balanced herself on the back of another chair to haul herself through. This second chair slipped beneath her shifting weight. The woman lost her balance and impaled herself on a large and unremoved shard of glass, hanging there helpless and dying as the flames blistered her legs.

One man, unwisely running against the flow of a crowd rather than with it, was knocked to the floor. Before he could rise to his feet, his hip bones were shattered by a falling table. In the midst of his agonized and probably pointless struggle to free himself, another mass of people ran over him and his left eye was put out by a teenager's stiletto heel. The fire took two minutes to kill him.

Fifty-seven people died within the inferno and five more joined them over the course of the next two days, having lingered for differing amounts of time in the ICU at Sefton General. A further forty suffered severe burns involving varying degrees of disfigurement, and three score more had to have some kind of medical attention.

The evening's main attraction didn't hang around to see the full results of his final number. Instead, like a star diving for the limo even as the band plays the coda, he exited early in the conflagration through the same fire door that his collaborators had used.

The musicians had already rushed to the front of the building to raise the alarm and offer assistance, so he was quite unimpeded as he walked through the car park and into the fields beyond, tie loosened and jacket hooked casually over one shoulder, humming a little tune to himself and staring at the moon.

5. Ebb Tide

It was during the sodomizing of the dead boy in the attic bedroom of an otherwise empty house that the creature told David it was going to leave.

It explained, as gently as possible, that it felt it had now tasted enough of the world and its pleasures. It had known laughter and debate, had induced rapture, veneration, terror, and death, had had sex with both kinds of people (*Men and women?* David had naively asked. "Living and dead," the creature had explained), and consequently had decided to move on in order to sample other experiences; chiefly that of being deceased. It intended, in short, to vacate Davids body via the orgasmic route and to take up residence in that of the dead teenager whom they were currently buggering vigorously.

But what about me? David asked, in a plaintive tone that was a curious mix of fright and possessiveness.

"Don't worry, David," the creature said. "I've made arrangements. You'll be well looked after."

What do you mean?

The creature's reply had that strange tone that parents use when explaining the rapid approach of something they know the child won't like but is, in their opinion, for its own good, like a spanking or a Boarding School. "Well," it said. "I took the Liberty of phoning the Police shortly after we broke in. They should be here any moment."

But there's nothing left inside me! David shouted, like a spurned lover or rejected child seizing at some pathetic practical objection when the true one—don't leave me!—is too shaming to voice.

"Oh, that!" said the creature. "Don't worry about that. I'll make sure there's enough substance left to perform the basic motor functions. No one will ever know, I promise. It'll be like I was never here. I'll even give you some eyes back."

David's panic was now approaching that of the condemned man who, within feet of the scaffold, begins to scream that he has left his room untidy, that he needs a drink, that he needs to make his bed, needs to piss, needs to put a book away, needs…

But how—

"David, the creature interrupted. "Surely it's clear to you by now that I can do anything?"

A world of possibilities seemed to be being snatched from David before he had had a chance to even consider them.

But I wanted to… I wanted… I—

"David, I can do anything, but I can't do *everything*. Better to go out on a high, I think. Ah, speaking of which—you're coming. And I'm going."

David's despairing scream was lost in a flurry of chemical and organic activity.

◆ ◆ ◆ ◆

When Inspector Anthony Murrow, the senior policeman on the case, arrived at the scene of the crime, the suspect was sitting quietly in the company of two uniformed officers.

Murrow had had fifteen years on the beat before his ten behind a desk and his instincts for criminal types was still pretty sharp. He could tell at a glance that the lad wasn't going to give them any trouble, despite the grotesque little trail he appeared to have blazed for himself over the last couple of days.

Murrow walked across the attic room to where the body of Leslie Castle, for such was the dead boy's name, lay awaiting the arrival of the coroner and the police photographer. He nodded at Hayes, the more experienced of the two constables, to join him and bring him up to speed.

Hayes told what little he knew of the facts and then ventured an opinion. "He's obviously off his head, Sir," he said. "He reckons as how it wasn't really him that did it."

"That so?" said Murrow, looking back at David for a moment.

"It was this... this thing inside him," said Hayes. "So he says, anyway. A monster. Made of *worms*. And he reckons he can prove it." Hayes paused significantly.

Murow let a second or two pass. "Are you expecting me to *guess*, constable?" he said.

"No, Sir. Sorry, Sir," Hayes said. "He says the thing's gone now, you see. Gone into the corpse instead. And Holloway says that if we keep watching, we'll see the worms come out of the body when... well, when this thing gets *bored*. Sir."

Murrow raised a slow eyebrow and then walked across the room to sit down opposite the suspect. In a not unkind voice, he asked a question. "This... this *thing*, David?" he said. "What does it *do*?"

The young man—Christ, *boy* really. What could he be? Twenty-two, twenty-three?—stared blankly at him for a few moments, but finally he spoke.

"Sometimes it sings," he said.

"Sometimes it sings," Murrow repeated, and slowly looked

across the room to the body. "Is it singing now?" he asked, in a voice skillfully devoid of disbelief, of contempt, of anything beyond honest enquiry.

David turned his head, following the inspector's gaze. Again, there was silence for a time as they both looked at the corpse, at its perfect stillness, and then David looked back at his interrogator and smiled.

He smiled in a manner that Murrow, for he was a man much given to words of resonance and much taken with the strange ambiguities of slaughter, would later describe to his wife as melancholic and wistful.

"Yes," said David. "It's singing now."

♦ ♦ ♦ ♦

Later, Leslie Castle would be buried beneath the ground, his people being old fashioned enough to shy away from cremation.

Later still, just as David had predicted, the worms would emerge from Leslie's body.

As to whether this second event succeeded the first by a matter of minutes or a matter of months, as to whether the worms poured forth prompted by the unnatural boredom of a monster or by the natural process of corruption, as to whether they emerged singly and simpleminded or bonded to each other and to a hideous guiding intelligence, as to all this...

Life and death have their secrets, the world has only guesses.

YOU ARE WHAT YOU EAT

—*click*—

"Okay, tape is running. For the record, I am Detective Lieutenant Consolata Meadows, and this is an informal debriefing, at the request of Internal Affairs, on case number 3472. Present, on a voluntary basis, is Detective Sergeant James Bertrand. Interview begins 9:45 am. Good morning, Detective."

"Lieutenant."

"You need anything? ... Yeah, that headshake's not going to record, Sergeant. I'll need all your responses verbally, please."

"Understood, Ma'am. Sorry."

"So... do you?"

"Ma'am?"

"Need anything?"

"Oh. No, I'm fine, Lieutenant. Thank you."

"You mind if I smoke?"

"No. But I didn't know you—"

"Habit I picked up recently. Very recently. From a perp we obtained. You know how it is."

"Yes, Ma'am. I do."

"Okay. Background data first. Your original DOB?"

"November 4th, 1989."

"And your HTZT date?"

"Human to Zombie Transformation?"

"Unless you know of another phrase that enjoys that un-likely acronym."

"No, Ma'am. Sorry. October 17th last year."

"And you were never just a Walker, right? You came back verbal? Sharp? Limber?"

"Second wave from the get-go, Ma'am."

"And—given your Police background in the Old World—you were pretty swiftly recruited to Security Enforcement?"

"Yes, Ma'am. October 31st."

"Really?"

"Yes, Ma'am."

"Happy Halloween."

"Ma'am?"

"Sorry. Humor. Something else I inherited from someone."

"Right. Strange, isn't it?"

"What is? Humor?"

"No. No, that thing. The… picking up of—"

"The YAWYE Syndrome."

"Yar-yuh?"

"That's what they're calling it. YAWYE. Another little ac-ronym for us to learn. You Are What You Eat. You might want to remember that if you talk to a lawyer."

"Do I need a lawyer?"

"Don't know. What do you think?

"Do we even *have* lawyers?"

"Second oldest profession, Detective Sergeant. New Order or Old. Now, shall we get on with why we're here?"

"Ma'am? With respect, I don't *know* why we're here."

"It's just a debriefing. Pretty routine."

"Is it?"

"Isn't it?"

"I don't know. I was given an assignment. I completed it. Filed a report. I'm not sure what the problem is."

"You think there's a problem, Detective Sergeant?"

"I don't know, Ma'am. Like I said."

"Like you said. Excuse me a moment."

"You're stubbing that thing out? You didn't even smoke half of it."

"Yeah, I know. It's weird. I feel the urge, act on it, but the smoking itself doesn't give me much of anything."

"So why do it?"

"Why not? What's it gonna do? Kill me?"

"Huh. That was humor, wasn't it?"

"Graveyard humor, Detective Sergeant. Best kind. Now, let's talk about the late Martin Gifford and his odd little hobby. We have his journal, as you know. Have it thanks to your investigation, in fact. And what illuminating reading it makes. For the tape, I'm reading an extract from ZIS Exhibit B478, a small spiral-bound notebook, pages unlined, entries undated: *Here's the thing; they make it easier than it used to be. When girls were girls, they were suspicious sometimes. Now they're eager to be approached. Because they're hungry. Silly little undead things. They have no idea they're not as hungry as me.* Well, he sounds just delightful, doesn't he?"

"Humor?"

"Kind of. Look, we'll come back to the journal. First, let's get some case background for the record. Correct me at any point if your recollection differs, Sergeant: Following the successful pacification of Los Angeles and the official end to any organized resistance movement by the Untransformed, the strict military supervision of sectors NW4, NW5, and C2 was replaced by a less numbers-intensive defense policy, and responsibility transferred to local Security Enforcement. Not much to disagree with so far, right?"

"Right."

"Right. Over the course of a month-and-a-half, various patrols in those sectors discovered six bodies. Well, I say 'discovered' but it's not like the bodies were *hidden* or anything. Not hidden at all. In fact, it was more like they were *displayed*, wouldn't you say?"

"Judging by the reports, Ma'am, yes. And the photos."

"Left in plain sight for us to find. Correct?"

"Correct."

"Like somebody was saying, 'Check *this* the fuck out.' Like somebody was messing with us, maybe. Taunting us. Having a bit of fun with us."

"You could put it that way, Ma'am, I suppose."

"Well, certainly we could say someone was showing a blatant and insolent disregard for the New Order we were in the business of imposing, couldn't we?"

"Central Command seemed to think so."

"Indeed. Sensing a pattern to the killings that produced those bodies—wonder how long it took 'em to work *that* out?— our superiors initiated an investigation, and the docket landed on your desk."

"That's right, Ma'am."

"Let's check back in with the dear departed Mister Gifford, shall we? Here's a choice bit: *Look, I know I'm fussy. I know I don't take every opportunity that presents itself. But I have certain barriers of taste. And—especially in this changing world—someone's got to maintain standards. That's what I say. So, while that means I can sometimes go a long time without a playmate, it also means that I don't bring home someone unsuitable for mother.* 'Unsuitable for Mother'. Huh. Not a bad title if he was thinking of publishing this thing as a memoir."

"Ma'am, I doubt he intended to—"

"Seriously? You know, I think I'm going to call someone I know at the Meat Farms. See if we can get you a bit of stand-up for lunch. Get us on the same page here."

"I had a late breakfast. No need to—"

"I was kidding, sergeant."

"So was I, Ma'am."

"Oh. Nice. Nicely played."

"No disrespect intended, Ma'am. I was just—"

"No, no. We're good. You returned the volley. That's okay. You saw what I was doing. Picked up on it. Did the same. And you didn't need to take a bite out of me to do it. No YAWYE necessary. Just good old-fashioned monkey-see, monkey-do. No disrespect intended, Sergeant."

"No offense taken, Lieutenant."

"Okay. Let's get back on track. So… Given your ten years' experience with the LAPD before your HTZT, you were assigned to investigate the matter of these murders and the showboating of the bodies. And—depending upon the results of that investigation—authorized to take any appropriate further action. Correct?"

"Yes, Ma'am."

"I'm getting tired of my own voice, Detective Sergeant Bertrand. Talk me through it, would you?"

"Okay, Ma'am."

"Whenever you're ready."

"Yes, Ma'am. Sorry. I... Well... Seemed to me there were certain inescapable conclusions from the get-go. For one thing, it was clear that the killings weren't the work of any of *us*."

"Us? You mean Security Enforcement?"

"No, Ma'am. I mean... our kind. First, none of the victims were human. They were all recent transforms. Extremely recent, in fact."

"Oh yeah. Our old friend Martin's *very* clear about that: *It's impossible to find one completely unmarked of course, but what I try and find is one with a single wound. Someone who was, for whatever reason, abandoned after the killing bite. Best of all, as I'm sure you can guess, is when I can get them before they wake. That's only happened once before. Last night's was even better.*"

"Yes, Ma'am. So first, like I say, no humans. And second, the final dispatch of the victims—after the... activities... that preceded it—was the driving through the forehead and frontal lobes of a sharp and heavy metal object. I verified with the M.E.'s office that the actual implement was an industrial chisel-blade."

"A-ha. Someone's little variation on 'Shoot 'em in the Brain', one of our forerunners' favored methods of putting us out of our misery. This particular someone being a someone who either didn't have a gun or, more likely, a someone who thought guns just weren't intimate enough."

"Precisely, Ma'am."

"But—gun, chisel, or whatever the fuck—brain-trauma

execution was the M.O., and so you figured the killer you were looking for was human."

"Correct."

"A human was hunting down newborns, destroying them, and displaying them ostentatiously for us to find."

"Correct."

"You know what I call that, Detective Sergeant?"

"No, Ma'am."

"I call that uppity."

"I don't believe the motive was insurgency, Ma'am."

"I was joking, Detective Sergeant. But, please, clarify."

"The victims were all female. The nature of the mutilations was clearly fetishistic. And the bodies were attired in various costumes that indicated psycho-sexual obsession. We weren't looking for a member of the resistance movement, Ma'am. We were looking for a predator."

"No shit, Sergeant. Just listen to this fucker: *The Zees usually work in packs, so I was very conscious of my good luck when I came across my latest friend. As usual, I'd been hunting on the fringes of the Echo Park ghetto, where the unconverted still feel free to wander, and the dumb ones feel free to wander alone. I spotted a certain foolish little miss—young, pretty, ripe—who was just about to learn her lesson: She'd gotten herself cornered, but only by one of them. I enjoyed her screams as he herded her into an alley, biding my time. I let him take his first bite—happened to be from her stomach, could've been anywhere, not something I can control—and then stabbed him through the back of the head. She looked really grateful, until I knocked her out. By the time she woke up, I'd been able to get everything ready. She was already strapped to the table and, more importantly, I'd been able to take my time selecting her wardrobe for our date.* Wow. 'Our date'. Wow."

"By triangulating the locations of the bodies and using a series of surveillance operations, I was able—"

"I've read your report, Sergeant. Your police-work was frankly exemplary, but we don't need to rehash the details. That's not what this is about. Let's move on to what happened once you'd determined who and where the perp was."

"Yes, Ma'am."

"You found that our guy was a human male, thirty-four-years-old—later identified, once you discovered his journal, as Martin Gifford—who'd escaped our military sweeps by taking up residence in a former industrial location somewhere near downtown Hollywood. Melrose and Gower, to be precise."

"Yes, Ma'am."

"Now, help me out here. You were fairly convinced that this was your killer? Beyond a reasonable doubt, say?"

"Yes, Ma'am."

"And yet you kept him under observation for quite some time."

"I did. I…"

"Go ahead, Detective."

"I was trying to understand what his trigger was. Where the hunger came from. What sent him out. But after a couple of weeks—"

"And two more victims."

"Yes, Ma'am. After a couple of weeks, I realized I'd been overthinking it. It was just… it was just something he did. Something he did on Monday nights."

"Every Monday night?"

"Yes, Ma'am."

"You verified this by surveillance?"

"I did."

"Just something he did on Monday nights. Like a poker game."

"Or Karaoke."

"Just a way to pass the time. A way to have a bit of fun. They really are strange creatures, aren't they?"

"You may be right, Ma'am, but I don't think Gifford's a particularly good example from which to generalize."

"Fair point. He was kind of special, I suppose. And when I say 'special', I mean 'a fucking monster'."

"They used to call *us* monsters, didn't they?"

"They did. And what's left of them still do. And, from their perspective... I mean, we eat living flesh, Sergeant. *Their* living flesh. So, you know. But we do it because we *have to*. It's some bizarre biological imperative that our scientists don't understand any better than theirs did. We do it to survive. We don't do it for pleasure, or for fucking entertainment. Gifford was a monster. And most of the pre-transformed would've thought he was a monster, too. Just like most of us would think that now. Most of us. Anyway, the thing is, Detective Sergeant, what we're having trouble understanding—what I'd like you to help me out with—isn't *his* behavior. It's *yours*."

"Ma'am?"

"I understand your curiosity, I really do. But, nevertheless, you identified and located him on—let me check my notes here—the Monday of what would turn out to be his penultimate attack, the fifth of six victims."

"Yes, Ma'am."

"Did you have reason to assume he was unfit for the meat farms?"

"No, Ma'am."

"But nor did you immediately terminate him."

"No, Ma'am."

"No. In fact, you didn't apprehend and detain him until the day after the killing of his *sixth* victim.

"That's correct, Ma'am."

"And you chose to detain him in his own base of operations rather than bring him in?"

"Yes, Ma'am."

"And—besides not notifying your Supervising Officer that to all intents and purposes you'd closed the case—it was apparently a further ten days before you took appropriate disciplinary action."

"Ha."

"Sergeant?"

"*Appropriate disciplinary action.*"

"I'm amusing you."

"No, Ma'am."

"But you find my choice of words... what? A little bureaucratic? A little clinical?"

"Euphemistic, I'd say. Ma'am."

"Oh. How very precise of you. Then by all means, Detective, let's call a spade a spade. You didn't eat the little fucker for a week and a goddam half. What's up with that?"

"Not entirely accurate, Ma'am."

"How so?"

"I didn't *finish* eating him for a week and a half."

"Correction noted, Sergeant. Thank you. Here's one of Mister Gifford's last journal entries: *She was even younger than I'd thought and quite remarkably pretty. Mother and father were delighted by her, and quite entranced by the Victorian Maiden look I'd selected for her to wear. It suited the newborn pallor, of course, and lent an engaging sense of outrage to her screams. It really was one of our best nights together as a family."*

"The 'industrial location' you mentioned, Ma'am—the place where he'd based himself—it was what used to be a movie studio. He'd set up a nest in what they used to call a back-lot, this particular one being a simulacrum of a middle-class street. In one of the houses, he'd created a mock family for himself. Mother and father—long dead, you understand, and I mean *dead* dead, not like us—were sat at a fully-dressed dinner table. Gifford would bring his dates home to meet the family and then have his parents watch as he… consummated… the relationship. In various ways. And then they'd all—in his head, at least—partake of the family meal."

"The dates were dinner."

"Yes, Ma'am. Parts of them, at least."

"Perhaps not so very different from us after all, Bertrand."

"It's different, Ma'am."

"Is it?"

"Yes. Like you said earlier. He didn't *have* to do that. He *wanted* to."

"Boy, did he ever. Way he saw it, and I quote, *it is not enough to kill. It is not enough to eat. I want to hunt. I want to trap. I want to terrify. The meat is seasoned by its fear.* So, yeah, you're right. It's different. Gifford was different. Special. Was that why your eventual execution of him was so punitive? So fucking *thorough*? I mean, you didn't leave a single morsel, am I right?"

"I didn't."

"Let's change tack a moment. Gifford's last killing was

Monday, November 11th. And he himself—after his nine-day adventure with you—finally departed this world on a Wednesday. So you can imagine our surprise, I'm sure, when another body turned up the following Monday?"

"Bodies are always turning up, Ma'am. It's a jungle out there."

"Bodies are always turning up, Sergeant, but not bodies dressed in a cheerleader uniform and mutilated in ways familiar to anyone with a passing knowledge of this case."

"That does sound… specific."

"I agree. And yet the one person we can be sure isn't responsible is Martin Gifford. Because there isn't a single physical trace of Martin Gifford left on this earth, thanks to you. 'Some of them just don't deserve to come back,' is that what you were thinking?"

"I suppose I must have been."

"You were feeling anger, maybe? Perhaps even empathy for his victims? It's possible. YAWYE syndrome. You could have picked those things up."

"I could have."

"But you don't feel them now, do you?"

"I…"

"Sergeant?"

"I…"

"You feel your perspective has shifted now? Like maybe you've picked up something other than empathy? Something different? Something special?"

"I thought this was a debriefing, Ma'am."

"Well. Debriefing. Interview. Interrogation. Let's not be picky. Excuse me one second… For the tape, we've been joined in the room by Officer Lundholm and Officer Taylor. Sergeant, your fellow officers here are not only armed, they are also in no way inclined to take any shit from anyone, particularly someone who disgraces the uniform. I assume you're smart enough to realize that I'm going to need your badge and your gun and that I'm placing you under arrest. You—"

"It was like your cigarette, Ma'am. I felt—"

"We haven't imported Miranda Rights from the old order, Sergeant, so I don't *have* to caution you to stop talking, but you might want to give it some thought."

"Understood, Ma'am. Thank you."

"Thank *you*, Sergeant. It's been… enlightening. For the tape, interview terminated 9:59 am."

—*click*—

THE WAY CHARLIE SAW IT

Look, even if there *was* a dog—and I'm not saying there was, it's just that I'm done fucking arguing with B—I still don't see how it could've saved us. Those assholes meant *business.*

We're sitting in an interview room and telling a uniformed lady cop all about it. I've seen enough TV shows to know that the fact we haven't been split up to give separate statements means they don't think we did anything wrong, which is good. But it also means that they think we're probably full of shit, which is bad. And which is also, by the way, *so* unfair. I guess two fifteen-year-old girls are automatically Little Drama Queens Who Make Stuff Up. Because patriarchy.

"And the guys who took you," Lady Cop is saying now, "They were wearing *costumes*?"

"Not costumes," B says.

"Definitely costumes," I say.

We say these things at pretty much the exact same time and, as soon as we have, our heads snap round to let us give each other our best are-you-fucking-joking-me-now faces.

Lady Cop cuts in before we can argue the point.

"Costumes or not," she says, "did you know them?"

"I don't know who they were and I don't know where they took us," I say, "but I don't think it was random. Don't see how it could've been. They must've been looking for B and me."

"B and *I*," says the grammar-policewoman formerly known as B.

"Actually, it *is* B and me," says the real policewoman. She tries to soften the correction with a friendly smile, but I don't think she's fully aware of just how little it takes to get your name on B's shit-list. "What's the B stand for, by the way?" she follows up, wiggling a pen over the yellow pad on the table like she's asking in case she needs to make a note. She's had the pen the whole time we've been talking, though I've yet to see her actually write anything down.

"My name's Lacie," B says. Just a hint of frost on it.

Lady Cop looks puzzled. "Then—?"

"The B's for Beehive," I say, to keep things moving.

B cocks her head at me like that's news to her. "Really?" she says. "*That's* why?"

I look at her like, duh, of *course* that's why. She's worn her hair in a beehive next best thing to forever, ever since she saw an ancient YouTube clip of Amy Winehouse, some dead singer her older brother dug way back when he was in High School.

"Why did you think?" I ask her.

B shrugs. "I didn't think," she says. "I liked it. Sounded cool." Then, giving me the big eyes, "Maybe I thought it was for Bestie."

"Aw," I say, hand on heart.

"Or Best-looking."

"You're so retarded."

"Let's stay on track, girls," the cop says. "So, you don't know where you were taken, but perhaps—?"

"*I* know where we were taken," B interrupts. "She doesn't."

"Why do *you* know?" Lady Cop asks.

"Because unlike her," B says, "I'm not a fucking heathen." But she throws me one of her best B smiles to me let me know she loves me anyway.

The cop's brow furrows at this apparent left turn but—I guess because she's a trained professional and all—she doesn't let it distract her from what she's actually asking.

"So where were you?" she says.

B's eye-roll lets us know she can't believe how resistant everybody is to the blindingly obvious, but she at least manages not to tut out loud.

"In Hell," she says.

◆ ◆ ◆ ◆

The way Charlie saw it was this. If a ball goes down a hole, you go down the hole after it. You don't stop to think about it, you go fetch. Otherwise, what kind of dog are you? Ball needs fetching, you fetch the ball. It's not rocket science.

Had Charlie in fact been a practitioner of rocket science or some similarly cerebral occupation rather than being a dog, he might have paused to wonder about the specific hole down which the ball had gone, might have registered that thirty seconds earlier said hole hadn't been there at all, might have taken a moment to ponder the implications. But Charlie, if pressed on the point, would confess to caring little for abstract rumination and so his response to the hole—other than to give it a warning growl in case it was thinking of pulling any shit—was to pound his way straight down it, no questions asked. Ball to be fetched.

◆ ◆ ◆ ◆

Lady Cop's gearing up to say something in response to B's we-were-in-Hell mic-drop when she gets a text. Her phone's lying on the table next to her yellow pad—still untroubled by anything resembling a statement—and she's got her notifications on mute, but I see the screen light up and the text balloon open. Lady Cop picks it up, looks at the text, looks puzzled, looks at us with a careful deadpan, and finally looks to the door of the interview room which, with perfect timing, is swung open by another uniformed cop who holds it wide and leans back to allow some guy who's not in a uniform to walk past him and into the room.

The two uniforms exchange a glance and Lady Cop stands up, gathering her virginal notepad and her pointless pen like maybe she hopes they'll all three get lucky in some other interview room, and is out of here, pausing only to give the non-uniformed newcomer the kind of friendly-but-cautious smile you might give to a tiger you've been assured is housebroken. The guy—no tiger far as I can see, fortyish maybe, but quite fond of himself given the fancy old-school suit complete with vest and pocket square—gestures at the chair which Lady Cop has left warm for him.

"Hello, ladies," he says. "James Arcadia." The accent's British and a bit more Prince Harry than Idris Elba. "Do you mind if I sit?"

I let B's shrug answer for both of us. What do we care if he sits? But I suppose it's nice to be asked, and he did call us ladies, and he is kind of good looking in a friend's-hot-dad way.

First thing he does once he's sitting is throw a glance at the camera mounted in a corner of the ceiling. Moment he does, the red recording light goes out, which seems odd. All he did was look at it, far as I can tell, but what do I know? Maybe somebody was monitoring it and read his glance as a signal.

Looking back at us, he smiles conspiratorially, like we're all playing the same game, and says, "So much more fun when things are off the record, don't you think?"

B and I share an instinctive glance, like each of our creep radars just gave a little blip. Only a little one, but still. I mean, he doesn't *look* like a creep, but then neither do a lot of creeps.

"Are you a cop?" B asks.

"I'm occasionally called in to do a bit of consulting," he says. "But no, I'm not a policeman."

"So what are you then?"

"Well, technically, my doctorate was in—" he starts to say.

"The EMTs already checked us out," B interrupts.

"Not that kind of doctor," he says.

A penny drops for me. I *knew* Lady Cop had her doubts about us. "Are you here to check if we're batshit?" I ask him.

Most adult smiles—even the best intentioned—have a kind of pat-you-on-the-head-for-your-adorable-precociousness element to them, but this guy's grin seems more of the hey-look-we're-in-the-same-gang variety. "On the contrary," he says. "I know you're both very far from batshit. I think, in fact, you're both commendably sane given your unpleasant adventure earlier today."

"Wait," B says. "You believe us?" Her voice is a little guarded, like she's waiting for the other shoe to drop.

"Of course I believe you," he says. "I sent the dog."

◆ ◆ ◆

The way Charlie sees it is this. The pack comes first. Coming second are pack-members who for some reason live elsewhere but visit often and then—vying for third place with mailmen who've finally learned their lesson—come young non-pack females who nevertheless live nearby and who have, on more than one occasion, been kind enough to provide illicit snacks. Charlie thinks illicit snacks are just terrific and, while he's a good dog and would listen politely if some Canine Behaviorist were to explain why illicit snacking is bad for dogs, his first question to the behaviorist once they'd finished their explaining would be this: Do you have any snacks?

Look, if Charlie's going to be honest about his ranking system, young neighborhood females who have provided snacks may not actually come third. They may come eighth. Or thirty-seventh. Because, truth be told, what does Charlie know from numbers? Numbers are not really a strong suit for Charlie, or for any dog. But here's what Charlie does know as he emerges, ball firmly in mouth, from the tunnel that the hole became into the sulfurous cavern to which it led; he knows who comes way last. And that would be multi-limbed flame-skinned assholes who choose to wave their pitchforks at Charlie's friend Snack-girl and her buddy.

◆ ◆ ◆

"You sent Charlie?" B says.

"Charlie?" I say.

"The neighbors' black lab?" B says in her try-to-keep-up voice. "Loves M&Ms?"

"I did send Charlie," this Arcadia guy says. "I'd arrived a

little too late to prevent the anomaly, and I knew Charlie'd be able to reach you a lot faster than I could once the dimensional gateway had actually opened."

We both just WTF stare at him.

"Look, here's the thing," he says. "Can we back-track for a moment? Just to clarify a couple of things for me. Did one of you by any chance make an unusual purchase at an estate sale recently?"

B gives me an accusatory look. "I *told* you that thing was creepy," she says.

"Ah," Arcadia says, "May I see it?"

I fish it from inside my top and slip the chain over my head, letting the little ornament rest in my palm.

"Wow," he says, sounding delighted in the way I imagine medical doctors sound delighted when you show up with something utterly terminal but fascinatingly rare. "Don't see many of *those* on Etsy, do you?"

"What is it?" I ask him.

"Well, I know it looks like it might be merely ornamental," he says, "but it's actually a tool of invocation. To be honest, I'm impressed that it still works—it was really meant to be regionally and temporally specific to its Babylonian origins. But, you know, old-school stuff. Built to last." He gives the thing another look. "Hats off," he says admiringly.

"Hats off?" says B.

"Respect," I say, translating from the medieval.

B still wants to know about her friend from the neighborhood. "How did you get Charlie to come after us?" she asks him.

Arcadia smiles again. "Threw him a ball to fetch," he says. "Well, not really a ball. More a sort of anti-matter dispersal tesseract in the *shape* of a ball, but Charlie was happy to chase it. And happy to drop it once he thought he needed to protect his friends. Which allowed it to do its stuff."

♦ ♦ ♦ ♦

The way Charlie saw it was that, reluctant as any self-respecting dog would be to drop a ball having gone to all this trouble to fetch it, there was clearly a lot of quite serious tearing-motherfuckers-to-pieces to be done and he'd best get to it.

The way Charlie saw it was that, as he leapt eagerly for the throat of his nearest enemy, the ball he'd dropped decided to stop being a ball and be instead, after briefly turning itself inside out, a massive and blinding pulse of white light that subsumed anything and everything around it before blinking out of existence and leaving behind it nothing but the strange consequence that everything that had happened had in fact not happened.

♦ ♦ ♦ ♦

Arcadia—almost reluctantly—takes his eyes away from the not-a-necklace-after-all and looks at me.

"Here's the important question," he says. "What on earth made you pick it up? Made you take it? There's usually a sort of don't-mess-with-me aura about these things that keeps civilians at bay."

I hold his gaze for a moment, ready to say something light but decide on the truth instead. "I don't know," I say. "I wanted it. I had an instinct that it would … prove interesting."

"Ah, yes," he says. "*That* feeling. I know that feeling." And he looks at me like he's having that feeling right now.

"Tell you what," he says, "I know a lead-lined vault on the

lowest level of a secret underground bunker that's just *dying* for the company of a pretty little trinket like this, so why don't I take it off your hands?" He scoops it up from my palm and drops it into his vest pocket. "And in return," he says, "I'm going to give you this remarkably impressive business card." It's a plain white business card and there's nothing remotely impressive about it, except the way it appears from nowhere between the fingers of his hand.

"Like magic," I say.

"Like magic," he agrees.

I glance at the card and put it in my purse.

"Look, go ahead and graduate from high school," he says, sounding like he thinks that's almost as dull an idea as I do. "And then, should you feel like it, give me a call."

I almost point out that the only thing on the card was his name but figure that, one way or another, channels of communication would probably become available if and when necessary.

Arcadia smiles, stands, and leaves, pausing one last time at the door to look back at us. "Oh, and B?" he says. "Charlie'd like you to know that he appreciates all the snacks and certainly hopes that your arrangement will continue for the foreseeable future."

"Right," says B, her natural snark pretty much back to full strength now that the interview seems to be over. "Because you speak Dog."

"Oh, Dog's easy," Arcadia says. "You should try Atlantean." He winks at both of us and then fixes his eyes on mine. "Perhaps you will," he says, and lets the door swing shut after him.

THE RETURN OF
BOY JUSTICE

Nearly gave him a fucking heart attack.

Out of nowhere, like a machine-gun, *bam-bam-bam-bam-bam* on the door of Alderton's seventh floor apartment.

Jesus Christ, what now? Seventy-eight years old. You'd think he could watch *America's Got Talent* in peace without some ass-hole rapping on his door like the whole damn building was on fire.

In theory, people weren't supposed to be able to surprise the tenants at their own apartment doors—needed to be buzzed in via the street door's intercom system—but the theory didn't allow for the fact that at least half the tenants were dicks, regularly wedging the street door open so as not to inconvenience their fucking drug dealers.

Bam-bam-bam-bam-bam.

Enough already. "Not interested!" Alderton shouted, but the rapping just increased in urgency at the sound of his voice and he cursed himself for showing signs of life.

He levered himself out of the armchair and grabbed his walking stick to help him across the room. If this was another

Jehovah's fucking Witness he'd tell them precisely where they could shove their *Watchtower* subscription. Reaching the door, he leant his weight on the walking stick—he'd need leverage if he had to slam the door against some mugger working the early shift—and opened up.

No mugger. No soldier of God. A kid, breathless and wide-eyed, black and maybe ten years old, who, the second the door was open, stepped into the apartment. Or tried to, till Alderton's walking stick pressed against his tiny chest and held him back.

"Whoa," Alderton said. "Where the hell you think you're going?"

"You gotta let me in," the kid said, part plaintive, part demanding. "They're coming for me. You have to save me."

"What?" Alderton said, and leaned his head over the boy to take a look up and down the corridor. "There's nobody coming, kid. Run off home. I'm all out of Halloween candy."

"Huh?" the kid said, mask of panic giving way briefly to a look somewhere between pity and contempt. "Halloween's not for three months."

Was that right? Jesus. He'd thought it was only a month or so since the last one. Older you get, faster it goes. *Time runs fleet-foot to the grave*, he thought, the picture of the sixth-grade schoolroom in which he'd first heard that line nearly seventy years ago clearer in his head than anything he'd seen in the last decade: Mrs. Mitchell in her powder-blue blouse, reading glasses hanging from her neck by the vanity-free twine with which she'd replaced the broken gold chain; Susan Johannson, floral print long faded on her hand-me-down dress but already a heartbreaker, rolling a pencil up and down the slope of her desk by the flicking of a restless forefinger; Paul Worrall, gazing out

the window and urging on recess, the sleeve of his green cam-
bric shirt interrupted by the tight black armband for his Ranger
brother, dead at Anzio.

"Hey!" the kid said, reclaiming Alderton's attention. "Help
me. Please. They're going to kill me."

"Kill you?" Alderton said. "Don't be so fucking dramatic."
Once upon a time he'd have bitten his tongue off, language like
that in front of a kid, but he'd watched the neighborhood go
slowly to hell for the last twenty years and knew that nobody
gave a shit about stuff like that anymore.

"I'm serious," the kid said. "I saw them do the other guy
back of Pickwick's. And they saw me."

"Pickwick's?" Alderton said. "What the hell were you doing
skulking around behind a bar?"

"*So* not relevant," the kid said, all but rolling his eyes, weary
at old people stupidity. Alderton didn't know whether to laugh
or smack him upside his little wiseass head.

"Why'd you come *here*?" Alderton said.

But the kid was done with back-story. "Help me," he said,
his voice flat and small. "I'm scared."

Shit. Alderton looked up and down the corridor again. Still
empty. The elevator was silent, too, and nor was there any sound of
someone rushing up the stairs. But the kid's face was convincing
in its lack of pantomime distress, in its stillness and surrender.

"Come in," Alderton said, ushering the kid past him with a
hand between his shoulder blades. "I guess I can call the Police."

"No! Not the Police," the kid said, spinning to face Alderton
as he closed his door. "You." And then, like it would help clinch
the deal, "You helped me last time."

Last time? Alderton looked more closely at the kid's face,

tried to place it. Seeing him in the context of Alderton's own apartment, the framed one-sheets on the wall behind him, helped for some reason. The kid gave his best shot at a smile, which helped more, and something clicked into place in Alderton's memory.

"Last time all you wanted was a damn autograph," he said.

♦ ♦ ♦ ♦

It had been a year or more ago, and the kid had been accompanied by his stepmother, or at least a white woman Alderton assumed to be his stepmother. A joyless stick of a thing who hadn't had a lot to say through their twenty-minute visit.

The kid was a talker, though. Savvy little fucker, precocious and smart. Soon as they walked in, he glanced around at the shithole Alderton called home and said, "They hadn't invented residuals back when you were working, huh?"

"Kid, they'd barely discovered fire," Alderton said, and wasted a wink on the mother, whose returned smile was that of someone who'd learned to imitate social responses without ever quite understanding or approving of them.

Meanwhile, the kid had already registered the paused VCR image on Alderton's TV. "Hey!" he said. "*Jeopardy.* The one *you're* on. Fast forward."

Alderton, surprised and a little creeped-out that the kid could be enough of an obsessive to recognize a specific episode of a daily quiz show from a freeze-frame of the host, made no move to the remote, so the kid grabbed it himself—had to be the only person his age who even knew what a VCR was anymore— and zapped through to where one of the contestants picked the $800 square in a category called *Who Was That Masked Man?*

"You watch this every day?" the woman said to Alderton. Well, those were the words she used. Her tone, and the unfriendly twinkle in her eye, made it clear that what she was actually saying was *Christ, you are so fucking into yourself.*

"No," Alderton said, intending an explanation that it was only their earlier phone call requesting this visit that had made him find the tape, but the kid shushed them before he could get it out.

"Here it comes," the kid said.

On the screen, a much younger Alex Trebek said, "Justice was child's play for this actor who portrayed the teenage sidekick of TV's vigilante hero The Blue Valentine," and Alderton felt the same stab of humiliation he always felt when not one of the three contestants buzzed in.

The kid gave a groan of disgust. "Morons," he said, and stabbed the pause button before Trebek could shake his head at the contestants and say, "No-one remembers Chucky Alderton?"

Christ, *Alderton* barely remembered him. Hadn't been Chucky for decades. Charles G Alderton was the name on the social security checks that were all that kept him from skid row, and he'd been Charles, not Chucky, in the handful of B-movies in which he'd appeared in the late fifties and early sixties, back before he and the public had quietly agreed that they should see other people.

But the kid, unbelievably, *did* remember. Remembered not only the Blue Valentine's sidekick, Boy Justice, but also the actor who'd played him for the show's single season from the fall of fifty-one through the spring of fifty-two. Hence the phone call and Alderton's bemused agreement that the kid could come by and get some stuff signed.

Alderton had met fans before, even done a couple of

in-person appearances at conventions organized by dealers in pulp fiction nostalgia, but this kid was different. For a start, he wasn't fat, white, and fifty—Christ alone knew how he'd ever discovered the show in the first place—but he also seemed alarmingly unclear about the lines of demarcation between TV heroes and the actors who portrayed them; Alderton had the not entirely comfortable impression that the kid believed he was visiting what was left of Boy Justice as much as what was left of Chucky Alderton.

But he was chatty and enthusiastic, loved action movies as much as Alderton did, and really knew his shit—they'd got into quite the smackdown about which Bond was best—and Alderton had happily scribbled his name on several Boy Justice items for him: grey market DVDs of the show, an ex-library copy of *The Encyclopedia of Pop Culture* (Boy Justice merited a five-line entry which managed to get two details of his costume wrong), and three—plainly very precious to the kid—actual pulp magazines from the thirties.

Not that Boy Justice had even appeared in the pulps. In the pages of *Strange Thrills*, The Blue Valentine had been strictly a one-man judge, jury, and executioner—a masked vigilante so merciless he made The Shadow and The Spider look like bleeding heart liberals—and it was only the insistent whim of a TV executive that had given him a teenage sidekick for his small-screen rebirth and granted Alderton what little enduring fame he had. Thirty-nine episodes, the last thirteen (filmed after a summer break) less popular with the fans because Alderton's voice had broken and he was suddenly as tall as Brooks Barrett, the handsome piece of wood who incarnated the Valentine himself.

♦ ♦ ♦ ♦

And now the kid was back in Alderton's apartment, and apparently in trouble.

"Come on, sit down," Alderton said. "Catch your breath. You want some coffee?" Oh, wait. Ten. "Can you drink coffee?"

"We won't have time," the kid said.

"Won't have time?"

"Here," the kid said. "You'll need this." He pulled something from his pocket and pressed it into Alderton's palm.

It was a souvenir pin, a cheap tin premium Alderton vaguely remembered them giving away in cereal boxes sometime back before the space age. Alderton's younger face, masked and smiling, with his own name lettered below and Boy Justice's name lettered above.

"Put it on," the kid said.

"This thing's probably worth money," Alderton said. "You should keep it, shove it up on eBay."

"Put it on!"

"Jesus Christ, relax already," Alderton said, sticking the stupid thing onto his shirt. "There. It's on. Now calm down. They weren't right behind you, so they're not going to know to look here."

"They'll have looked you up," the kid said.

"Looked me up?"

The kid pulled a cell phone from the pocket of his jeans and waggled it at Alderton. "Hello?" he said, in his best earth-to-idiot voice. "Twenty-first century. Apps. IMDB. Street Directory."

"You're missing the point," Alderton said, trying to keep the right-back-atcha exasperation out of his voice. Ten years old, cut him some slack. "What would they be looking up to start with?"

"*Boy Justice*," the kid said, like it was obvious. "I told them you'd protect me."

"Jesus Christ, kid! You couldn't just fucking *run*?"

"I *was* running," the kid said. "Shouted it back at them. Thought it might stop them." Not even sheepish. Like he *still* thought that.

"You're completely delusional," Alderton said. "You need to be on some serious fucking medication, swear to God. What the hell do you think's going to happen if they show up here?"

The kid shrugged. "You'll protect me," he said.

And it was exactly then—with the kind of timing Alderton had thought possible only on his ridiculous TV show—that his apartment door was kicked in and everything became suddenly and alarmingly real.

◆ ◆ ◆ ◆

There were two of them, and the one who came in first was holding a gun. Not pointing it at anyone, just letting everyone know it was available should circumstance require.

"Look out, he's got a gun," he said conversationally, waving the piece around a little in case they'd failed to spot it.

While his partner did a poor job of closing the broken apartment door and the kid ran instinctively behind Alderton to huddle into a protective crouch on the La-Z-Boy, the one with the gun strode further into the room, checking it out briefly and dismissively before settling his gaze on Alderton.

He sniffed twice, theatrically, as his partner ambled up to join him. "Hey," he said, as if to an invisible audience. "Old guy smell. It *is* real."

Little prick. Alderton would have told him as much but

he was too busy being afraid. They were little more than kids themselves—maybe twenty, maybe not even—and it was only as Alderton took in their polyester tracksuits and sneakers that he realized he'd been expecting pinstripes and fedoras, been expecting stock hoods from his fucking show. One would have been called Lefty and the other would have been called something Italian. You know, to add authenticity.

But the one with the mouth was unmistakably Irish, and his shaved-head partner was who-the fuck-knew. Iron Curtain escapee, it looked like. Armenian? Russian? Some thug too dumb to pass the KGB entrance exam exploring the free-market opportunities of the new world?

"You must be Boy Justice," Irish said, the grin mocking, the tone contemptuous. "Some kind of super hero? Some kind of Dark Knight shit?"

"I'd've been Robin, at best," Alderton said. "But no, I wasn't any kind of hero. I was an actor." He knew that this wasn't news to Irish, that the bastard was just fucking with him, but still his hand gestured pathetically at the one-sheets on his wall as if to offer proof, like this little thug gave a crap.

Irish looked at the posters briefly, then back at Alderton. "Glad we got that straightened out," he said. "I was all set to shit my pants."

As if to point up just how very far from frightening he found Alderton to be, he tucked the gun into the tracksuit's waistband at the small of his back, and then displayed his empty hands, palms out, at his sides. Smiled, too. All friends here. Reasonable men capable of coming to a reasonable understanding.

"Look, Pops," he said, "if you play smart, we can get this done without ruining the rest of your retirement. All you gotta do is convince me you're someone who knows when to keep his fucking mouth shut and we'll be out of your hair." He threw an insolent glance at Alderton's balding head. "No offense," he added, and tossed a grin at KGB, who gave an unpleasant bark in response that Alderton figured was meant to be laughter.

"What about him?" Alderton said, gesturing behind him.

"Who, the kid?" Irish said. "We'll be taking the kid." Thing is, he didn't use the word *kid*.

"What did you call him?" Alderton said.

"Huh?" Irish said, cocking his head a little, as if mildly surprised at anything even resembling a challenge.

"The kid," Alderton said. "What did you call him?"

Irish said it again. Conversational. Like the word was nothing. Like the kid was nothing.

"Watch your damn mouth," Alderton said.

His voice wasn't as steady as he'd have liked it to be, but still he felt the air suck out of the room and everything come to a bright and trembling focus as Irish took a step nearer to him.

"Watch my mouth?" Irish said. "Watch my *mouth*? Why don't you watch it for me? Watch it bite your fucking face off."

He snapped his teeth together, jutting his head forward, and grinned with satisfaction as Alderton flinched and took a step backwards, wobbling and having to steady himself with his stick. He'd all but bumped into the La-Z-Boy, from where the kid's frightened breath was for the moment the loudest thing in the room.

"I'm not going to let you take him," Alderton said.

Irish cupped a hand to his ear and leant his head forward. "One more time?" he said.

"You're not taking him anywhere," Alderton said. "I'm not going to let you."

"Well, well," Irish said, smiling like he was delighted with the way this was going. He turned to KGB, make sure he was getting this. "Look what we got here," he said. "A Mexican standoff."

KGB looked around the room, as if checking. "No Mexicans," he said.

"No standoff," said Irish, and smashed Alderton in the face with a tight little fist that drove him to the floor and dropped him into blackness.

◆ ◆ ◆ ◆

The basement door's padlock had opened easily once Boy Justice had selected the right size pick from his utility belt's collection, despite the strangely thick oil that coated the lock and made his fingers' work slippery.

Now, as he stepped cautiously over the threshold into what lay beyond, the young crime-fighter wondered, with a brief thrill of alarm, if he had in fact stepped over the very threshold of time itself. For the room in which Boy Justice found himself was no simple basement, but more akin to some terrible medieval dungeon!

Great vaulted arches seemed to lead into infinite shadowed spaces beyond this first chamber in which he stood, and said chamber was lit only by a dozen flaming torches—torches which illuminated a huddled body lying on its cold stone floor.

Glancing around with care to ensure that the motionless figure was indeed his sole companion in this eerie place, Boy Justice then crossed the room determinedly to uncover the mystery of this latest example of the evil workings of the Scarlet Claw and his minions.

Kneeling, he turned the prone figure over so that the flaming torches of the dank dungeon could illuminate its face—and a cry of anguish erupted from the youngster's throat!

"No!" he cried. "It can't be!"

The pale and lifeless face was one he knew all too well. The figure lying motionless on the dungeon floor, its blue domino mask removed by whoever had done this terrible deed, was none other than Valentine Dyson himself.

The Blue Valentine was dead!

Boy Justice stared with profound horror at the charred edges of the bullet-hole in the breast pocket of the Valentine's midnight-blue suit, still reluctant to believe the evidence of his own eyes.

Suddenly, evil laughter rang out as if from everywhere, echoing off the dank walls of the basement dungeon and, as if from some unseen control device, all the torches extinguished themselves at once, plunging Boy Justice into blackness!

The youthful hero leaped to his feet, readying himself for whatever new horrors the vicious crime-lord had planned for him.

Was that a movement behind him? A sudden movement, as of something rising from the shadows? Boy Justice span around, fists raised and ready despite the all-encompassing darkness in which he was contained.

"Do your worst!" he shouted defiantly. "I'll go down fighting!"

"That's the spirit," a voice said from the black void. "But let us hope it shan't be necessary."

That voice! Was it? Could it be? Boy Justice held his breath, afraid to hope, until a match was struck in the blackness revealing someone he had not hoped to see again this side of eternity.

"Val!" Boy Justice shouted in ecstasy. "You're alive!"

"I do wish you wouldn't use that diminutive of my name, young fellow," said the Blue Valentine. "Rather tends to undercut my dignity."

The Valentine put the match to one of the torches and then,

flipping open his sterling silver cigarette case with an elegant gesture, he withdrew one of the black Russian cigarettes he favored and lit it from the flame of the torch.

"But how...," Boy Justice uttered in confusion. "You were..."

The Valentine smiled, and held out the now-closed cigarette case in order to let Boy Justice see the flattened bullet embedded in the center of its filigree design.

"Lined with adamantium," he said. "And always worn over my heart."

In the same movement that replaced the case in his inside pocket, the Valentine produced another blue domino mask and affixed it to his face. "I don't suppose you happened to notice my topper anywhere before that rather melodramatic dousing of the lights?" *he said.*

Boy Justice, still reeling from the shock of his mentor's rebirth, pointed to where the blue silk opera hat lay on the stone floor.

"Well spotted, sir," *said the Valentine and, retrieving the hat, placed it atop his head at the slightly rakish angle he preferred.*

"Better?" *he said.*

"Better," *the lad replied.*

The Valentine put out his hand, and Boy Justice, returning the gesture, gripped it fervently.

"The Oath?" *he asked.*

"The Oath," *said the Valentine, and, together, they repeated the words that had come to be feared by wrongdoers everywhere:*

"Where Evil lurks, it shall not live:

The Valentine does not forgive."

The Valentine nodded, smiled, and removed the flaming torch from its wall-holder. "The work awaits," *he said.* "Let us explore the labyrinth. We have criminals to kill, and innocents to rescue."

With no further ado, the Blue Valentine set out beneath one of the vaulted arches to whatever mysteries lay beyond.

Boy Justice stared after him, watching until the midnight blue of the Valentine's costume could no longer be distinguished from the shadows surrounding it. Any moment now, *the lad thought.* Any moment now, I'll start after him. *Yes. Any moment now. But why weren't his legs moving? Why did he suddenly feel so tired, so weak, so old? Why couldn't he open his mouth to call after his friend?*

Without understanding why, he felt his thumb rubbing against the first two fingers of his hand. The fingers that had worked the padlock—the padlock that had been coated with a mysterious oily substance...

Poison!

Boy Justice tried to shout, tried to move, but it was too late. He was powerless against the sudden wave of dizzying unconsciousness that raced through his body, slamming into him like a tight little fist that drove him to the floor and dropped him into blackness.

◆ ◆ ◆ ◆

Alderton blinked his eyes open.

A grinning face was looking down at him.

"How'd *that* feel, Pops?" Irish said.

Alderton, still on his back on the floor, opened his mouth to answer but started spluttering on the blood that flowed in from his shattered nose. He felt like he was going to choke, felt the accompanying panic rise, and forced himself to take slow shallow breaths until his body decided it wasn't going to die right that minute. He twisted his head on the floor to look around.

He couldn't have been out long because nothing else seemed

to have happened. The kid was still huddled, petrified, on the chair, and KGB was still standing a few feet behind Irish, passing the time by doing a little browsing of Alderton's poorly-stocked bookshelf. He ran his finger along the spines of the thrift-store paperbacks as he turned to look down at Alderton.

"You read all these?" he asked.

All these? Christ almighty, there were probably twenty-five books in total. "No," Alderton said. "I just keep them there to impress my dates." He finally managed to get himself up onto one elbow. "Little help here?" he said to Irish, extending his other hand for a lift.

"Fuckoff," Irish said.

Nice. Alderton grabbed at his stick, lying beside him, to help himself up but Irish snatched it away from him. "Don't want you getting ambitious," he said, and broke the stick in two over his knee, letting the broken halves fall back to the floor.

"Huh?" Alderton said, then got it. "Oh, right," he said, picking up the longer half of the broken stick, and levering himself awkwardly up on to one knee. "Your chosen profession has taught you to exercise caution, even in the least likely of situations."

Irish curled his lip. "Speak fucking English," he said.

"You're being careful," Alderton said. "Perfectly understandable. You're fearful, lest an old cripple give you a nasty tap with a thin piece of wood."

KGB laughed, with what sounded like actual pleasure. "*Lest*," he said, voice cracking on the word with amused delight. Alderton had always enjoyed an appreciative audience, but he wished KGB had kept his admiration to himself. Because Irish plainly felt slighted by his partner's laughter, felt a tiny slip in his command of the room, and was going to have to do something about that.

He glared at Alderton. "You think you're better than me?" he said.

Alderton—still on one knee, his arm trembling as it tried to lift his miserable old body, the shattered end of the broken walking stick all but buckling on the floor—stared up at him, at the rage in his dark little eyes, and saw the future. Saw the absence of reason, the absence of mercy, saw himself and the kid dead at the hands of this stupid thug, and thought *fuck it.*

"Better than you?" he said. "I've passed *turds* that are better than you, you rancid little motherfucker."

Irish's face creased in primal fury and he flung himself down toward Alderton.

Moron, Alderton thought, and wished he had time to say it.

But he didn't. What he had time to do was raise the stick and keep it as stiff as his atrophied muscles allowed.

The idiot's momentum did the rest. The sharp end of the shattered walking stick slid easily through his left eye and plunged deep inside his skull. Alderton gave a further twisting thrust until he knew he'd skewered the fucker's brain and then flipped the body aside.

"Jesus Christ!" KGB shouted, shock freezing him in place. "Alan!"

Alan? The fuck kind of gangster name was that? Alderton watched KGB finally raise his hands into fists like he was going to do something. But KGB wasn't going to do shit. Alderton was. He reached over Alan's twitching body and yanked the gun out of his waistband.

KGB was running at him now, but Alderton felt like he had all the time in the world. Too young for Korea, too old for Vietnam, but two years in the service and plenty of target practice. He cocked the gun, held his breath, and fired.

Like riding a fucking bike. The bullet went exactly where Alderton wanted. KGB's kneecap exploded in a shower of blood and bone and Alderton watched him hit the floor screaming.

Behind him, he heard the kid exhale loudly, part gasp, part sigh of relief, and Alderton forced himself upright with the other half of his stick. He limped a step or two toward KGB. Fuck the limp. Fuck Time's fleet-foot run to the grave. Fuck everything, especially this whimpering bully and his dead or dying asshole friend. Alderton's blood was up and something resembling the memory of an erection was stirring in his pants. He leveled the gun in the direction of KGB's face and watched him splutter and sob.

"Georgie Balloons," Alderton said. "Joey Rats. *Those* are fucking gangster names, you pissant little bitch."

His finger tightened on the trigger.

KGB closed his eyes in terror.

The Valentine does not forgive, said a voice in Alderton's head. The kid's voice. Brooks Barrett's voice. The voice of Alderton's rage at all that had been lost. The voice of the dark. The voice of the Valentine himself, primal and merciless.

But the Valentine wasn't here. It wasn't his call anymore.

Alderton waited a moment. Took a breath. Let the adrenaline rush recede.

KGB opened his eyes, squinting, unsure, afraid to hope.

Alderton lowered the gun. Slightly. "One word," he said. "One wrong move."

KGB nodded, carefully.

"Call the cops, kid," Alderton said. "Use that fancy phone of yours. Use a fucking app, if you like. Knock yourself out."

But the kid wasn't listening. "*Boy Justice*," he was whispering. "*Boy Justice*." Like a mantra. Like a prayer. Like everything he'd needed to be true in the world suddenly was.

◆ ◆ ◆

Later, after the cops had come and gone and a woman from Social Services was on her way to take the kid home, the kid asked Alderton what happened now.

"You go home to your mother," Alderton said.

"She's not my mother."

"Does she feed you?"

"Yeah."

"Wash your clothes? Get you to school on time?"

A shrug, a reluctant nod.

"She ever smack you around?"

"No."

"Then she's meeting minimum requirements," Alderton said. "The rest of it you're going to have to find for yourself. It's there if you look. Be good to your friends. If they're not good to you, find better friends."

"Most of my friends are idiots," the kid said.

"That's life in the big city."

The kid cocked his head, looked at Alderton appraisingly. "You're quoting *Robocop*," he said.

"Oh," Alderton said. "Check out the big brain on Brad."

"*Pulp Fiction*," the kid said.

"See?" said Alderton. "Not *all* your friends are idiots."

The kid just looked at him. Life had already taught the poor little bastard not to ask.

"Saturday afternoons," Alderton said. "Provided it's alright with your mother. We'll watch movies, get drunk, and smoke cigarettes."

The kid's mouth fell open.

"Jesus," Alderton said. "What are you, retarded? No booze, no cigarettes. Learn to recognize a joke, for Christ's sake."

The kid smiled at him.

Alderton felt his heart jump in his chest. Not the arrhythmia for once, thank Christ, but something older, something waking from a long sleep.

He hoped that somewhere, in whatever unlikely area of heaven God reserved for people born not of flesh and blood but of imagination and desire, the Blue Valentine was proud of him. *The work awaits*, he'd said in Alderton's dream. *We have criminals to kill, and innocents to rescue.*

Well, it was going to be slow, and it was unlikely to be spectacular, but a rescue was nevertheless underway.

As he felt his own mouth return the kid's smile, though, Alderton found himself wondering just for a moment which of them it was who was being rescued.

THE THING ABOUT CATS

Manhattan, 1979

Turns out that by town car the trip to the Upper West Side is going to take us nearly forty minutes. Travis, our usual driver, isn't to blame. He's doing his best—and his best is about as good as it gets—but there's a Reagan rally in midtown and it's screwing up traffic everywhere.

About twenty minutes in, Mr. James chooses to point out that he told me we'd have been quicker taking the subway. And so *I* choose to point out that I married him for his money and that gold-diggers are not as a rule expected to ride subways.

"Besides," I add, "This Arthur Hillibrand character will still be dead whatever time we get to his penthouse."

"Well, you *say* that ..." Mr. James says, and I have to admit he's got me there. If I had a nickel for every corpse we've had to re-kill for the department in the last three and a half years, I'd have ... well, I'd only have about 65 cents, but you get my point.

"Apparently Mr. James and I could have taken the subway, Travis," I say through the open partition to the front seat. "You could have had the afternoon off. Mixed yourself a cocktail and watched *Donahue* or something. Would you have liked that?"

Travis finds my eyes in the rear-view. "What?" he says, shaking his head. "And miss seeing you in that dress, Mrs. J?"

I smile at him and turn to my husband. "There," I say, because matters have clearly been settled. "Why us, by the way? Why not the cops?"

"Circumstances," Mr. James says. "And associations."

"Ah," I say. "So, Mister Arthur Hillibrand is a person not unknown to the Bureau." I fish a cigarette out of my purse and waggle it for my husband's attention. "Who is he, anyway?"

The zippo's in his hand already, bless him. "Hillibrand?" he says. "He was a poet."

"Christ," I say, drawing in the flame and taking a first drag. "No wonder somebody killed him."

◆ ◆ ◆ ◆

The private express elevator—into which the building's doorman had ushered us before tapping out an access code on one of those newfangled keypad thingies—takes me and Mr. James speedily up to the top floor where it opens directly onto the reception area of the late Mr. Hillibrand's penthouse suite.

I whistle. I assume the Vatican and Buckingham Palace have got this place beat, but I know a few embassies and country houses that are clearly going to need to up their game.

I give my husband a look. "I thought you said he was a poet," I say, because come on.

"Family money," Mr. James explains, nodding at the framed photographs of earlier and more respectable Hillibrands— bank owners, railroad barons, or whatever—and their stern and well-upholstered wives, before extending his hand to the stout fellow in Jeeves drag who's walking out of the living room to meet us. "I'm Mr. James," says Mr. James. "This is Tabitha. Was it you who called?"

Jeeves shakes the proffered hand, though his slightly pained expression makes it clear he's wondering whether Mr. James has any idea at all about the proper way to interact with household staff. Mr. James is perfectly familiar with the proper way to interact with household staff. He doesn't care for it.

"My name is Kilgallen, sir," says the late gentleman's gentleman. "I did indeed place the initial call to the Bureau, using a number with which Mr. Hillibrand had entrusted me, but I don't believe you and I spoke directly." Look, you can certainly choose to remember that his name is Kilgallen if that's what floats your boat but I'm just going to keep calling him Jeeves. It's not going to bother him—I'm not going to say it out *loud*—and, besides, at the moment he's already busy being bothered by the fact that whoever answered his phone call hasn't shown up in person, which makes me wonder whether Jeeves has any idea at all about the proper way to interact with the FBI.

"If you don't mind my asking, sir," he says. "What is it that you do at the Bureau?"

"I investigate," Mr. James says, and gives Jeeves the benefit of his most charming, most confident smile. Somewhat placated, Jeeves grants him a nod before turning his still-not-sure-about-all-this gaze on me.

"And I do his dirty work," I say, without waiting for whatever insulting question it is that he's attempting to formulate. I'm really not sure that Jeeves and I are going to get along.

My husband gestures to the living room. "Shall we?" he

says. He waits till Jeeves has turned around before treating me to one of his best *behave yourself* looks as we follow the valet to the crime scene.

There's a dead body alright and—despite the aforementioned checkered history which Mr. James and I have had with dead bodies—this one is convincingly dead; very cold and very still and already starting to discolor.

Oh, and missing its head.

The curious thing about the body—you know, apart from *that*—is that it seems to have greeted its demise with an impressive degree of aplomb. It's sitting upright, legs casually crossed, in a tall straight-backed antique chair made from the kind of dark heavy wood usually reserved exclusively for churches of the really miserable denominations. An ascot or cravat or something equally ridiculous is laid out on an occasional table beside the chair and the corpse's white shirt is unbuttoned, revealing a hairless chest which boasts several carefully incised runic markings, though none of them appear to be recent. Both hands rest, seemingly at ease, in the body's lap.

"His legs are crossed," I say to Mr. James, because I suppose that's what strikes me the most. I mean, who sits cross-legged and unperturbed through their own decapitation?

"And in dress pants," Mr. James says. His voice is as respectful as he can make it—doing his best to spare Jeeves's feelings, I'm sure—but I can still pick up the undertone of dry amusement at this confluence of elegance and atrocity. He turns his head to the valet and keeps his voice gentle. "And we're quite sure, Mr. Kilgallen, that this *is* Arthur Hillibrand?" he says.

"You know, on account of the no head thing," I offer helpfully. Yeah, I know—saucer of milk for Ms. Tabitha—but I'm still pissed about that whole implicit and-what-do-*you*-do-other-than-look-pretty crap.

"Mister Hillibrand's fingerprints are, I believe, on file should it be necessary to check, sir," Jeeves says. "But I'm … quite certain."

We follow his gaze as he looks pointedly down at the corpse's left hand. It's a moneyed hand, delicate and un-calloused, its fingernails manicured and subtly polished. And the fingers themselves are long and elegant. All six of them.

"Huh," I say. "Would you look at that?"

Mr. James, though, is already done looking at that. He's looking instead at the set of glass-paneled double doors off to the side of the living room's Baronial fireplace. Striding over to them, he pushes them open to take a quick glance into the dining room. I sneak a peek too. As dining rooms go, it perhaps wouldn't look like much in the Waldorf Astoria nor have turned heads on the first-class deck of the *Titanic* but it seems perfectly up to the task of serving bacon and eggs to everybody who'd want some should an Emperor and his entire retinue happen to drop by. But Mr. James doesn't appear to be interested in counting the twenty-four place settings or admiring the 18th century silverware and 14th century tapestries. He has that look of someone less interested in what they *are* seeing than in what they're *not*. He lets the doors swing shut—bit of a squeak to be honest, Jeeves perhaps not quite up to date with his WD40 duties—and takes a step or two back into the living room.

"Sir?" Jeeves asks, off his quizzical look and his silence.

"I'm very curious about the cats," Mr. James says.

"What cats?" I say, before Jeeves can answer him. "There *aren't* any cats."

"Precisely what I'm curious about," my husband tells me,

clearly weighing the possibilities of accompanying the comment with a smug smile. As *I*, however, am clearly weighing the possibilities of a drop kick to his solar plexus, he elects to restrain himself.

"Here's the thing," he says. "To the majority of his neighbors in this building, Arthur Hillibrand was commonly known—and far from affectionately—as The Catman."

"Wait a minute," I say. "Is this going to involve a rooftop mounted signal from a Police Commissioner and a suspiciously fetishistic costume?"

"No," he says. "It's going to involve a suspiciously terrible racket, which by all accounts emanates from this penthouse every night at midnight. The concerted screeching, wailing, howling, and hissing of what sounds like a thousand cats."

"Jesus," I say. "And all the neighbors could come up with was a disapproving *nickname*? Why the hell didn't they try to get him thrown out?"

"It'd be a tough eviction," Mr. James says. "He owns the building."

"Owned," I say, a correction of tense which I grant you is rather petty, but he keeps pulling out all these annoying *facts*—which he could have shared with me on the car ride over here instead of wasting his time cheerleading for the fucking subway—and it's getting on my nerves. "Also," I add, "at the risk of repeating myself, there aren't any cats."

A small discreet cough from Jeeves catches our attention and we see that he's taken the opportunity to trot the mile or so over to one of the room's several floor-to-ceiling bookcases. "The cats are in here, sir," he says, pressing the spine of a leather-bound book on one of the shelves.

◆ ◆ ◆ ◆

Well, it's a secret room of course and, sure enough, it's packed to bursting with cats. No actual *cats*, you understand—unless you choose to count the few dozen mummified Egyptian ones scattered here and there throughout the collection—but instead what amounts to a museum's worth of feline representation through the ages: Paintings, sculptures, tapestries, photographs; children's toys, board games, revolting Victorian napkins with cutesy kittens in baby clothes; VHS tapes of *The Black Cat, That Darn Cat, The Aristocats*, and *Island of Lost Souls*; signed photographs of Anne Francis as Honey West brandishing her ocelot, and of all three of TV's Catwomen (that half-rhyme of *To Arthur, from Eartha* must have irritated his poet's ear, I'd have thought). High culture, low culture, ancient and modern, priceless masterpieces, tatty junk. A first edition of T. S. Eliot's *Old Possum's Book of Practical Cats*, a battered paperback of Enid Blyton's *The Mystery of the Disappearing Cat*. Clearly, if you were in possession of anything with a cat on it or in it and were looking to unload, Arthur Hillibrand and his bottomless checkbook had been your go-to guy.

"God," Mr. James says. "Look at the eyes on that one."

He's standing in front of a large portrait in oils of the Ancient Egyptian cat-goddess Bast. It's late nineteenth century and looks to be by one of the Symbolists for sure; if not Jean Delville himself, then certainly School Of. While Bast's human body is a pale and voluptuous *fin-de-siecle* dream of femininity, her fully feline head is sleek and black and striking, and Mr. James has got a point about the eyes. They stare directly out at the world—cruel, confident, amused.

"What do you think she's saying to us?" he says.

I have no doubt in my mind. "*You're all mice*," I say.

"Brrr," Mr. James says, and averts his gaze from her alarming splendor. "Still, it's fairly clear that neither she nor any of her fellow works of art here are likely to be responsible for these reported midnight wailings."

"No fooling you," I say.

"I'm a detective," he says, with a modest nod.

"If I may, sir ..." says Jeeves, and we see that he's now brandishing an old 78 RPM record, pulled from a cabinet behind him. "I believe *this* to have been the source of the neighbors' irritation."

There's a floor-standing antique Victrola in front of the cabinet and Jeeves lifts the lid, cranks the handle, lays the disc on the turntable and applies the needle.

The noise is certainly horrendous—the collective screeching, wailing, howling, and hissing of what does indeed sound like a thousand cats—but it's also astonishingly loud. Wall-shakingly loud. No Wonder the Neighbors Fucking Hate You loud. Mr. James waves at Jeeves to stop it and, once the valet's lifted the needle-arm from out the grooves and put it back in its housing, stabs a finger towards the large metal horn protruding from the Victrola.

"There's no way all that sound was coming from *that*," he says.

"No indeed, sir," says Jeeves proudly. "The master had it wired up to his recently installed quadraphonic sound system."

"Jesus Christ," I say. "What was *wrong* with him?"

"Mister Arthur was an enthusiast of the unusual," Jeeves says, his sweeping gesture taking in the whole room. "A connoisseur of the curious. Goes without saying."

"Yet there you go, saying it," I say.

He cocks his head, mask of servility slipping just a little. "I'm sorry?"

"Apology accepted."

"Tabitha…" says my husband, in that rein-it-in tone which he always thinks is going to work.

Before Jeeves and I can investigate our antipathy further, something else claims our attention. Off to the left of the Victrola is a free-standing plinth, atop of which is a life-size statuette of a Siamese cat. I really don't know what happens to make all three of us turn to look at it at the same time—perhaps we sense a great disturbance in the Force or something—but I do know that as soon as we *do* turn to look at it the statuette steps elegantly from the plinth onto the lid of the Victrola and from there to the floor.

"Good Lord," Jeeves says, staring down at the cat. The cat stares back at him briefly and then, lest he should think it gives a shit, starts licking its front paw as if it may have picked up something unpleasant from Arthur Hillibrand's rug.

Mr. James treats Jeeves to a raised eyebrow. "Not an item from the collection with which you were previously familiar, Mister Kilgallen?" he says, and the valet shakes his head, long and slow.

The cat—yellow eyes, long sharp teeth, tail flicking rhythmically, precise as a metronome—turns her face to me. Not Siamese at all, I see now.

We hold each other's gaze for a moment and then, slowly, she inclines her head. Regal but respectful, like a formal nod of greeting.

"It's been a long time," the cat says. "Good to see you again, *moya sestra*."

Mr. James looks from the cat to me—of course he does, who wouldn't in the circumstances?—but I'm glad to say I married a professional; there's no trace of a double-take, and it's no more than a second before he's turning to Jeeves with a smile that appears entirely uncompromised by the presence of a cat who's just spoken to his wife in Serbian.

"I understand you've had quite the day, Mr. Killgallen," he says, "but I wonder if I might trouble you for a glass of water?"

Now while I have little doubt that Jeeves hears this as the obvious code for *I need a word with my wife in private* that it is, I have to say he plays his part well. "Of course, sir," he says, with just the right degree of unflappable. "Anything for the lady?"

"Tabitha?" Mr. James asks me.

"How are you with Singapore Slings?" I ask Jeeves.

"Not entirely unfamiliar, Madam," he says, "though one hates to boast."

I still doubt that Jeeves and I will end up as coffee-date companions at any point in the near future, but it seems his jib has some cut after all and it wins a small smile from me before he makes his way to the kitchen.

Which leaves me, my husband, and the cat.

"Well, I knew you had a mysterious past," says Mr. James. "But—"

"We should talk about that at home," I say, already planning what to wear in order to turn his mind to finer things. "Don't we have a murder to solve?"

Mr. James smiles, fishes in his pocket, brings out a quarter, and rests it on the back of his thumb.

"Tell you what," he says. "Tails you introduce me to your sister. Heads you don't."

He flips the coin into the air, and I watch it as it rises. Then I watch it as it peaks. And then I watch it as it fails to fall, watch it as it freezes in place a good couple of feet above our heads.

Mr. James, when I look back at him, is equally motionless—head tilted, eyes on the quarter, palm out ready to catch it, not moving, not blinking, not breathing—and I assume that, somewhere in the kitchen, Jeeves too is currently not doing anything at all and that my Singapore Sling is paused partway between being and becoming.

I'm not going to pretend that this state of affairs isn't disconcerting, because of course it is, but I'm already beginning to calm down. Coin and drink, valet and detective, are perfectly fine, I realize. They are not frozen in time and space. Nothing alarming is happening to them. Nothing is happening to them at all. It's happening to me.

I've not been folded through the continuum for several years, and it remains as disturbing an experience as I remember. I keep my eyes on the almost-fixed point of the cat's flicking tail as I follow her between the worlds, through the emptinesses and the vastnesses and the alternating coruscations of colors that last had names before the oceans drank Atlantis.

It is every bit as impressive as you'd expect it to be and I'm sure it would all look fabulously psychedelic in a Stanley Kubrick movie or a Jack Kirby comic book but I have to tell you that, in real life, one's enjoyment of it is significantly undercut by the nausea—three parts motion sickness and seven parts metaphysical dread—that invariably accompanies it.

But, as ever, it's just at that dreadful moment when you become convinced your psyche is about to be permanently shredded to nothingness by the dream winds, that you blink, raise your head, and find that you are merely somewhere else, which is distinctly preferable to being in all the somewheres at once.

Not that the somewhere I find myself this time isn't impressive. When I open my eyes, I'm standing in an antechamber of the throne room of the dreamlands and the cat, perched elegantly on a plinth of carved alabaster, is looking at me patiently, allowing me the necessary moment to anchor myself in this reality stream.

"Princess," I say, dipping my head, and she flicks her tail in response.

It had been kind of the Lady Atalal to call me sister. But the truth is I'm barely of her species, let alone of the royal line. My mother, far from a full-blood herself, had further diluted the line twenty-five years ago by the romantic but ridiculous step of letting her thirty-two-year old self get pregnant by a forty-seven-year old private detective from San Francisco. There is, I gather, no actual rule about such matters in the dreamlands but Mom's earthbound dalliance is probably still a topic of discussion in certain quarters of the kingdom.

Christ, I suddenly think, is that why I'm here?

"Your husband is hardly our concern," the Princess says, as if I'd asked her a question out loud. Oh, right. The mind-reading thing. A trick that's missing from my quarter-breed's deck. Not that it's actually *mind* reading they do, at least not the way we usually think of it. Atalal and her kind are creatures of dream; they don't read thoughts so much as they read emotions and the pictures that accompany them. Hence the Princess's confusion. She received the impression that I was thinking of my husband, a detective in his forties, while in fact I was thinking of my father, a detective in his forties. Yes, Sigmund Freud, I know. Calm the hell down. Sometimes a pipe is just a pipe.

"Something is about to awaken," Atalal says. "Already its dreams disturb our realm—mutating the territories, breeding monsters from dream flesh, quenching the very stars in their courses. Great Kadath is already fallen and, over the scorched earth of Trefondaine, the flayed skins of princelings flap in tatters."

"Still not big on small talk, then?" I say, risking a suggestion of a smile, and she rewards me with that slow narrowing of the eyes that her kind use to signify amused tolerance. At least, I *think* that's what it signifies. Hard to be entirely sure, because it's pretty much the same expression they use when sucking the marrow from the bones of their slaughtered enemies.

"There's a war going on in the invisible world, my sister," she says, "though I assure you that its consequences, should we fail, will be all too visible. Battles are being waged on many fronts. In your world, for example, there are parties who work avidly to hasten the rising, seeking nothing so much as the eternal oblivion that they believe it promises. Your masters are already learning that there is another sleeper, one who lingers in the chambers of the dream sea, and all our auguries can as yet not tell in which direction his waking will tip the scales. With such a delicate balance, there is no room for tolerance of trouble-making dilettantes who merely seek power in their own right. The idiot in whose nest I found you—"

"Arthur Hillibrand," I say, not so much interrupting as showing I'd been paying attention. Her contempt for him comes as no surprise to me. Her kind don't care for creatures who get magic wrong, and humans get magic wrong all the fucking time, especially the rich and stupid ones. "And there was me thinking he was driving his neighbors crazy just out of bloody-mindedness," I say. "No. He was trying to summon you."

"His ridiculous and barely understood ritual did him little good," Atalal says, "though he did manage to gain access to the kingdoms on a few occasions. He thought he could gain power in the world of the spirits but found instead, as all find who venture here unwisely, merely the transmutation of the flesh."

"Ah," I say, in my best Mr. James manner. "The sixth finger."

"Sixth finger?" she says, amused. "That's nothing. You should see what his insides are like."

"I'm guessing I'd rather not."

"But you might have to, surely?" she says, like I'm missing the point. "Though I suppose it depends on your choice of method."

"Choice of method?"

"For killing him," she says, clearly glad to have had the confusion cleared up. "As I say, current circumstances regrettably allow no tolerance for interfering opportunists. He won't be expecting you, but nor will he be surprised that we sent someone. He's learned of our displeasure and has been trying to undo his rituals."

I'm missing something here. "Are you sure there hasn't been a double booking at your end?" I say. "Because, judging by appearances, that mission's already been assigned."

"What?"

"Arthur Hillibrand's dead," I say. "Severely dead."

Atalal tips her head, like something's confusing her or taking her by surprise. "You should be getting back," she says, and there's an unusual undertone of urgency in her voice.

"How much of this will I remember? I ask. "I've never been great at remembering things from my dreams."

"Don't be silly," the lady Atalal says. "You're not dreaming.

I'm dreaming. And for now, I'm done with my dream of you."

I hardly have the time to take half a step forward and incline my head in goodbye …

… before I'm completing the step in the secret collection room in Arthur Hillibrand's penthouse suite and looking up, just in time to see the quarter flipped by Mr. James begin its descent.

He catches it smoothly, claps it onto the back of his other hand, and reveals it with a flourish.

"Tails," he says, without looking. "I win."

A tiny hint of confusion clouds his eyes for a second, like he can't remember exactly what it was he'd been playing for, or why. "*Did* I win?"

"Well," I say, "a: It's your double-tailed coin so, you know, duh. And, b: As I've explained to you on more than one occasion, what more could you possibly be looking to win? You've already got *me*."

"Yes, yes," he says. His tone, to be honest, is a little cavalier for my money. "A state of affairs I find more than acceptable," he adds, "as I trust you know. But wasn't there something…? Weren't we…?"

He looks to the plinth beside Mr. Hillibrand's Victrola and at the rather nice but perfectly ordinary Siamese cat statuette that sits atop it. Mr. James is opposed on principle to the creasing of brows—"It's *indicating*," he's been known to say. "Something a bad actor does."—but I think a mild furrow might at this point be itching to make itself evident on his forehead as he grapples with the unfamiliar feeling of being unable to not quite remember something that might not quite have happened.

Looking past the plinth and its lack of answers to whatever it is that's itching him, he looks to the wall beside the secret door and its row of small and not very good paintings of cats in anthropomorphic guises; sailor cats, mailman cats, cowboy cats, baseball player cats, guitar-slinging cats in grey suits who are supposed to be maybe The Beatles in their Ed Sullivan days or something equally stupid. Just awful, the whole set. Dull as hell, as poorly rendered as they are imagined, and—painted as they are on canvas rather than on black velvet—not even able to lay claim to the dubious virtue of high-end *kitsch*. And yet Mr. James is staring at them as if fascinated.

"Pictures," he says, practically to himself. "Pictures all in a row."

"There are better ones…" I say, gesturing tentatively back at the imposing Symbolist portrait of Bast and at the Boris and Bela movie posters, vaguely worried that my husband may have had a stroke while waiting for his coin to come down.

"No, no," he says, "I mean the *other* pictures …" He waves me forward with him as he heads for the door and out through the living room to the reception area where we first met Jeeves.

No Jeeves there right now—he must be a man who takes very seriously the preparation of Singapore Slings, I'm thinking—as Mr. James stops in front of the family portrait gallery we'd glimpsed when we arrived.

"Take a look at them," Mr. James says.

I take a look at him instead. "This better not be a test," I say.

"Indulge me," he says. "I'm testing an idea, not you."

I look at the pictures. Parents probably, grandparents presumably, great grandparents possibly. All in matching frames all in a row, all mounted on the reception area wall and set between a couple of those narrow doors that lead to linen closets or whatever.

"What do you see?" Mr. James says.

"Several generations of sourpusses in extremely uncomfortable clothes," I say, fairly confident that he's not going to find much room for argument there.

"It's a good job you're lethal," he says. "Because you see, but you do not observe."

"Yeah, well you play your fiddle and I'll play mine," I say. "What's up with the pictures?"

"It's not the pictures, it's the display," he says, sweeping his hand through the air along the row of frames to end between the last one and the closet door.

I see it now. Though I am, I confess, somewhat underwhelmed. There's a significantly larger gap between frame and door at that end of the row than there is at the other.

"Clearly a household that needs to fire whoever's responsible for hanging its pictures," I say. "Oh, wait. Do you think it's Jeeves himself? Because those dining-room doors squeaked too, remember? It's probably a drinking problem. It usually is. He might well be drinking my sling right now."

"It isn't a picture-hanging issue," Mr. James says. "There was another picture here, obviously. And it's been removed. I'm guessing fairly recently."

"Okay," I say. "So a snap's gone missing. But isn't it a more pressing matter that so has Hillibrand's head?"

Mr. James gets that quietly pleased look he gets whenever he realizes what a clever boy he is.

"Actually," he says, "I don't think that's the head we're looking for at all."

The kitchen—which is at the far side of the dining room and which is where Mr. James leads us now at a slow sprint—is unsurprisingly huge, though most of it is frankly little more than show-off space. In all that square footage, for example, there's only the one fridge.

And, in that fridge, there's only the one head.

"The late Mr. Hillibrand," I say.

But Mr. James begs to differ. "The late Mr. Kilgallen," he says.

"Jeeves?" I say, because this sad, shocked, and ice-flecked face is not the one I've come to know and have mixed feelings about.

"That missing picture in the hall?" Mr. James says. "Fair to assume, wouldn't you say, that it'd be of the latest scion of the house of Hillibrand? Couldn't be left out there in plain sight if said scion was about to pretend to be his own valet. And neither, unfortunately, could the valet."

"But that's not quite right," I say. "I have it on the best authority that the sixth finger proves the body is Hillibrand. A souvenir of all his occult dabbling. Transmutation of the flesh, if you want to be technical about it."

"Ah," says Mr. James. "Then the situation is perhaps a little more complicated than it first appears. I think we'd best be on guard."

He doesn't have to tell me twice. I'd already picked up on the creaking floorboard from behind the pantry door, and I'm spinning in its direction as it bursts open and Jeeves races at us, a stunningly large cleaver raised in both hands above his head, and rage twisting his face. And by his face I apparently mean, if my husband is to be believed, Arthur Hillbrand's face.

Whichever iteration of himself he is, he appears to think he may have the drop on us. But I'm spectacularly good from a standing start, and I've been fired up for the sport ever since this guy first gave me attitude.

Humans are so slow. I don't know what the hell this Hillibrand hybrid thinks he's dealing with, but he's about to learn. I'm sweeping beneath the clumsy swing of his cleaver and slamming a stiletto heel into his crotch before he even sees me hitch my dress to mid-thigh—a sight, let me tell you, that would put most would-be murderers into a frozen and vulnerable moment of erotic adoration, transmutated flesh or no transmutated flesh.

He doubles over in the usual manner, allowing me the luxury of a glance across the work surfaces. A kitchen is full of useful tools for any conscientious assassin and the bread knife's in my hand and busy opening three of his vital arteries before he fully straightens up. Disconcertingly, though, he does in fact straighten up. What he *doesn't* seem to be doing is in any way slowing down yet.

Mr. James is leaning back against the Corinthian Marble countertop of the kitchen's work island and lighting one of those *Gauloises Vertes* which he insists he smokes for the taste and not the demi-monde affectation. "We can assume it was the *real* Kilgallen who made the call," he says, "after Hillibrand appeared to have killed himself to avoid the consequences of his wizardly shenanigans." My husband has apparently decided he can best use this time in the tying up of loose ends, lest worrying about them should distract me from the fight.

Hillibrand makes an impressive back-handed slice with the cleaver which could really do some significant damage were I to choose to stay in place and let it connect. All things considered, my step to the side and downward sweep of the bread knife is the better call, doing enough damage to his hand to make him drop the cleaver.

Mr. James takes a nice slow drag of his smoke. "But suicide wasn't really Arthur's thing," he says. "Not when there was a perfectly good act of ritual magic waiting to save him. Mr. Kilgallen didn't realize that he was about to become part of the ultimate master servant relationship."

Heads seem to have been the focal point of most of today's activities, so I decide my best plan is to remove the one that's currently busy snarling at me. I'm trying to find the right angle of attack to do precisely that when Hillibrand elects to do the job for me.

Thumbs tight beneath his jaw below each of his ears, fingers tight at each of his temples, he gives something between an upward push and a sideways twist, and the head pops up and off like heads were always supposed to work that way. Most of the blood is gone in a single sickening cascade, but the severed trachea and the first few inches of spinal column dangle and twitch unpleasantly as one of the hands moves the head across to plant it squishily in the palm of the other.

"*Phtaq selumarnis aklo! Aklo!*" the head screams at me, which I'm going to hazard a guess—if the fury and hatred in the eyes is anything to go by—is probably *Die, bitch, die* in eldritch vernacular. Seems like big talk from a severed head resting on a hand and I'm about to say so until it raises itself four feet above Jeeves' palm courtesy of the twitching limbs that are suddenly sprouting from the neck, branching out from the dangling spinal column like one of those step-frame movies of plants blooming in speed-dial. Within seconds it's an ambulant fucking triffid, spider-crawling its way off its former host and heading my way.

"Ah," Mr. James says. "Makes sense now." He points his cigarette at the monster like a professor jabbing a stick towards a whiteboard. "Bodies just flesh-puppets. Head full of dream-lands ectoplasm. Hence the ability to make the initial swap."

Hillibrand's jaw drops open and the eyes roll up in the head and—though I don't quite see how the vocal chords still have a sound-chamber with which to work—a horrific and deafening screech lets whatever neighbors may be listening know that the Catman's not yet done fucking with their sleep patterns.

The mutating limbs, and the mutating sub-limbs blooming from within them by the second, are multiplying wildly, spiraling out into the room like some crystalline spider web foaming into overdrive, fractal nightmare upon fractal nightmare. Chicken-like feet or claws are hatching from the ends of some of them now and skittering along the walls to help heave the head at the center of the web in my general direction.

The mouth—still shrieking—is also masticating and drooling like it can already taste the smorgasbord of viscera that used to be the hottest housewife on Fifth Avenue. It is fast, it is furious, and it is, in case I'm not painting a vivid enough picture for you all, absolutely fucking terrifying.

But I've still got some cat in me, despite the interbreeding, and the thing about cats is that, once the game's on, we don't scare any more easily than we can be moved to pity. Whether you're cowering against the skirting board wondering how the hell we got between you and your mousehole or swaggering at us with your fright mask and your Halloween screeching, it doesn't mean shit to us. We're coming in for the kill.

I dive directly at Hillibrand's head as it skitters toward me on its nightmare legs and I drive my knife in through the eye at an upward angle into the brain like a cross between a trans-orbital lobotomy and a bullet to the head. I feel it die around the blade, feel all that rage and energy, all that sound and fury, simply cease to be.

The multiplying limbs, the cascading fleshy horrors of a moment before are suddenly motionless and pale, just abandoned spook show decorations, frighteners from a derelict ghost train. Within seconds they're drying out like dead vegetation, desiccated and fragile, snapping like dead twigs beneath Mr. James' tread as he crosses the kitchen floor to me.

He brushes a few of them off his jacket and pulls one or two from my hair before slipping his arms around my waist.

"Still no sign of that damn Singapore Sling," I say, patting his cheek. "Would you be a darling? I need to find the vanity. I think I may have broken a nail."

He's barely located the gin before we both hear the buzzing in his jacket pocket. Mr. James takes a quick look at the text message on his pager and then shows it to me.

I feel a small tingle of excitement. Though I have no idea what *temporal anomaly carnegie hall* may turn out to mean, I have a pleasant sense that the day has not yet ceased to prove interesting.

Mr. James smiles at me. "I'll have Travis bring the car around," he says.

I take the drink to go.

APPENDIX I
STORY NOTES
& ACKNOWLEDGEMENTS

Though I'll almost certainly mention their names again in the story-specific notes which follow, let me first list and thank the editors of the various anthologies, magazines, or chapbooks in which the stories collected here first appeared. They are, in alphabetical order:

Mike Baker, Michael Brown, Dan Chichester, Mike Chinn, Stephen Jones, Conrad Williams, Stephen Woodworth, and William Wu.

Thanks, too, to Mark Miller of Encyclopocalypse Publications for the e-book and audiobook editions of the collection and to Robert Barr of Shadowridge Press for giving it a home in print.

The Stuff that Dreams are Made of

Firstly, yes, I know the title's a misquote, so don't fucking @ me. Also, to split hairs, it's only a misquote if you think you're quoting *The Tempest*. If you're actually quoting *The Maltese Falcon*, which I am, then it's not a misquote; it's a perfectly accurate quote of John Huston's misquote (Huston's, by the way, not Hammett's; the line's only in the movie).

This story is the second longest one in the book, and conventional wisdom would have it that opening a collection with one of its longest stories is a really stupid idea. But conventional wisdom seems to be under the impression that just because a story is placed first in a collection people are actually going to *read* it first. But who's conventional wisdom trying to kid? You don't do that, do you? Nobody does that. You scan the table of contents for either a short page-count or a title which you find intriguing, and you start there. Don't feel bad. We all do it. (What you *should* feel bad about is if you're reading any of these story notes before the story to which they refer, because you're extremely likely to encounter spoilers. So, you know, *caveat lector.*)

I'd like to thank my fellow writers and dear friends Steve Woodworth and Kelly Dunn for the kind loan of their first names for my detective and my *femme fatale.* The story—novelette, actually, if you want to get all technical about it*—was written for *The Lovecraft Squad: Waiting,* the first anthology in the series created by editor Stephen Jones. I took the opportunity to make it a prequel to an earlier piece of mine, 'Intricate Green Figurines', by retro-engineering an introduction to three particularly unpleasant people who'd first appeared in that story. As the observant reader will no doubt have noticed, Constantine Garland, Jerome Cadiz, and Miss Woodman constitute a mashup/homage to two of my favorite evil trios of fiction, being modelled not only on Caspar Gutman, Joel Cairo, and Miss Wonderly (from the *Falcon*), but also on Miss Lally and her two alarming accomplices from Arthur Machen's *The Three Impostors.* 'Intricate Green Figurines' itself—which can be found in my previous collection *Rumors of the Marvelous*—sees my troika of little scamps move their disturbing activities from San Francisco in the 1940s to Liverpool in the 1980s. You'll find they've not aged a day.

More than a century ago now, magazine editors and publishers created sub-categories for stories based on word-count. Depending on the magazine, the decade, or the genre, the parameters can shift slightly, but a ballpark consensus would be that anything up to 7000 words is a short story, 7001-14,000 words is a novelette, 14,001-40,000 words is a novella, and anything from 40,001 words up is a novel. These were magazine definitions, by the way; try telling a book publisher that your 40,001 words constitute a novel and see what happens.

Z.O.A.

This story first appeared in the third volume of the *Zombie Apocalypse* books, a series once again masterminded by Stephen Jones. The title—and the protagonist's predicament—is a riff on *D.O.A.*, a movie first made in 1950 and remade in 1988. The name of my protagonist—Denny O'Brian—is a nod to the male leads of both versions, Edmond O'Brian and Dennis Quaid. If you've seen either of those movies, you'll remember that those guys had twenty-four hours to solve the mystery of who was trying to murder them before the slow poison in their bodies killed them. My guy's got about the same amount of time to rescue his daughter from a bunch of armed religious lunatics before the slow infection in his body turns him into a zombie.

ALL OUR HEARTS ARE GHOSTS

The title of this story is an example of what scholars have recently started calling Mondegreens, possibly because it sounds more elegant than 'misheard lyrics', which is what it means. I say recently—the word seems to have edged its way deeper into popular consciousness in the last decade or so—but it was actually coined all the way back in 1954 by Sylvia Wright who misheard "laid him on the green" as "Lady Mondegreen" when listening to an old ballad. The most famous example of a mondegreen—at least for a generation or so either side of me—is "Scuse me while I kiss this guy," from Jimi Hendrix's 'Purple Haze'. That's what pretty much everybody thought they heard, but Jimi wasn't in fact exploring non-binary possibilities in his sexual future, he was instead exploring the visions of an acid trip and what he was actually saying was "Scuse me while I kiss the sky." Similarly, a few decades later, what Pink was actually saying in her song 'Raise Your Glass' was "all my underdogs," and not, as I misheard, "all our hearts are ghosts." I'd nevertheless like to thank her—and my faulty ears—for the title.

As well as mishearing Pink's lyric, I was also guilty of misunderstanding the brief. When Conrad Williams was kind enough to invite me into his 2011 anthology, *Gutshot*, I somehow formed the impression that he was looking for honest-to-God western stories, not Weird Westerns (an existing sub-genre, and one which anybody but an idiot like me would have recognized as the one which made much more sense, given both my and Conrad's track record). But even though I went ahead and wrote a mainstream story about the twilight days of an old gunfighter, the tiniest bit of weird crept in right at the end*, which is how come it can show its face in this book, ostensibly a collection of horror stories. Because it's not a horror story, of course. It's barely even a ghost story. Being barely even a ghost story, it's a very inappropriate choice for the title story of the book. But it is the most appropriate *title* to be the title of the book, so shut the fuck up.

If you are shot through the heart, it's extremely unlikely that you can then shoot your opponent through the head, even if you're as cool as Addison Steele**. Which means he was dead when he did it.

Who I totally picture as looking like Lee Van Cleef, by the way.*

****Who was Mrs. Harlan Ellison's Hall Pass, as she once drunkenly confided to me.*

Postcards from Abroad

The first draft of this story had a somewhat milder ending; rather than a zombie in a basement, my nameless investigator found a body in a bedroom. The moment that he did, the mysterious banshee-like howls which had first roused the neighbors to complain started up again from below and, reaching a conclusion about the nature of the nice old lady to whom he'd been chatting, our man from The Department went downstairs to explain things to her gently.

While I was polishing the story, though, I got a phone call from my friend Peter Schneider, a legendary figure in New York publishing* with whom I'd worked at both Stealth Press and Hill

House. During our conversation, he told me about an idea he was playing around with that could be the basis for a series of some kind, whether in books, movies, or TV. I thought then—and still think now—that it was a million-dollar idea so I'm not going to spoil it by spelling it out here, but I immediately asked if I could borrow one of its underlying concepts to add a bit of liveliness to my story's climax. Peter gave me his blessing, and it was thanks to his generosity that I could trade out a dead body in a bedroom for an undead body in a coal cellar.

The story was first published in 2013's *The Impostor's Monocle*, the penultimate chapbook in the *Rolling Darkness Revue* series that the great Glen Hirshberg and I produced and edited for Earthling Publications, and was republished by Her Infernal Highness Paula Guran in *The Year's Best Dark Fantasy & Horror 2014*.

*Peter's the guy who—when Stephen King pointed out that 'Richard Bachman' couldn't sign the limited edition of The Regulators *on account of being dead—came up with the idea of including in each copy a unique cancelled check from Bachman's checkbook, each signed by the celebrated pseudonym before his untimely death. "Okay, you got me," King said, and happily forged Bachman's signature on each of them.*

LORD BYRON'S THE NOVEL OF THE FRAGMENTS

Appearing in *One Night in the Villa Diodati*, a chapbook edited by Stephen Woodworth, 'The Novel of the Fragments'—the title is a flip of the real Lord Byron's 'Fragment of a Novel'—was written as part of Steve's fun tribute to the 200th anniversary of the real night in the Villa Diodati, the night in 1816 when, argu-ably, both science fiction and horror fiction were born thanks to an eighteen-year-old girl. Mary Goodwin (she was already calling herself Mrs. Shelley, though she didn't actually marry the guy until six months later) was one of four friends who took part in a Ghost Story contest to amuse themselves one dark and stormy night during their stay at the Villa. I think we can all agree she won.

For the chapbook Steve had me, Kelly Dunn, and himself write four new stories in the guises of the original four partici-pants: Kelly channeled Mary, Steve manfully took on both John Polidori and Percy Shelley, and I got his Lordship.

I should also note that 'Only Death, Sir,' one of the epon-ymous fragments, is repurposed, having originally appeared in *Horrors! 365 Scary Stories*, edited by Stefan Dziemianowicz, Robert Weinberg, and Marty Greenberg. It was a big book, and it really did contain 365 stories, though they were all examples of what was then awkwardly known as the 'short-short' and would today be called Flash- or Micro-Fiction.

Eternal Delight

Not only the longest story in the collection, but also by far the oldest. It was written in 1986 but not published until 1994, when it appeared in the first issue of the late Mike Baker's fic-tion magazine *Skull*. Mike was already losing his shirt on his non-fiction news-zine *Afraid*, but apparently decided that he wasn't losing it fast enough.

Being as old as it is, it's perhaps not surprising that the story* required me to slap a content warning on it for 2022 readers. The warning is because of a sexual encounter that reads as if it's an assault (though it turns out to be a piece of consensual role-play). The story also contains what is now clearly an ableist slur, which I elected to leave in because it reflects—accurately if unpleasantly—how Mouthy Young Brits Who Think They're Funny spoke in the 1980s.

Novella, if you want to split hairs. See the story-notes for The Stuff that Dreams are Made of *for clarification.*

You Are What You Eat

This story appears here in slightly different form than in its original appearance in the second volume of Steve Jones's *Zombie Apocalypse* series. All the stories in that series were presented as one form or another of the 'found-documents' style: letters, diary-entries, articles, transcripts, and the like. Here, I've revised it to consist only of dialogue, with no narrative description whatsoever. I'm far from the first person to have a bash at that, but I fancied trying it.

The Way Charlie Saw It

William Wu, bookseller and magician, began publishing his *Scales and Tales* anthologies for animal charities some years back and I wrote this story following Bill's kind invitation to do something for his 2018 chapbook. 'The Way Charlie Saw it' is the second story in the collection to feature James Arcadia (who was also in two stories in my previous collection, *Rumors of the Marvelous*). Or, rather, it's the second of two that feature him by name. He's also clearly the unnamed bartender engaged on His Majesty's Secret Service in 'The Things that Dreams are Made of', and—in a weird parallel universe kind of way—he pops up again in its semi-sequel, 'The Thing About Cats', which closes out the book.

THE RETURN OF BOY JUSTICE

2012's *The Alchemy Press Book of Pulp Heroes* was an anthology in which contemporary writers were encouraged to celebrate, invoke, imitate—maybe even affectionately satirize—the masked adventurers of the pulp magazines of the 1930s, characters such as The Shadow, Doc Savage, The Spider, Zorro, The Phantom Detective*, and other ancestors of the comic-book superhero. When publisher Peter Coleborn and editor Mike Chinn generously invited me to be part of the fun, I thought I had a ready-made springboard because I'd already invented both a pulp writer, Norbert Read, and his pulp hero creation, The Blue Valentine, in my 1997 novel *Big Thunder*. I figured I could maybe knock off a quick pastiche of one of Norbert's stories, a previously unrecorded adventure of his vigilante hero. But the muse is a weird mistress, and 'The Return of Boy Justice' ended up being less about The Blue Valentine and more about the miserable old bastard who'd briefly played his sidekick on TV.

*Yes. Fully aware that only about half of those fellas wore masks, thanks. Just trying to keep it moving here.

The Thing About Cats

First published in 2020's *The Lovecraft Squad: Rising*, 'The Thing About Cats' features Tabitha, the daughter of Steve Donnelly (the protagonist of 'The Stuff that Dreams are Made of'), alongside her husband Mr. James, who's sort of an avatar of James Arcadia (from "Postcards from Abroad' and 'The Way Charlie Saw it'). Tabby will eventually be the mother of Kitty Donnelly, my reluctant Occult Detective from three stories in *Rumors of the Marvelous*, and I'm alarmed to realize at this late stage that Kitty's use of the matrilineal surname suggests my unconscious might have death or divorce in mind for Mr. James at some unfortunate point in the future.

The naming of Mr. James, by the way, was partly a visual joke: I wanted to make sure that the master of the English ghost story, M R James, had his name plastered subliminally all over the place in a book named for H P Lovecraft, master of American cosmic horror. Kind of like Tagging in a rival gang's neighborhood if the gangs were, you know, sexually repressed scholarly types in respectable suits and sensible shoes.

Songs of Metal & Flesh

And, finally, notes for a story that you haven't yet read. But it's coming up right now, and—despite being possibly my most popular story, at least based on sales numbers—is separated out as an appendix because it isn't a piece of prose fiction. 'Songs of Metal and Flesh' was written for issue three of Marvel's *Hellraiser* comic book, for editor Dan Chichester. What's presented here, in the sad absence of Dave Dorman & Lurene Haines's glorious and gory illustrations, is my script.

If you've never read a comic-book script before and have no particular desire to read this one, then don't worry, you don't have to; this book (to my astonishment) managed to limp its way to 55,000 words without it, so has already met minimum basic requirements for a book-length volume. Think of this as a DVD or Blu-Ray extra, which you can check out if you like, but which isn't part of the theatrical cut.

Children of Fire

Sorry, did I say 'finally'? In the words of Lieutenant Columbo, just one more thing...

This piece, too, is an appendix rather than being included in the regular contents because, like "Songs of Metal and Flesh", it isn't really a *story*, though this one at least is in prose. It was written at Mike Brown's request for his magazine *Dread* and was intended as a little side-order for my movie *Hellraiser III: Hell on Earth*, which had just been released. Each of its three chapters serves as a back-story/biography for the three supporting characters in the film who were transmutated into pseudo-Cenobites by Pinhead. I took the opportunity to suggest a pre-narrative link between all of them by means of their connections—substantial or tangential—to a book of poems published in 1913, thus making this tiny little thing an example of that sub-genre of supernatural fiction which deals with haunted or cursed books. The title of the poetry collection itself is a recursive call-back to the comic-book script, of course, and the fictional author of that fictional collection—John William Adams—is also an off-screen presence in my novel *Big Thunder*, where extracts from his poems provide an epigraph or two.

APPENDIX II
SONGS OF METAL AND FLESH

PANEL LAYOUT: Five bands each occupying the full width of the page and each of increasing depth, the first about an inch deep. The last band is divided into two panels of equal size. (i.e., six panels in all)

PANEL ONE: Framed against a white background, there is a five-line musical stave divided up by bar lines and with colon-like Repeat Dots at each end. Scrawled in a manic hand in blood-red ink across the length of the stave is the title: SONGS OF METAL AND FLESH. A few spare drops of blood decorate the surrounding area.

PANEL TWO: CLOSE UP on a widely staring human eye. Because the panel stretches the full width of the page and we are about to get successively closer to this eye, some detail of the rest of the face will be in frame. It should be heavily shadowed so that our interest is exclusively on the eye. At the bottom of the panel is a CAPTION.

CAPTION
Beauty comes in at the eye. That's what they tell you.

PANEL THREE: TIGHTER CLOSE UP, as if we are TRACKING in on the eye. It all but fills the panel now. There is a CAPTION at the upper left of the panel and another to the lower right.

CAPTION 1
But that really undersells the world's generosity, don't you think? Dwell for a moment on the *smell* of a beautiful woman...

CAPTION 2
Concentrate on the *feel* of the rose petal. Think on the *taste* of the beloved's tongue...

PANEL FOUR: EVEN TIGHTER C.U., so that we are just looking at curved bands of white, speckled color, and jet black (white, iris, pupil). Within the shiny black of the pupil there is just the suggestion of a reflection — some kind of mass or hill, perhaps, but shown far too obliquely for us to guess.

CAPTION
And, most of all, *listen*. Listen to the
world as it sings to you…

PANEL FIVE: EXTREME CLOSE UP on the Pupil of
the eye with just a hint of the colored iris at
each corner of the panel. The reflection, too,
is now a little clearer, but still oblique; is
it a mass of people? Is something horrible happening to them? A pile of corpses, perhaps?

CAPTION
Enjoy. Enjoy. I know I used to. For me now
it's different. For me now it's true…

PANEL SIX: Jet-black, not even a hint of the
reflection—as if we were so close to the pupil
that any closer would involve molecular study.
Bottom right, a CAPTION.

CAPTION
Beauty comes in at the eye.

PAGE TWO

PANEL LAYOUT: A symmetrical nine-panel grid.

PANEL ONE: Jet-black panel like the last but with a pinpoint of yellow light in its centre and thin beams of light radiating from it. At the top of the panel, a CAPTION.

CAPTION
Which is pretty ironic, given my history…

At the bottom of the panel, in a different type-face, is a sub-title like CAPTION.

CAPTION/TITLE
Thirty Years Ago.

PANEL TWO: In the foreground we see the profile of a young boy, JASON MARLOWE, and a thin beam of light being shone into his eye from a pen-light in the hand of an OPTOMETRIST (only his hand is visible). In the background, on a chair by a wall decorated with framed diplomas, sits JASON's worried MOTHER, an attractive woman of about thirty.

PANEL THREE: JASON's head is still in foreground but is now facing the reader. He is about five years old and has a pleasant unremarkable face, except that his eyes are rolled slightly up in their sockets and have a milky, washed-out look. The OPTOMETRIST, a man in his early forties whose income just about disguises his natural seediness, has his hand on JASON's skull and stands behind him, looking out of frame to the unseen MOTHER.

> OPTOMETRIST
>
> I'm sorry, Mrs. Marlowe. There's no change. No change at all. Nor is there likely to be.

PANEL FOUR: The crown of JASON's skull is visible in the foreground as the OPTOMETRIST crosses the room towards the MOTHER, his head turned back in JASON's direction. The MOTHER has turned slightly in her chair and has one despairing hand raised to cover her face.

> OPTOMETRIST
>
> Your son… Jason… He's blind, Mrs. Marlowe. And he'll be blind for the rest of his life.

At the bottom of the panel, beside JASON's head, is a CAPTION.

> CAPTION
>
> Big news.

PANEL FIVE: TWO-SHOT on the OPTOMETRIST and the MOTHER. She has turned to face him, her eyes a little wet. He stands over her, a little closer than he needs to be, a trust-me-I'm-a-doctor look on his face that flirts between competence, compassion, and condescension.

> OPTOMETRIST
>
> But, you know, his other senses *will* compensate. Have probably already begun to.

There's a CAPTION at the bottom of the panel.

> CAPTION
>
> He didn't know the half of it. I was hardly even listening. I was busy sucking in the sensual details of the world.

PANEL SIX: CLOSE UP on the corner of the OPTOMETRIST's desk, showing a decanter of water, two glasses, and a small pile of documents.

Two CAPTIONS, one towards the top, one towards the bottom.

> CAPTION 1
>
> Tiny rustles of paper and glass as breezes undetectable by most entered his room through gaps in his glazier's efficiency.

> CAPTION 2
>
> Subtle tingles on my tongue as traces of his chemicals mated with my taste buds.

PANEL SEVEN: ANOTHER ANGLE on MRS. MARLOWE and the OPTOMETRIST. She has now crossed her legs.

He has his hands casually in his pockets and a less-than-professional glint in his eye. He clearly finds this woman attractive.

                    CAPTION 1
    I could hear the rustle of their under-
    wear as they spoke.

                    CAPTION 2
    I could smell the undercurrent of arous-
    al in his response to my mother…

PANEL EIGHT: CLOSER on MRS MARLOWE and OPTOME-
TRIST as they lean in slightly toward each other.

There's a CAPTION at the top of the panel.

                    CAPTION
    …could hear the contractions in his
    throat as he tried to gulp it into hid-
    ing, could almost feel the heat from his
    flushing cheeks.

The expression on the OPTOMETRIST's face, though subtle and disguised, confirms JASON's reading. MRS MARLOWE's face, however, betrays only a sad concern for her son.

                    MRS MARLOWE
    It's just… it's just that it *hurts*. When I

think of all he'll miss. When I think of all he's *missing*…

PANEL NINE: CLOSE UP on JASON's face, his sightless milky eyes rolled up but his expression calm and satisfied. Background is in half-tones, as if fading to invisibility or insignificance.

CAPTION 1
What was I missing? Redundant illustrations
of things I already knew.

CAPTION 2
I had all I needed.

CAPTION 3
Smell. Sound. Touch. Taste…

PAGE THREE

PANEL LAYOUT: Nine-panel grid.

PANEL ONE: JASON is sitting cross-legged surrounded only by white space. Musical notes swirl and dance in the air around him. His eyes are glassy, but his face is ecstatic.

CAPTION 1

...and MUSIC!

CAPTION 2

I could hear music.

PANEL TWO: JASON against the white background again but now his boyish fingers snatch at the air attempting to grasp at the swirling notes as if he perceives them as objects, things to be caught, touched, tasted.

CAPTION 1

I could *feel* music. I could almost *smell* it.

CAPTION 2

It displaces the air, you know. It changes reality.

PANEL THREE: JASON in exactly the same position as PANEL TWO but now with the background filled in. He is cross-legged on the floor of his sitting room. The music he hears stems from a hi-fi in the room. MRS MARLOWE stands in an open doorway with a worried look on her face. (NB: remember this is about 1959 — the room should be depicted accordingly. 'Hi-Fi' is probably a Dansette.)

CAPTION

It's solid. It takes up space. I needed to *touch* it...

PANEL FOUR: The same sitting room but with a new addition to the furniture; an upright piano. JASON sits at it, his small hands stroking the keys.

CAPTION
...to *make* it... to *find* it...

PANEL FIVE: TOP-SHOT, looking from overhead down onto a piano keyboard and two hands on it. Because of continuity, this is clearly JASON — but the hands are older, the hands of a nineteen-year-old.

CAPTION 1
They called me a prodigy. They called me inventive. I wasn't in*vent*ing. I was un*cov*ering.

CAPTION 2
I was capturing for the deprived world the hidden melodies it was too deaf to hear for itself.

PANEL SIX: WIDE-SHOT of the nineteen-year-old JASON sitting at a Grand Piano in front of an audience of people his own age. The presence of a blackboard behind him and a lectern to his side suggests we are in an academic establishment.

CAPTION
And the more I found, the more I knew was

still hidden. The more I sensed a vast
sonic truth waiting to be revealed.

PANEL SEVEN: SPLIT-SCREEN EFFECT — many hands
applauding in one half of the panel as JASON's
hands in CLOSE UP lift themselves off the keys
as if he has just finished playing.

PANEL EIGHT: MEDIUM CLOSE UP of an older man's
hand on JASON's shoulder, squeezing it in con-
gratulation. It is the hand of the college
PRINCIPAL. What we can see of JASON's face is
completely impassive.

PRINCIPAL

And I trust none of us need any more
convincing of why Jason Marlowe has been
accepted into our scholarship program…

PANEL NINE: JASON's head and shoulders against
a white background with musical notes in half-
tones around his head. A small private smile is
on JASON's face.

CAPTION

I didn't listen to the flannel. I didn't
need it. He was right. But the ghosts of
the notes dying around me were infinitely
more interesting.

PAGE FOUR

PANEL LAYOUT: Nine panel grid in format but the bottom strip is divided into FIVE small panels, not three normal ones, to imitate a CAMERA PAN.

PANEL ONE: Head and shoulders shot of DEBORAH, a beautiful teenage girl with dangerous eyes, who's cradling a violin and giving a half-smile as if she has just finished playing and knows she is being paid attention to.

CAPTION
The Academy was good for me. At first. Not just music, but friends. More than friends. There was Deborah.

PANEL TWO: LONG SHOT of the exterior of a Sorority House in moonlight. DEBORAH, in the open doorway, has her hand on JASON's arm and is clearly persuading him to come in.

DEBORAH
It's safe. Be with me.

CAPTION
She sounded sweeter than running water through reeds.

PANEL THREE: TIGHT CLOSE UP of bodies making

love. A female hand pressed tight against a naked male back.

CAPTION
She smelt more beautiful than meadows
after spring rain.

PANEL FOUR: Another TIGHT C.U. A tongue licking
at the hollow of a neck.

CAPTION
The taste of her shamed honey.

PANEL FIVE: Another TIGHT C.U. A male hand
pressing against a female breast.

CAPTION
Touching her was like pressing your hand
to the beaches of heaven.

PANEL SIX: LOW ANGLE C.U. on JASON's face, as
if from DEBORAH's POV as she lies beneath him.
Except that we're in JASON's reality, not hers
— he is surrounded by the white space and notes
again, which makes his ecstatic expression more
ambiguous than straightforwardly orgasmic.

CAPTION
And the sounds of her pleasure were the
nearest song could come to those hidden

melodies, those mysterious harmonies that
I knew circled somewhere between our
world and the next.

PANELS SEVEN to ELEVEN: DEBORAH and JASON are
lying in her bed after making love. JASON is
asleep. DEBORAH is not. Her eyes are fixed on
a framed photo on her bedside table. Her face
is fixed and impassive. We can't guess at her
emotions.

The 'movement' through this series of small
panels is imitative of a camera simultaneously
PANNING round and TRACKING in. We start behind
the bedside table so that only the back of the
photo is visible, with DEBORAH and JASON in
the background. Then we move gradually round
and in, concentrating on the revelation of the
framed photo so that by the last panel the photo fills the panel. It is a black and white head
and shoulders portrait of STEPHEN MIDDLETON, an
alarmingly good-looking fellow student.

PAGE FIVE

PANEL LAYOUT: Nine panel grid.

PANEL ONE: A color duplicate of the b/w photo
of STEPHEN from the last panel but instead of

the photographer's blank backdrop we see the far wall of the Academy's concert room.

CAPTION

I learned other things at the Academy, too…

PANEL TWO: STEPHEN in similar pose but a WIDER SHOT including the front end of a piano at which he sits.

CAPTION

Rivalry… Jealousy…

PANEL THREE: EVEN WIDER SHOT of STEPHEN at the piano. Unlike JASON's mix of impassivity and ecstasy when he plays, STEPHEN's expression is one of intense concentration. His hair has fallen across his brow. Maybe he even sweats a little.

CAPTION

Stephen Middleton was the best the Academy had. Apart from me.

PANEL FOUR: MEDIUM-LONG SHOT on the coffee room in the Academy. JASON, DEBORAH, and STEPHEN sit on easy chairs, smoking, drinking coffee, talking. DEBORAH sits midway between the two men, curled up on her chair. Her body is angled toward JASON but her face, complete with secret smile, is turned to STEPHEN.

In the background of the room is a coffee counter, a TV, maybe a small bookcase, and a practice piano — an old upright.

> CAPTION
> His envious hatred swam in the air around him each time we spoke, despite his friendly words.

> STEPHEN
> You really are something special, Jason. Something quite different from the rest of us.

PANEL FIVE: CLOSER THREE-SHOT.

> JASON
> That's nonsense. You're good.

> STEPHEN
> It's true. I am. I'm extremely good. But you're… different. You make it all seem… natural. Easy.

> JASON
> It *is* easy. That's the *point*. It's not *about* work, it's… let me show you.

PANEL SIX: DIFFERENT ANGLE as JASON crosses the room to the practice piano. Although JASON is speaking, DEBORAH and STEPHEN are looking directly at each other rather than him.

                    JASON
   You see, you think of it as something you
   have to make out of nothing. No. It's *all
   there*. Just let it all out and then catch
   what you want…

PANEL SEVEN: OVERHEAD SHOT, CLOSE on the keyboard as JASON's hand is pulled across it (movement lines and depressed keys showing he's run across the whole keyboard).

                    JASON
   Just let it all out. Just listen. Listen
   and snatch.

PANEL EIGHT: WIDE THREE-SHOT, JASON at piano in foreground, DEBORAH and STEPHEN now standing in background. They're standing very close and STEPHEN's arm is round her shoulder. They're looking at JASON.

                    STEPHEN
   Fascinating… I think I'm beginning to
   understand.

PANEL NINE: CLOSER THREE-SHOT. STEPHEN has pulled DEBORAH even closer to him. His free hand is arrogantly fondling her breast. DEBORAH's head is tipped back slightly in pleasure. JASON has a strange half-smile on his face as he continues to play.

CAPTION 1
They thought they had a little secret. But I knew. I could hear them. I could smell their cruel excitement.

CAPTION 2
But I played along.

PAGE SIX

PANEL LAYOUT: Nine panel grid.

PANEL ONE: DEBORAH's bedroom. OVERHEAD SHOT looking down at the bed, which contains a naked DEBORAH and JASON. They are embracing, lit only by moonlight.

CAPTION
So did she.

DEBORAH
I want to see. I want the light on.

PANEL TWO: JASON's room. CLOSE UP on STEPHEN's hand holding a flashlight and sending a yellow beam into the darkness that fills the rest of the panel.

PANEL THREE: DEBORAH's room. CLOSER TWO SHOT on DEBORAH and JASON. They are still in an embrace, but DEBORAH is easing herself out of it, a smile of arousal on her face. (The light is now on)

                    DEBORAH
      Wait. I want to play. Let's play
      something.

PANEL FOUR: JASON's room. WIDER SHOT of STEPHEN standing and his flashlight beam finding JASON's piano.

                    CAPTION
      We played. While the real game went on
      elsewhere. While we were at her place,
      Stephen was at mine. She must have given
      him the key.

PANEL FIVE: DEBORAH's room. CLOSE UP on JASON's arm, wrist, and hand. He is tied to the bedpost by one of DEBORAH's silk stockings.

PANEL SIX: JASON's room. HIGH-ANGLE SHOT look-

ing down at STEPHEN crouched in front of the
piano. He's doing something at the keyboard but
the lid is up so we don't know what it is.

PANEL SEVEN: DEBORAH's room. OVERHEAD SHOT down
on the bed (same angle as panel one). Now JA-
SON is on his back, his arms spread-eagled and
tied to the bedposts by her stockings. DEBORAH
crouches on top of him. One arm is tucked down
in front of her. We can't see what it's doing
but considering where she's sitting it's a fair
bet she's masturbating either JASON or herself
or both. The other hand, though, is in plain
view. It's stretched out towards JASON's chest
and it's wielding a knife. She has made several small scratches on his chest. (NB: this is
perverted love-play, not mutilation — there's
very little blood.) JASON's expression is one of
tense excitement, not fear.

> DEBORAH

It excites you, doesn't it? It makes you
hard. You love it.

PANEL EIGHT: JASON's room. LONG SHOT with piano in foreground and STEPHEN exiting through
the door in the background. The flashlight is
off. It's the light through the open door that
semi-illuminates the room and shows us the piano
lid is down. We still don't know what he's done.

PANEL NINE: DEBORAH's room. MEDIUM-CLOSE on JA-
SON, his arms
stretched out. But he's surrounded by his white
space and notes are dancing around him. The
notes are two-tone now—there are red notes
among the black. His face is ecstatic.

> CAPTION
>
> The song was better than ever. She'd
> given me more clues to the hidden sona-
> tas. This mix of pain, pleasure, and se-
> cret agendas was the closest I'd got.

PAGE SEVEN

PANEL LAYOUT: 3 regular panels across the top
of the page and then a big splash/montage panel
taking up two-thirds of the page.

PANEL ONE: JASON's room. Same angle as panel
eight, page six. It's now dawn. JASON is enter-
ing through the doorway.

> CAPTION 1
>
> It was dawn when I got home.

> CAPTION 2
>
> I should have known.

CAPTION 3
Should have smelt that guilty cocktail of
sweat and rust.

PANEL TWO: ANOTHER ANGLE as JASON crosses to
the piano and lifts the lid.

CAPTION 1
Should have felt how the piano's discom-
fort prefigured my pain.

CAPTION 2
But Deborah'd left me exhausted and inspired.

PANEL THREE: HIGH ANGLE CLOSE SHOT on a section of the piano keyboard.   Now we can see
what STEPHEN did. In between every key is a
slightly protruding razor blade.

CAPTION
A dangerous combination.

PANEL FOUR: A big, impressionistic mix of images. A montage of different but simultaneous
aspects of one event.
What actually happens is that, as JASON runs
his hand down the keyboard in his usual loosen-
ing-up glissando (as he demonstrated to STEPHEN
in the coffee room), his fingers are sliced to
ribbons by the razor blades.

So what we want is a series of striking and deeply unpleasant images: the hand starting to be pulled across and leaving a finger-tip or two behind; trails of blood along the white keys; a mutilated hand held high and spouting blood; very tight close-ups of the protruding razor blades; and — probably the main image and located in the lower right hand of the page — JASON's screaming, contorted face, surrounded by white space, broken notes in blood-red ink whirling spastically around it, mingling with his screams.

PAGE EIGHT

PANEL LAYOUT: Nine panel grid.

NB: panels one to three are identical in angle and location, but each panel is darker, as if night is falling. Let's assume panel one is four in the afternoon, panel two eight in the evening, and panel three midnight.

PANEL ONE: HIGH ANGLE MEDIUM-WIDE looking down on a hospital bed containing JASON. His heavily bandaged hand is on a support rail to the side of the bed and there are a couple of drip-bags pumping away into his arm. His eyes are open, his face impassive.

CAPTION 1

Nothing was proved. I didn't want it to
be. They'd given me a lot to think about.
I was very grateful.

CAPTION 2

Deborah even visited. That was especially
good.

PANEL TWO: Identical to panel one except that
it's darker (twilight, not night) and DEBORAH is
sitting beside the bed. JASON is rendered exactly the same as in panel one — ie. he has no
apparent response to her visit. DEBORAH's face
is a mask of prepared concern.

CAPTION 1

The counterpoint between her mouth's
platitudes and her body's excitement was
magnificent; like putting an A natural in
a D sharp minor, like biting into a
strawberry and finding an angry wasp.

At the bottom of the panel another caption
bridges panels two and three.

CAPTION 2

I could smell it. I could taste it. My
body bathed in the sweet satisfaction
that my maiming brought her.

PANEL THREE: Identical to panel one except that night has fallen. JASON has still not changed expression or moved position.

(Wider margin than normal between top row and second row, to signify a TIME CUT.)

PANEL FOUR: VERY WIDE SHOT. Prestigious concert hall, masses of people. STEPHEN on stage at grand piano. (Orchestra behind him if they can be fitted in.)

CAPTION 1
Our worlds diverged.

CAPTION 2
Stephen got the glamour. The tours. The recordings.

PANEL FIVE: TWO-SHOT. STEPHEN and FAN at cocktail reception. The FAN, an achingly beautiful seventeen-year-old girl, stares up at STEPHEN with adoring eyes and proffered autograph book. STEPHEN, now about thirty years old, looks down at her with a fire in his eyes fuelled in equal part by lust and contempt.

CAPTION
He betrayed Deborah in every town he performed in. I liked that.

PANEL SIX: HIGH-ANGLE MEDIUM WIDE looking down on a hospital bed. The scene is reminiscent in staging of panels 1-3, but it's a different hospital and it's DEBORAH who's in the bed, with JASON sitting beside it. DEBORAH is ill, drawn and terrified. She looks, and is, very near death. JASON is angled away from us so that we can't tell what he's feeling.

CAPTION 1
Deborah got cancer and died.

CAPTION 2
I visited. She smelt fabulous. Fear and pain fought for dominance in harmonies of anguish.

PANEL SEVEN: LOW ANGLE MEDIUM WIDE. JASON sits behind a desk in an academic office. The room is PACKED with books and records. The desk before him has many open books — his hand is pressed onto one of them as if reading braille — and sheets of music manuscript paper. His other hand, resting on the desk, is covered by a black leather glove to disguise its disfigurement. JASON is now in his early thirties.

CAPTION
I got what I needed — and from which a concert career may have distracted me;

space and time to research and compose.
I had to pursue the insights I'd been
given.

PANEL EIGHT: MEDIUM WIDE on outside of office
door. It is clearly Night — the college corridor
is in darkness — but light escapes from beneath
JASON's door, which is closed. The signs on the
door read DEPT. OF ETHNO-MUSICOLOGY and PROFES-
SOR JASON MARLOWE.

CAPTION

I worked long hours but not lonely ones.
I had my books in braille, my books on
tape. I had centuries of hidden knowledge
to keep me company.

PANEL NINE: OVERHEAD SHOT, CLOSE on desk surface
(as if JASON's POV). We are focused on the cover of a book, on which JASON's black-gloved hand
rests. The cover reads "AURELIA" by GERARD DE
NERVAL. In the background, the spines of other
books are visible and we can see some authors'
names, such as DE ROBATAILLE and ROCCO PEVERELLI.

CAPTION 1

The Parisian lunatic, Gerard de Nerval
a poet who took lobsters for walks and
hanged himself with an apron — unlocked
one door:

CAPTION 2 (different type-face)
"Let us recompose the dissonant scale and
we will gain power in the world of the
spirits"

PAGE NINE

PANEL LAYOUT: The whole page is a sheet of music manuscript paper viewed from a canted angle. It's professionally printed rather than a
mss. of JASON's and looks entirely conventional
except that the instructions printed over the
staves (the things that normally read "andan-
te" or "pizzicato") are unusual Italian phrases
like "Poco Sangramente", "Como Uno Stilletto",
and "Allegro e Lacrimante".

Laid over this background are three panels and
four separate caption boxes. Panel one is top
centre of the page with a caption box to either
side. Panel two is middle right of the page and
is wider than panel one with one caption box
to the left. Panel three is bottom left of the
page, wider again, with one caption box to the
right.

PANEL ONE: MEDIUM CLOSE on JASON at his desk.
Manuscript paper lies in front of him. Despite
his blindness, he is composing directly onto

the paper, one of his hands holding a ruler or some kind of measuring device to guide the other hand which wields the pen.

CAPTION 1 (left of panel)
He was right. Music was a puzzle. A vast incomprehensible mystery which allowed initiates at best a glimpse of the manic world it hinted at. There were new scales to discover, new conjunctions of notes to reveal. Melodies of universal malice. Symphonies of suffering.

CAPTION 2 (right of panel)
Every time we found something consonant and sweet and thought we glimpsed the face of God, we'd been side-tracked and fooled into easy solutions. There was a bigger music. A darker song of terrible beauty. I would open the ears of the world to the screams of mountains in torment, to the death-cries of Dragons, to the eternal moans of the universe as its wounds split open to bleed space and ooze planets.

PANEL TWO: WIDER SHOT of JASON in a similar position to panel one but surrounded by his white space. As well as the black and bloody notes that circle his head, the white space also now contains to either side of him ethereal shapes in blue, like floating spirits.

> CAPTION 3 (left of panel)
> I knew the puzzle was solvable. I knew I would find the cluster of notes that would open the door to the occult. I had help. Spirit guides would come to me from the world of dreams. Blue angels singing the songs of metal and flesh, wordless and sublime.

PANEL THREE: EVEN WIDER SHOT of JASON but now we're back in the "real" world and can see the reality of his spirit guides: A CENOBITE stands to either side of his desk. They occupy exactly the same spatial relationship to JASON as the ethereal blue things in panel two in order to make it quite clear to the reader what is now guiding JASON.

The CENOBITES, BRAINS and HOPPER, share the usual hellish aesthetic of decorative mutilation. BRAINS has had his scalp peeled open so that his brain pulses visibly, the gathered flesh of his scalp sewn into clusters around his temples and brow. HOPPER has only one leg, but it is placed symmetrically right in the middle so that his waist flows neatly into it. BRAINS is from the PINHEAD school; tall, austere, and knowing. HOPPER is more like BUTTERBALL; a stupid ugly fuck.

There is no disruption to the room — BRAINS and HOPPER simply stand there, knowing that JASON is proceeding quite nicely down their ordained path without any pyrotechnics from them. Equally, JASON is in the same working position as the last two panels and seemingly quite unaware of the CENOBITES' physical presence.

      CAPTION 4 (right of panel)
  But always the real world would intrude, always the music of power would slip by me again. It was terrible. I knew the score was within me… I just had to let it out.

PAGE TEN

PANEL LAYOUT: Five page-wide bands. Bands 1, 3, and 5 are narrower than bands 2 and 4 and are sub-divided into five very small panels each.

BAND ONE (PANELS 1-5): Five very small and very CLOSE images, all glimpses of one environment which we'll see fully in Band Two. Panel one; JASON's hand lights a candle. Panel two; a sheet of blank music paper lies on a bare wooden floor.

Panel three; a hammer knocks a double-pointed nail into a piece of wood. Panel four; discarded pants fall to the floor, with JASON's naked leg also in shot. Panel five; A section of a large piece of wood, bristling with nails, barbed hooks, and razor blades.

CAPTION (bridging panels 2 & 3)
Then one day I understood.

BAND TWO (PANEL 6): HIGH WIDE ANGLE on a room in JASON's house. The room is stripped of furniture and decoration. The floor is bare boards. JASON, naked, sits cross-legged in the center of the room. Some candles — presumably for ambient smell, not light — burn here and there. Scattered in a rough semi-circle around JASON are many sheets of music manuscript paper, all blank. Behind him is a large piece of wood (probably an old door) propped upright. It is studded and scarred with razors, hooks, and nails.

CAPTION
I had to move beyond composition. Beyond study. To an act of faith…

BAND THREE (PANELS 7-11): Five very small panels like band one. This sequence of five images is like a perverse piece of Muybridge footage; we follow JASON sequentially as, now on

his feet, he twists, turns, and drags himself
across the board of blades, his face alternate-
ly pain-wracked and serene, his body increas-
ingly slashed and torn.

    CAPTION (bridging panels 8, 9, 10)
  To unlock the puzzle, I had to unlock
  myself.

BAND FOUR (PANEL TWELVE): Same angle as Band
Two. JASON is on his feet, caught mid-step in
a whirling dervish dance which sends sprays of
his blood flying furiously through the room.

BAND FIVE (PANELS 13-17): Sequence of five small
images; various sheets of mss. paper (one per
frame) at different angles all being splashed by
drops of JASON's blood. The drops, almost magi-
cally, land within stave lines rather than the
white spaces between.

PAGE ELEVEN

PANEL LAYOUT: Six panel grid - except that the
top row is divided into five small panels not
two big ones. (Nine panels in all)

Panels 1-5 are a PULL BACK sequence from mss.
paper

PANEL ONE: Entirely blood-red.

PANEL TWO: Big blood-red circular splodge surrounded by white space with a thin black line
emerging from either side of the splodge.

PANEL THREE: White space with three parallel
black lines running across the panel. In the
middle of the second line is the red splodge.
Now we see it has a blue line joined to its
right side which runs up the panel.

PANEL FOUR: Now it makes sense: We see a section of a five-line musical stave with two joined
notes (quavers) on it. The tails of the notes
and the connecting line are in blue ink, the
heads of the notes are red blood.

PANEL FIVE: Now we see the whole piece of paper
with JASON's hands on it, one hand feeling for
the blood-drops, the other adding tails and
shit.

Running right across the bottom of these panels, separating them from the four that follow,
is a caption box.

                    CAPTION
      A decade of research and composition
      had swelled my reputation if not my bank

balance. I knew I could get it performed.
And I knew who I wanted to perform it.

PANEL SIX: Crowd shot of a seated, well-dressed
audience waiting expectantly, facing the reader.

CAPTION

The audience was full of the informed and
the fashionable. People that I knew, in
one way or another, would appreciate what
they were being offered tonight.

PANEL SEVEN: CLOSER on crowd, picking out JASON
in a prominent seat.

CAPTION

I was very excited. Tonight, the world
was to have its blinkers removed, its
earplugs taken out. Tonight, the veil
between Life and the Real was to be
shredded.

PANEL EIGHT: REVERSE ANGLE (crowd's POV). Stage
with orchestra and, in front of them, a grand
piano and a waving STEPHEN, acknowledging the
crowd's welcoming applause.

CAPTION

The piece hadn't been rehearsed. I'd
had them prepare with what I called

related pieces. I'd fed the media some
conceptualist bullshit reason for that.
They lapped it up.

PANEL NINE: CLOSE on piano keyboard, with STE-
PHEN's hands perched in mid-air ready to begin
playing.

CAPTION
Now it would begin.

PAGE TWELVE

PANEL LAYOUT: Nine panel grid. (NB: Every panel
has a blue wash over it to place it in Cenobite
reality)

PANEL ONE: Same angle as last on previous page.
STEPHEN's hands have slammed down on the keys.

CAPTION
Crisp attack.

PANEL TWO: Head and shoulders shot of STEPHEN
facing the reader. Two chains have flown in
from the bottom corners of the panel — as if
shooting up from the keyboard — and have buried themselves deep in each of his eyes. Blood
jets away from his face. His mouth is open in

a terrified scream of pain. We should see some
background, but we don't. Realism is hardly the
issue here.

CAPTION
Good tone.

PANEL THREE: Same angle as panel one but WIDER
shot as STEPHEN falls backwards, clawing at the
chains. The keyboard, in foreground, still has
several keys depressed - in other words, the
music is continuing without his help.

CAPTION
My, he was playing well.

PANEL FOUR: WIDE on Auditorium. To left of panel
is an aisle. Framed in the doorway at the end
of it is BRAINS. To right of panel are the rows
of seats. The audience are panicking, standing,
screaming, trying to leave.

PANEL FIVE: WIDE on Auditorium. Like a reverse
of the previous panel: to the right is an aisle
with HOPPER in the doorway, to the left are rows
of distraught audience. (ie; in effect, panels
four and five are like the left and right-hand
sides of a Cinemascope frame with the middle
bit — more audience — cut out.)

PANEL SIX: CLOSE on four or five chains flying through the air from various intersecting angles.

A caption bridges panels five and six.

> CAPTION
> The audience's enthusiasm could only just be restrained.

PANEL SEVEN: MEDIUM-LONG on HOPPER. He's grinning. He's holding three severed heads. The heads are screaming.

PANEL EIGHT: MEDIUM-LONG on three headless violinists, their necks gouting blood, their fingers playing furiously.

PANEL NINE: MEDIUM-LONG on BRAINS. He is conducting with a bloodied baton.

A caption bridges panels eight and nine.

> CAPTION
> The band played like men possessed.

PAGE THIRTEEN

PANEL LAYOUT: One big splash panel takes up

three-quarters of the page and then there's a
bottom row of four small panels. (Five panels
in all)

PANEL ONE (SPLASH): Big MASTER SHOT of the apocalypse in the concert hall. We're looking out
from the stage. Hooks, chains, steaming piles
of viscera, the works. The audience are dead
or insane. Mostly dead. Speared in their seats,
hooked and slashed. In some cases, brains have
exploded out through ears that have heard the
forbidden. In others, whole bodies have spontaneously combusted. It's a hell of a mess. Except
that, right in the middle of it, still sitting
in his chair, still calm, still unharmed, is
JASON.

CAPTION
Everything was perfect.

PANEL TWO: Head and shoulder shot of JASON,
surrounded by his usual white aura (no notes
in the air).

CAPTION
Everything was pure.

PANEL THREE: Exactly the same as panel two, except that now the aura is bright red.

CAPTION
Everything had passion.

PANEL FOUR: Exactly the same, except that the aura is cenobitic blue.

CAPTION
Everything was calm.

PANEL FIVE: A jet-black panel.

CAPTION
Then everything went away.

PAGE FOURTEEN

PANEL LAYOUT: Four page-wide bands, the top one split into two panels. (Five panels in all).

The page layout is effectively a reverse of page one (minus the title panel); we are now pulling out from the eye instead of tracking into it.

PANEL ONE: Jet-black panel.

CAPTION
Everything went to Hell.

PANEL TWO: VERY TIGHT CLOSE UP on the black pupil of JASON's eye with just some hints of white beyond the curvature of the pupil in the four corners. As on page one, there is an oblique reflection in the eye.

CAPTION 1
I'm alive, I think.

CAPTION 2
I can see.

PANEL THREE: TIGHT CLOSE UP on JASON's eye. Because we've now switched to the full width of the page, we see more detail. We've also TRACKED out a bit, but we're still very close.

CAPTION
I'm paralyzed. I'm bereft of taste,
touch, and smell.

PANEL FOUR: CLOSE UP on the eye, but now there is some facial detail around it. It's slightly to the left of the panel and the right side is heavily shadowed.

CAPTION 1
I'm deaf.

CAPTION 2
(A touch of exquisite cruelty, that)

PANEL FIVE: CLOSE UP on JASON's eyes. The one we've been TRACKING out from is to the left and sharply lit, the bridge of the nose and the other eye are to the right and all but lost in shadow.

CAPTION 1
I'm here for Eternity.

CAPTION 2
And all I can do is watch...

PAGE FIFTEEN

PANEL LAYOUT: Splash page.

PANEL: VERY WIDE, JASON's POV. In a cavernous space in Hell, we see what has become of the orchestra. It is a huge Boschian nightmare. In the same way that CENOBITES are fused and sewn to their costumes and weapons, so have the orchestra become one with their instruments. Limbs are replaced by sounding boards and strings. Cruelly exposed bones have had holes drilled in them to act as infernal flutes. Brainless crania become tom-toms. In some cases, these people play themselves. The more elaborately transformed are played by disembodied limbs or bows hooked up to perpetual motion machines. From

the screams of agony on all the distressed faces, it's clear that their transformation hasn't
robbed the bodies of sensitivity; each finger-
ing, each stroking, each blowing or plucking is
a new torture for them.

STEPHEN occupies centre stage, just as he did
in the concert hall. His flesh has been peeled
from his torso, allowing his ribcage to be used
as a xylophone. His sinews are stretched taut
from his belly to his wrists, offering service
as a harp. His trachea and lungs have become a
wind instrument.

JASON's last caption is placed to the top left
of the page.

CAPTION
...as beauty comes in at the eye.

At the bottom right is another caption in a
different typeface.

CAPTION
In a certain corridor in the 40011th sec-
tor of Leviathan's Labyrinth is a room
devoted to the chastisement of many but
the torture of one. Jason Marlowe should
be flattered. He has the largest private
room in Hell. Where 10,000 years is but

the blink of a suppurating eye, but a
millisecond can contain the nausea of a
lifetime, he sits and watches the orchestra of the damned. Everything he ever
heard was a pale foreshadowing of the
music of their pain. He can see them
shake, quiver, and despair as they make
the song of the spheres. All around him
is the sound his spirit yearned for. All
around him is the silence of an indif-
ferent God. All Hail Leviathan, Lord of
Irony! Long may his cancers bloom! Long
may his mysteries fester!

APPENDIX III
CHILDREN OF FIRE

...in the shadows of Babylon's ruin
We harvest the roses of Twilight.
Sundered, dishonored, the heirs of desire;
Orphans of ecstasy, children of fire.

—John William Adams (1879-1913)

ONE

Richard Bloodstone was born in Hackney (a district of London, England) in 1955.

His father's name was John Cooper. He was a visiting seaman from Canada, and he never knew that he had fathered a child on the nineteen-year-old chorus girl whom his exotic accent, new world glamor, and bulging pay-packet had enticed into the bed of the unprepossessing hotel room in which he was staying.

Cooper shipped home to Alberta four days after Richard's conception and gave no more thought to England or to chorus girls' kisses until a late afternoon in 1987 when a man he had never seen before walked into the dim light of a sports bar in

Medicine Hat. Cooper, ten years divorced and two unemployed, was sitting at a rear booth nursing a beer. The dark-haired and strangely familiar man approached the booth, said "Hello, Dad," took out an automatic pistol, and shot him three times through the left eye. The police were expecting a quiet day and couldn't respond to the manager's call for nearly forty minutes. Nobody in Medicine Hat ever saw the killer again.

Richard's mother was Flora Pender on her birth certificate, Natalie Silver on her Equity card, and Ginger Rogers in her dreams. John Cooper was not the first man in her life, so her young heart was not broken when he failed to return for the Saturday matinee at the Piccadilly theatre, but she was disappointed. Six weeks later, when she knew she'd missed her second period, she was furious; She'd been offered a six-month extension on her contract and this little keepsake from Canada meant the end of that. Too much of her parents' Catholicism was still in her blood for her to countenance an abortion, and too much West End propriety was in the minds of the producers for them to countenance an overtly pregnant chorine. She left the show behind, she left London behind, she left behind her dreams of single-spotlight stardom.

Richard was born in the duchy of Cornwall in a small cottage near Tintagel. The cottage belonged to Flora's maternal grandmother's sister, Great-Aunt Sissy. Sissy, a lapsed bohemian, was the only relative who had wholeheartedly supported Flora's choice of career. She had spent an absinthe winter in London three years before the Great War of 1914 as the favorite companion of an aging and minor symbolist poet whose one slim volume of verse, *Songs of Metal and Flesh*, was dedicated to her. When the scandal about his involvement with a radical off-shoot of the Order of The Golden Dawn broke in the salons and the newspapers, Sissy had been summoned home by her parents. Since then, she had outlived two thoroughly respectable husbands and, childless, had inherited the cottage from her second. She welcomed Flora into her home and, seven months later, personally delivered Richard into the world in the very early hours of a cold September morning.

On a Tuesday in April 1961, Sissy came downstairs early to start the fire and found a note from Flora. She read it through once and then flung it onto the grate among the small logs and coal-nuggets. An hour or so later, she woke the five-year old Richard with a cup of tea and the news that his mother wouldn't be coming back.

Sissy lived until 1969. The cancer that killed her had begun its slow internal feasting more than six years earlier but the fierce and unexpected love for the child that fate and her family had given to her kept her from surrender until just after his fourteenth birthday.

The authorities took forever to find Flora and it was only in early 1974, when Richard was legally an adult, that he saw his mother again. Their meeting was in a railway station cafeteria and Flora, now Natalie Edwards, was as delicate as she could be in framing her request that Richard refrain from further contact with her. Her husband was a young turk Member of Parliament who fully expected a cabinet post in the next reshuffle, and the sudden emergence of a long-lost and illegitimate son of his wife's could cost him dear. Richard could always go and find his father in America, she said (her grasp of geography being as reliable as her commitment to motherhood). Richard shook her hand awkwardly and left. The News of The World paid him ten thousand pounds for the story, and he used it to finance his trip across the Atlantic.

His only reading material on the QE2 was Sissy's treasured copy of her long-dead lover's book of poems. Richard was particularly drawn to an unrhymed sonnet entitled 'Orchid for a Dishonoured Prince', and began a lifelong habit of muttering under his breath the closing sextet:

The room is dimmer now. The thirteenth comes.
The philosophic stone is steeped in blood.
The petals of the black rose part like wounds,
And razor tongues within sing slow pavanes.
Now strikes the filial hand (unholy joy!),
And scarlet rivers ease the pain of years.

In the thirteen years between his arrival in New York and his appointment with his father, Richard took various jobs across the length and breadth of the North American continent. Many were interesting, many were not. What emerged as his favorite form of employment was bar-work. He was surprised at this. He'd always assumed he'd eventually discover within himself a vocation for something significant—medicine, literature, politics, whatever—but no. It was bar-work. He liked it. It was very straightforward. Very honest. People stated their needs. You satisfied them. They rewarded you. It was as simple as life should be.

After his encounter in Medicine Hat, Rick (as he'd been calling himself ever since first seeing *Casablanca* and realizing he shared a first name with the coolest bar-owner of all time) returned to New York and found work in the main bar of The Boiler Room, a nightspot owned and operated by JP Monroe, a man with whom he had little in common save patricide and (eventually) transmutation.

TWO

Daniel Erwin "Doc" Fisher had two formative experiences as a boy: seeing *Shane* at his local drive-in, and being given an 8mm movie camera by his uncle Mort.

In the absence of a father (Ray Fisher was killed in a drunk-driving incident when Doc was three years old), he grew up with Alan Ladd's mysterious mythopoeic gunfighter as his male role-model. He wanted to be strong, silent, and sad. He wanted to save people. He wanted other men's women to fall in love with him and he wanted to be too decent to do anything about it.

In the absence of a stable life (his mother took him from school to school as she moved from town to town, job to job, man to man), he grew up obsessed with capturing life on film. He pointed his camera at reality, and it became more manageable. He could frame it, compose it, give it a beginning and an end. He could make it make sense.

By the time he was in his twenties, he had already combined these two obsessions. He was a professional TV cameraman (he had wept for the death of celluloid newsreel at the hands of television but had made peace with the enemy, had come to terms with tape) who wore his hair and clothes like a frontier ghost. Buffalo Bill with a Sony, he either ignored or genuinely didn't notice his colleagues' sniggers at the hip-holstered cellphone, the monosyllabic slow-talk, the fringe-sleeve buckskin coats.

By the time Doc came to take his job with Channel 8 and begin his association with Joey Summerskill, his résumé was very impressive and very detailed. There was, however, one curious three-month gap in late 1977. The man who conducted the interview for Channel 8 asked what Doc had been doing through that early winter. "I have no idea," was Doc's answer and his perfectly blank stare discouraged his interviewer from probing further. Doc got the job anyway. Speculation among his colleagues about this three-month sabbatical ranged from covert government work to ten weeks in de-tox. Nobody got it right.

In October 1977, having just returned from an assignment in Europe, Doc received a phone call from a contact in the industry asking if he was up for some quick freelancing. Doc called the number his friend gave him and found himself listening to an enthusiastic but elderly voice.

◆ ◆ ◆ ◆

Woodrow Penman III was the sixty-three-year-old inheritor of a vast family fortune. That fortune, and the businesses that fed it, were now administered totally by hired men. All Penman had to do to fill his days was find interesting ways to spend money.

A lifelong bibliophile, Penman had for the last seven years specialized in collecting obscure works of an occult nature. His initial interest in rarity of text was slowly succeeded by an obsession with depravity of content. He made contacts in the secret world of Magick and began to be involved in a small way in the staging of occasional rituals. The drive to be top dog which had taken Woodrow Penman I from copyboy to press baron was still there in the blood of his grandson. The aging billionaire yearned to win the respect of his latest peer-group by an act of summoning that was both novel and awe-inspiring. After much research, he believed he had found his means. As with many great discoveries, it was via a happy accident of coincidence in what he had believed to be two different avenues of research that Penman came to a great discovery of his own.

He had been sifting through his manuscript collection and had been flicking past some examples of the Arthur Machen - A E Waite correspondence when a set of initials in one of Machen's postscripts caught his eye. The PS read, "I see JWA's capers with our misguided brethren have lost him Fleet Street's favour. What flesh, I wonder, will sing his songs now?" The oblique reference in the second sentence confirmed for Penman that the man under discussion was the poet John William Adams but what was exciting was that he had never before made an association between the poet and the JWA whose initials appeared regularly in the papers of The Brethren of The Sundered Body, an obscure and short-lived occultist group of Edwardian England.

Three hours later Penman was trying to control the tremors of incipient glory that coursed through his body: by careful cross-referencing of clues, portents, and hidden instructions in the Brethren papers with certain lines from certain poems in Adams' book, he was convinced that he had unearthed a buried invocation to a Power. The Power was unnamed in any of the texts except by circumlocutory phrases like *He who Dwells in the Deep*, but Penman cared little for names—he knew from his studies how one author's Astaroth is another's Isis, how Beelzebub is sometimes Lucifer and sometimes not. Names were human guesses and were unimportant. There were Powers. They could be summoned. That was all.

◆ ◆ ◆ ◆

"And you can leave the camera running? It'll record everything?"

Doc smiled at the eagerness and the naiveté in the billionaire's voice. Yes, he could leave it running. Yes, it would record everything.

Three days later, on the stroke of midnight, he pressed the record button on his camera and left the 30th floor apartment on Eighty-Sixth Street in Manhattan. He'd framed it, focused it, color-compensated for the candlelight, and knew he could leave the rest to technological inevitability.

He didn't think much about it after his second pre-sleep bourbon though he'd chuckled once or twice on his drive back to Queens. The old guy in his faggy white robe. The other people sitting cross-legged at each point of that five-pronged star painted on the floor of the big empty room. The way Penman had had each of them say something weird while Doc checked the audio-feed and had glanced nervously round the place if two or more of them spoke at once. Lifestyles of the rich and famous. Jesus.

Doc rose at 7:30 the next morning and went back to collect the camera. He'd offered to stay over but Penman had said it wouldn't be appropriate. He exited the elevator outside Penman's place a few minutes before nine and let himself in through the unlocked front door.

♦ ♦ ♦ ♦

It was five hours before the Police arrived. Doc was sitting propped against a wall, his eyes glassy, his mouth slack and drooling. Naturally, the authorities took the camera away, but the tape proved worthless. It had fed through the camera alright but was completely blank, leaving the investigative team with no clue as to what precisely it was that had taken the six people who had passed the night in the room and spread them over the walls and ceiling like lumpy and steaming purée.

Doc was institutionalized for nearly three weeks. He took a long holiday after that. When he returned, his court-appointed psychiatrist, a Dr. Phillip Channard, was disappointed—but not surprised—to discover that Doc had completely forgotten the whole episode and had no further light to shed. He took Doc off his books but kept the police photographs of the catastrophe. He had several private files among which such pictures might find an appropriate home.

THREE

Jimmy "See-Dee" Hammerstein was born the year *Sgt. Pepper* came out. His tenth birthday party was marred by the death of Elvis Presley. On the day he graduated high school, Massive White Bias, his favorite thrashers, went gold for the first time. He dropped out of college to concentrate full-time on organizing underground Rave parties on the same day that Bobby Corvino, once retired 'fifties idol, began his series of come-back collaborations with dancemeister Hophouse Jack. Jimmy and music were in sync. He loved it. He lived it.

He began his reign as DJ at the Boiler Room when he was twenty-four years old. The kids loved him both for his impeccable sense of dance floor zeitgeist and for the ease with which he could obtain whatever their drug-of-choice might be. Ecstasy was the big hit of the moment but, though Jimmy was happy to acquire it for anybody upon request, he no longer indulged in the stuff himself. He always avoided the question why.

About eight months before JP Monroe added a certain ornate and grotesque pillar to his in-club collection of esoteric art,

Jimmy—or See-Dee, the sobriquet he had insisted on ever since staging his ticket-only dance floor burning of his entire vinyl collection—had been crashing at the apartment of Slither, his lead-guitarist friend from Thanatos. They, along with Slither's girlfriend Lamia and any passing guests, had been doing a lot of E. For the last few days Slither himself hadn't shown his face much. He was hanging in his bedroom working at his eight-track home studio.

Unlike Slither's usual in-your-face self-trumpeting, his manner about whatever he was currently working on was secretive. His eyes began to project a kind of knowing pride, as if he was privy to some hidden wisdom that the rest of the world was too blinkered to get. It was a look like the look of the guys who *really* knew who killed Kennedy, the look of the upbeat and stupid side of paranoia.

See-Dee'd been there about a week when he brought The Fan back from the club to meet Slither. The Fan had actually paid him a hundred dollars for the privilege—Slither didn't let fans into his home so See-Dee had agreed to introduce the guy as an old friend of his. It had all been cool at first, but See-Dee had begun to worry when, after a little drug-taking, The Fan started to show his true colors by pressing Slither on his current project. See-Dee and Lamia had exchanged an oh-shit look but, surprisingly, Slither went with the flow—which was great for See-Dee, because the cocktail of intoxicants he'd ingested over the last three hours was shutting him down and he didn't think he could keep his eyes open much longer, let alone throw the guy out if Slither had freaked. He leant his head back against the wall and drifted into sleep as their conversation washed over him.

"Has it got a name yet?"

"Sure. *Orphans of Ecstasy, Children of Fire.*"

"Way cool."

"Yeah. It's the title of this poem from way back. But, you know, I, like, *chose* it."

"Right."

"The whole thing is like based on this book. This English guy, man. He *knew*. He was out there. And this is *way* back. Before rock n roll. Before everything."

"And the fish that hides in stone."

"Three cycles back, and the eye in your hand."

"Before the sky was blue."

"Babylon's cauldron, and eighty to go."

See-Dee smiled in his dreams at the nonsense his mind was making of what his ears were ceasing to hear.

◆ ◆ ◆ ◆

He woke with a start at about four in the morning. He was alone in the room. He assumed The Fan had left and that Slither and Lamia had gone to bed. He was about to pull out the sofa-cushions to crash himself when he noticed that their bedroom door was slightly ajar. There was a strange flickering light coming from the room and he could hear a low rhythmic pulse and the high tinny sound of cymbals through headphones. He went over and inched the door open a little more.

Both naked, Slither and Lamia were fucking. Slither was standing up and Lamia was bent over in front of him, her elbows resting on the foot of the bed. They were both wearing headphones which were plugged into Slither's eight-track porta-studio.

The Fan was wearing headphones too. He was spread-eagled naked on the bed, ankles and wrists tied to the posts. A score of deep and bloody gashes had been opened all over his body and long thin candles had been thrust into every wound. Each candle was burning and the light from them threw crazy shadows on the wall of the room as The Fan's body twitched in time to the music all three were hearing. Lamia still had the knife in her hand and was making small delicate cuts in the sole of The Fan's left foot as Slither moved in and out of her.

Slither caught sight of See-Dee in the doorway and gestured his hand to a fourth set of headphones. See-Dee looked back at The Fan—at the animal ecstasy in his idiot eyes, at his tongue licking at the air as if servicing some unseen lover—and shook his head, no thanks. Slither shrugged, no biggie, and turned his attention back to the fun.

See-Dee closed the door carefully, collected his stuff from the main room, let himself out into the New York night, and caught a cab to the Club.

SHADOWRIDGE PRESS

shadowridgepress.com

Made in the USA
Columbia, SC
28 October 2022

70131986R00169